Cast Out of Darkness

Cast Out of Darkness

Timothy C Sayer

Edited by Jonathan Starke at The Artful Editor

www.artfuleditor.com

Combat Fly Fishing, LLC
2016

First Printing: 2016

ISBN 978-0-9976497-2-7

Combat Fly Fishing, LLC
Sedalia, CO

www.combatflyfishing.com

Ordering Information:
Special discounts are available on quantity purchases by corporations, associations, educators, and others. For details, contact the publisher at the below listed e-mail address.

U.S. trade bookstores and wholesalers: Contact Combat Fly Fishing, LLC
tim@combatflyfishing.com

Dedication

To my lovely wife Chelsea.

Thank you. Without your support, guidance, and patience, I would have never completed this book.

Thanks for always being there...especially when times got tough.

Contents

Acknowledgements

I would like to thank all of my friends who poured over the pages of this book and gave me their personal insights on how to improve the story. Of those, there were a select few that truly did more work than I could have expected and I would like to thank them by name.

Marie, thank you for the extended time you spent reviewing my manuscript. Your insight as a fervent reader was invaluable and helped me polish the fishing chapters so they would be more enjoyable to the non-angler.

Rob, thanks for using your fly fishing expertise to check over some of the more technical angling portions of my book.

Lally, thank you for carefully proofreading the final draft of my manuscript. Your suggestions and corrections helped immensely. I hope we remain fishing buddies for a long time to come.

Doug, you gave me a unique insight into the world of a United States Marine. Your knowledge of the Corps and your experiences during your time of service helped me to shape believable characters and dialog. Thank you. I hope my representation of the Marine Corps is true and honorable like the men and women who belong to this elite branch of our military.

I would like to acknowledge the U.S. Marine Corps website at www.marines.com which helped me research many of the procedural aspects of the Marine Corps to include training procedures and deployment history.

I would also like to acknowledge thewalkingdead.org where I was able to research the history of First Battalion, Ninth Marine Regiment, especially during their time in Vietnam.

I would like to express my sincere appreciation to the Marines who serve or have served in the Second Battalion, Fourth Marines and the First Battalion, Ninth Marines. Learning the history of your battalion's courage and sacrifice while conducting research for my book, was truly humbling. May your stories of service never be forgotten.

A special thanks to Kris, Lyle, and John, who have been loyal fishing buddies over the years and helped to inspire several of the fishing stories in this book.

I'd also like to thank my friends Al, Paul, DB, Chuck, Kurt, Jim, Max, John and Troy who have stood by me though the toughest situations I've ever experienced and taught me the value and rarity of unflinching friendship. The brotherhood that we developed over the years helped inspire many of the characters in this book.

Finally, to my wife Chelsea, thank you for finding consistency flaws in my story, giving me honest criticism, and spending loving time reading and then rereading over the same material as many times as it took until I got it right. You truly are my best friend and I can't imagine a life without you. You are my *Allison*.

Preface

Sixteen years of law enforcement has exposed me to death more times than I can remember. Some of those incidents were natural, some homicidal, some accidental, and some suicidal. Of those encounters, it was the suicidal incidents that often left me wondering why. Why this person? What made their situation so different from anyone else, that they would feel the only course of action was to end their life? Was there anything that could have brought them back from the precipice of this darkness?

More and more I hear of our service men and women being plagued by this darkness and after surviving some of the most unimaginable hardships overseas, they come home only to take their own lives.

Now I want to be clear; I don't subscribe to the myth that combat veterans are somehow weak and mentally unstable because of their experiences and I know that not all veteran suicide is directly linked to combat service. I do think that for the ones out there that are suffering and contemplating suicide, it's important for you to know that there are people out there willing to help and that your life in this world holds so much more value than you might think. Don't allow the veil of darkness to hide the light your life shines on others.

The story you're about to read and the characters portrayed in it are fictional. It is not based off of any particular person and although the combat scenes and stories are based off of real conflicts, the combat events are fictional. It's simply a story about a U.S. Marine who uses his love for the outdoors and of fly fishing to help battle the demons of loss, post-traumatic stress, and survivor's remorse as I imagined he would. Thank you for reading my book and I hope you enjoy it.

-Tim

CHAPTER ONE

Al Anbar Province, Iraq April 19, 2004

Marine Lance Corporal Blake Jacobs could hardly see a foot in front of his face. The air was filled with a brown sandy dust that had engulfed him like a thick fog. The taste of burning rubber scorched his throat as he choked on the thick fumes. He could hear muffled yelling, almost like someone was cupping their hands over his ears. There was a steady high pitch tone like feedback from a microphone interrupting his ability to make out the yelling. His head was spinning out of control. His heart was pounding in his chest. Unable to recover his equilibrium, he frantically threw his arms out in front of him and to his sides like a child searching for a light switch in a dark room. Blake's fingers connected with the edge of something metallic and sharp. It was the jagged teeth of the rail system attached to the hand guard of his M4 rifle. He feverishly moved his hand down toward the butt stock. Like a blind man reading a braille book, he felt around the rifle until he located the pistol-grip handle and with his left hand, grabbed onto it with a strangling hold. His right hand fumbled and bounced around as he desperately searched for the front passenger door handle of the up-armored Humvee that he was trapped in. Blake found the handle and pushed down on it. The latch popped and Blake pushed against the door, but he could only open it about six inches before the heavy armor, assisted by gravity's force, shoved him back into the Humvee and closed once again. Blake braced his feet against the center console and lowered his right shoulder against the door. With a simultaneous crank of the handle, coupled with a thrust of his legs, it opened. With a short violent fall, Blake collided face first onto the sand dusted blacktop street below. The door swung back onto his hip and legs that were still hanging from the frame, pinching them in place. In anguish, he crawled forward on his elbows, pulling his legs and feet free of the Humvee's heavy iron door.

Blake made it to his knees but still struggled to regain his balance. The haze from the dust had begun to dissipate, and he could see a plume of black smoke near the front of the four-vehicle motorcade that he had been traveling in only minutes earlier. Blake looked back at his Humvee, which was the third vehicle from the front. The now empty Humvee was lodged in a two-foot trench on the left side of the street. Both tires on the right were flat, and the skin of the Humvee was peppered with divots that had chipped the tan exterior. The bullet-resistant windshield and the passenger side-door windows were cracked and splintered but intact.

Blake was starting to recover his hearing, and he could make out his name being called from somewhere behind him. "Jacobs! Jacobs!"

Blake turned around and saw his squad leader, Sergeant Earl Tomlin. "Wake the fuck up, Jacobs! We've got wounded at the lead Humvee! Get up there and set security around the motorcade!" Without another word, Tomlin sprinted toward the front of the convoy.

Blake stood up and took two steps before his legs gave out causing him to fall on his face. Blake screamed at himself, "Damn you! Get! Up!" Blake stood back up as the adrenaline rushing through his veins erased any muscle fatigue from moments earlier. He ran toward the front of the motorcade as the forth Humvee in the convoy, the only vehicle still operable, drove past him and stopped parallel to the the second Humvee. The vehicle positioning, created a pocket of cover for the Marines who now consolidated their remaining forces between the two vehicles.

Sgt. Tomlin was calling for help on the radio when Blake arrived at the scene. Tomlin broke from using the radio to point at the left front corner of the second Humvee. "Set security there, Jacobs! Help's on the way!"

Blake scanned the surrounding area while taking a knee at his assigned post. He could see that the first Humvee in the motorcade was the source of the black plume of smoke he had seen earlier. The rear axle, along with the rear passenger compartment, had been completely blown off, and the rest of the vehicle was fully engulfed in flames. The echo of loud pops from exploding rounds could be heard as the ordinance located inside of the cab cooked in the blaze. Blake was horrified; he knew from the severity of the damage that no Marine riding in that vehicle could have survived.

The second Humvee in the convoy suffered serious damage as well but had not caught fire. The hood and the right front wheel well panel had been blown apart exposing the Humvee's engine block. The upper front passenger doorframe had a basketball-size hole blown through it. Smaller fist-sized shrapnel punctures had penetrated the Humvee's armor like a shotgun blast and cut through the cab killing the two Marines riding in the front. What was left of their mangled bodies remained in the front seats of the battered wreckage.

The other three Marines in the Humvee had all been pulled out of the left rear door and were lying in the street on their backs. Navy Corpsman Brandon "Doc" Wells, who had been riding in Blake's Humvee at the time of the attack, was in the process of placing tourniquets on Marine Private John Petting, who had been manning the 50-caliber belt-fed machine gun inside the turret of the Humvee.

Petting was barely conscious and was missing both legs just above the knees. Doc Wells, who was known for his ability to work amazingly well under combat stress, had dug both of his knees into the upper inside thigh area of each of Petting's stumps and was using his body weight to cut off the flow of blood that had been pouring out of Petting's exposed femoral arteries. Doc Wells took out a combat tourniquet, which was nothing more than a one-inch-wide piece of black nylon. The nylon strap had been fed through a metal buckle to make a loop and had a thin six-inch metal cylinder attached to it to act as a windlass. Wells carefully placed the tourniquet over and around the torn meat and shattered bone of Petting's right stump. Once clear of the wounded area, he quickly ran the tourniquet high near Petting's crotch and pulled the nylon tight through the buckle. Doc Wells twisted the windlass, which synched the nylon tight around Petting's leg, compressing the femoral artery against the bone and muscle of Petting's thigh. The tight compression choked off the flow of blood, keeping the wound from draining. Doc Wells locked the windlass in place and released the pressure from his knee to see if the hemorrhaging had stopped. The tourniquet was successful, and Doc Wells pulled another one from his medical pack and repeated the procedure on Petting's left leg.

Once Doc Wells had set both tourniquets on Petting, he moved to the other two Marines. He determined quickly that one was dead, probably killed instantly by the initial blast, and the other was unconscious and suffering from massive internal injuries. The surviving Marine needed to be on an operating room table as soon as possible. Doc Wells placed a clear plastic tube down the Marine's throat to keep his airway open. He stabilized the tube by running white medical tape from the base of where the tube entered the Marine's mouth, around the back of the Marine's head, and over his jaw in a crosshatch fashion. He repeated this until the tube was held firmly in place. Doc Wells would check on the Marine's breathing and pulse from time to time, but there wasn't much more he could do.

Blake noticed a blast pattern that originated from the right side of the road. The street was littered with pieces of metal shrapnel and chunks of asphalt and dirt. Dark charcoal-colored striations scarred the street, starting from the blast point and streaking toward the motorcade. A one-foot crater about the size of a pickup was at the origin of the blast, which had dropped half of a two-story building. Blake knew immediately that the motorcade had been hit by a Vehicle Born Improvised Explosive Devise, commonly known as a VBIED, incorrectly pronounced *veebid* by the Marines. Blake had been briefed about these kinds of attacks before, but this was the first time he had ever been involved. The Iraqi insurgents would pack a vehicle with enough explosives and shrapnel-producing metal debris to disable an entire convoy. The insurgents would either park the VBIED on the side of the road and detonate it as the convoy drove past or a suicide bomber would try to blend in with traffic and drive the VBIED up close to detonate the bomb.

The street was empty of people, and no civilian bodies were lying around the blast site. The convoy had been driving through a dangerous neighborhood at the time of the attack, and Blake remembered that it had been eerily quiet right before the explosion. This was an indication that the local populous knew the bombing was coming and probably assisted with the attack. Blake feared that a secondary ambush was certain. With half of the Marine patrol killed or wounded and only one operable vehicle, the remaining Marines did not have the ability to break from the ambush point. They would have to hold out until the Quick Reaction Force, or QRF, arrived.

The QRF was made up of 10 Marines who were on standby to act as an immediate rescue force for military patrols that came under attack. They would stage themselves at military Forward Operating Bases or FOBs, which were small military outposts strategically placed throughout the Anbar Province. In the event of an attack, the nearest QRF team would deploy from the FOB using three up-armored Humvees with turret-mounted machine guns and would rush to support the downed convoy. Once on the scene, the QRF would determine if more assets were needed to evacuate the wounded or to transport personnel to safety. They would then either handle the evacuation themselves or call for additional reinforcements, if necessary. Blake knew that the convoy was only three or four miles from the nearest base and that it would only take them a few minutes to arrive. Blake thought, *As long as there isn't a follow-up attack, the wounded should be back at the FOB in 15 to 20 minutes.*

As Blake was working out the timeline of their rescue, the sight of a shadowy figure coming from an alleyway across the street interrupted his thoughts. Blake pointed his rifle at the alleyway, and the silhouette slowed to a creep as it got closer to the street. He could see the unmistakable shape of an RPG 7. RPG was an acronym for *Rocket Propelled Grenade*, a portable antitank weapon first designed by the Soviets to be carried by infantrymen. The rocket launcher could hit a target from 200 meters away. The RPG was designed to be shoulder-fired and quickly reloaded. It was a major threat to U.S. up-armored Humvees and could easily penetrate the already weakened armor of the vehicle Blake was using as cover. One direct hit could take out the remaining Marines.

Blake raised his rifle and took aim at the center of the figure. He used his right thumb to push down on the selector switch. With a metallic click, he disengaged the safety and engaged the semiautomatic firing feature. Blake placed his index finger on the trigger just as the olive cone-shaped point of the RPG's warhead exposed itself in the daylight of the street. Blake took a deep breath and held it as he pressed the trigger. He felt the rifle's recoil jostle his cheek as a spent 5.56mm brass bullet casing popped out of the ejection port as a round shot out the end of his barrel. A sharp deafening crack echoed in the street. Then Blake settled back into the rifle and fired three more well-aimed shots into the menacing silhouette. The RPG shot wildly into the air after Blake's rounds impacted the target.

The rocket's burning propellant hissed as it flew over the convoy, leaving an air-distorting vapor trail as it exploded into a rooftop on the opposite side of the street. Small chunks of debris rained down around the convoy. "Contact right! Contact right!" Blake yelled to the other Marines. A hailstorm of small-arms fire irrupted onto the convoy from the right side of the street. Bright flickers of light came from the muzzle flashes of the insurgents' AK-47s. They were coming from the windows, alleyways, and rooftops—the ambush Blake had feared.

CHAPTER TWO

Silver Dollar Lake

It was the morning of September 11, 2001. The sun had not quite peeked over the eastern plains, and Blake was up early having a quick bite while packing a lunch for a fishing trip. His mother was still sound asleep, and he was trying to be as quiet as possible. He stood over the kitchen counter eating a bowl of oatmeal. Between bites he sloppily slapped together a ham and cheese sandwich. Then he grabbed an apple from the fruit bowl and threw the sandwich and apple into a plastic grocery bag. He had to hurry; Aaron would be there any minute.

Raised a devout Christian, Aaron Grady was a funny, clean cut, adventurous young man. He and Blake were both only children who grew up together and had recently graduated from high school in Littleton, Colorado. They had been best buddies since kindergarten and did everything together. In fact, they were together so often that many people assumed they were brothers.

Growing up, Blake spent most of his time over at the Grady house, just down the street. Blake's parents had divorced when he was six, and he didn't see much of his father. Blake's mother was very loving but had to support them by working long hours during the week and a second job on the weekends. She counted on the kindness of the Grady's to watch over Blake in the evenings until she returned home from work.

As boys, Blake and Aaron would sit around the Grady's dining room table finishing up homework and eating a meal that Mrs. Grady had prepared for the family. During dinner, Blake and Aaron would pester Mr. Grady to tell them stories of his experiences in the wild. Mr. Grady was an avid outdoorsman and never missed an opportunity to go camping, hunting, hiking, or fishing. Almost every weekend he had some adventure planned on the Colorado Front Range or beyond. Most of the time he took the boys with him on these outings, and Blake and Aaron inherited Mr. Grady's love and passion for the outdoors.

On a late spring day, when Blake and Aaron were 10 years old, Mr. Grady had taken them hiking above the tree line to a high mountain lake near the Continental Divide called Silver Dollar Lake. This gin-clear snow-fed lake was only accessible by a small foot trail just off of Guanella Pass near George Town, Colorado. The trail was two and a half miles long, and the climb was mildly arduous starting out with steep hairpin switchbacks that cut through a spruce pine forest. The trees at the start of the trailhead were over 50 feet tall, but they would gradually reduce in height the higher in elevation they would climb. As if there was an invisible line drawn at about twelve 12,000 feet in elevation, the now eight-foot-tall trees had reached the limit of their ability to survive the cold, thinly oxygenated atmosphere. Only dwarf shrubs, dark green moss, brightly colored wild flowers, and short thin blades of grass dared to grow in this ecosystem known as the Alpine Tundra.

Blake and Aaron were in awe at the vastness of the area. They marveled at the dark gray rocky peaks of the snow-capped mountains that lined the horizon to the west. The enormous mountain range was lightly silhouetted against the deep blue Colorado sky. Mr. Grady stopped and took a long look at the majestic scenery before suggesting that he get a photo of Aaron and Blake together using the Rocky Mountains as the backdrop. With Blake and Aaron side by side, authentic smiles and each with an arm draped over the other's shoulder, Mr. Grady snapped a photo with a disposable 35mm Kodak camera that he had purchased at a gas station earlier that morning. Little did they know, that simple camera captured a moment in time that would mark a milestone in Blake and Aaron's lives.

They continued down the trail that straightened out and continued west along a sedate uphill grade. After about 20 more minutes of hiking, the trail started to slope slightly downhill. Soon the view of a small dirt foot trail ending at the ridge line of a hill, gradually gave way to the clear deep blue waters of Silver Dollar Lake.

The lake was nestled under a large snow-spotted mountaintop that stood about two thousand feet to the southwest side from the base of the lake. Grass-covered rolling hills surrounded the lake to the east and north. The lake wasn't huge, only about the size of a professional baseball field. Beneath the surface was a knee-deep rock-covered shelf that extended from the northern shore out 20 feet toward the center of the lake. At the end of the submerged shelf was a drop-off that was so deep that no visual indication of the bottom could be seen.

As Blake walked past the lake he could see a fish trolling just off the shoreline. He yelled, "Mr. Grady! What kind of fish is that?"

"That's a trout, Blake."

Blake heard an unfamiliar voice clarify, "A cutthroat trout."

Blake looked beyond Mr. Grady a few feet up the trail. A middle-aged man was sitting on a hillside just south of the trail. He was wearing a long-brimmed hat, blue jeans, and had an olive green vest over a red flannel shirt. He was looking into a small tin box that opened like a book. He had an unusually long fishing pole lying next to him.

"Fishin' today, huh?" Mr. Grady asked.

The man said, "Yep, fly fishing. Although I can't figure out for the life of me what they're biting on."

"Well, I wish I could help, but it's been years since I've been fly fishing, and to be honest…I was never any good at it."

"I'll figure out the riddle here pretty soon. They're just being a little picky this morning."

Mr. Grady hiked down the trail a little ways and sat up on the hill where he and the boys could overlook the lake. He said, "Let's take a break and watch him fish for a bit."

As Aaron sat down on the hillside, he asked, "Dad, what's fly fishing?"

"Well, instead of using bait or spinning lures the way we typically fish, a fly fisherman uses artificial bugs made out of thread, feathers, and animal hair that are tied to a hook." Mr. Grady pointed to the man. "See that long rod he's got there?"

"Yeah, Dad, I see it."

"Well, he uses that rod to cast a special nylon line that's coated in a flexible plastic type coating that helps the line float. He ties a clear line, known as a leader, to the end of the nylon line, and then he can tie on the bug he made, or the *fly*, to the other end. He casts the fly out onto the water and hopes the fish eat it…and basically that's fly fishing."

Aaron, still looking a little confused, nodded.

"Just watch, son. You'll see."

Aaron and Blake studied the man as he stood up and walked to the edge of the lake. He began by pulling line from a circular reel on the bottom of a nine-foot fiberglass rod. The man was holding onto a cork handle that was about 10 inches long; it wrapped around the rod just above the reel. The line was bright green, and he continued to pull the line from the reel until there was a pile of line at his feet. He began his cast by clinching the handle of the rod with his right hand and bending his wrist forward, which forced the handle of the fly rod to become parallel to his right forearm. He seemed to fuse the rod in that position, and then with his left hand he picked up the loose end of the fly line between the pile at his feet and the eyelets of his rod and pinched the line between his thumb and index finger.

The man began the cast by pulling back on the rod and then stopping the rod tip a couple feet behind his head. The fly line drifted behind him before he would smoothly thrust the rod tip forward again. He continued these back-and-forth motions, never letting the line touch the water. He started out with about eight feet of line but with every false cast would allow more and more of the line that was piled at his feet to feed through the eyelets of his rod until he had an impressive length of line floating through the air. With one firm tug of the line as he was thrusting forward after a back cast, he released the line from his fingertips, and the remainder of his line shot through the eyelets of the rod. He pulled up on the rod slightly once all the line had tension with the reel, and the line gently landed on the surface of the water, along with the leader and the fly.

The man focused intently on the fly that was floating on the surface, watching it bob up and down in the riffles of the wind-blown lake. Suddenly the water surface was breached by a violent splash near the fly. The man firmly but gently thrust the rod back toward his left shoulder. The rod tip immediately bent toward the location of the splash. The line went tight against the reel, and the cylinder of the reel began spinning and releasing line through the eyelets. The man put pressure on the spinning reel with the palm of his hand, slowing the amount of line that was being pulled into the water. As soon as the line stopped, a beautiful cutthroat trout jumped out of the water and dove back into the lake.

Keeping his rod tip high, the man began reeling line back from the trout until the fish had reached the shore. With a small wood-handled net, the man reached down to the water and scooped up the trout. He dunked his hands into the lake to get them wet before handling his prize, and then he reached down into the net and dislodged the fly from the trout's mouth. He looked over at Blake and Aaron and asked them if they wanted to see the catch.

Blake and Aaron ran over to the man as he picked the 15-inch cutthroat out of the net. He held the fish gently in the palm of his hand, carefully cupping the trout just below the pectoral fins and only lifting him a few inches from the surface of the water. The trout was dark green on top and blended into a light olive toward the middle. A brilliant bright red stripe ran from the gill plate all the way down the middle. The trout was thinly speckled with black spots that started out very sparse near its head and became bigger and thicker near the tail fin. The belly and lower jaw popped with sharp-white brilliance. The trout's mouth and gills were pulsing and would quickly open and slowly close. Using both hands, the man gently turned the trout upside down to reveal two skinny dark red markings pigmented on both sides under the jaw. He explained that the markings were the reason behind the name *cutthroat*. The man then held the trout under the surface until it started processing the oxygen-rich water through its gills once again. The trout swayed back and forth, and with a swift thrust of its tail fin, it broke free of the man's light grip and swam off unharmed.

From that point on, Blake and Aaron were fascinated with fly fishing. Mr. Grady, who once dabbled in the sport, dug through his basement and found all of his old fly fishing equipment and gave it to the boys. While other kids played baseball and football, Blake and Aaron would spend hours in the front yard practicing the art of fly casting. They bought an old fly tying vise along with a bunch of material from a garage sale and learned to tie their own flies. They would pester their science teachers for information and books concerning the study of insects, otherwise known as *entomology*, in hopes of gaining an upper hand on the river. On weekend outings Mr. Grady would always try to plan a trip to a river, stream, or lake that the boys had not yet been to. It almost seemed there wasn't a body of public water in the great state of Colorado that the boys had not tried to pull a fish out of.

Over the years they became extremely accomplished anglers and set out on regular fishing adventures together. Today's trip would be no different from the countless other trips they had taken. Blake and Aaron would be heading to one of their favorite spots, a tail-water stretch of the South Platte River known as Cheesman Canyon.

As Blake stuffed his bag lunch into a worn-out backpack, he could see the headlights of Aaron's Jeep shining through the living room window as he pulled into the driveway. Blake went out to the garage to gather his fishing gear and opened the garage door. He walked around the dark gray Jeep Cherokee and opened the hatchback using an old broomstick handle. The Jeep had seen better days. Blake loaded his gear then opened the squeaky front passenger side door and slammed it to make sure it was securely shut. Aaron put the Jeep in reverse while Blake was putting on his seat belt.

"You ready?" Aaron asked.

"As ready as I'll ever be. Let's do this!"

The two best friends headed off on their fishing adventure. Little did they know what tragedy and chaos the United States would suffer on that heartbreaking September day and how it would change their lives forever.

CHAPTER THREE

Cheesman Canyon September 11, 2001

A s Aaron turned southbound onto Santa Fe Boulevard toward the town of Sedalia, there were only a couple of cars out on the otherwise deserted highway. The sun was still not up, and the streetlights were still glowing a shade of yellowish orange as they approached the city limits. Their destination would be the first three miles of the South Platte River running north out of Cheesman Reservoir. This gold-medal stretch of the South Platte River flowed through a boulder-filled cliff-lined drainage known as Cheesman Canyon. This stretch of river was only accessible from a dirt footpath known as the Gill Trail. The Gill Trail started just off the east side of a single lane county road and continued over three miles south through the canyon and ended at Cheesman Dam. Their plan was to hike south from the road about two miles to a small creek confluence with the South Platte known as Cow's Crossing.

Blake reached for the stereo. He turned the main knob, but nothing happened.

"Radio's not working, bud. It shorted out last week."

"Does anything in this piece of shit work?"

Blake didn't even own a car and only had limited access to his mother's sedan, so Aaron said, "Feel free to ride your bike to the river next time."

With a confident sarcastic-looking smirk, Blake said, "Please! If it weren't for my share of the gas money this thing couldn't make it out of the neighborhood, let alone to the river. Face it, you need my gas money just as much as I need this crapper."

Aaron laughed and replied in a fake deep voice, "Touché, good sir! Well played."

They headed west at Sedalia and turned onto Highway 67 toward the foothills. Winding through the narrow mountain roads, Aaron and Blake joked about things that had happened on past fishing trips. Deprived of a radio, they exchanged playful banter and recited hilarious movie quotes that helped pass the time. Before they knew it they were going south, driving along the famed South Platte River. They followed the road that paralleled the river for 10 miles until they reached the town of Deckers.

Deckers was not a town in the traditional sense. Mainly known as a fly fishing destination, the town was made up of a little country store, a few cabins for rent, and a famous fly shop called Flies & Lies. Flies & Lies was more of an institution than a fly shop. Visited by thousands of fishing enthusiasts every year, this tiny shop had its finger on the pulse of the South Platte. If an angler wanted to know what flies were working, he made sure he popped in before setting out on the river. Even though Blake and Aaron typically tied their own flies, it was considered bad form to get information about the river from the shop and leave without buying anything. On most trips they would usually hang out for a few minutes and buy a few flies or some tippet after trading stories and getting a couple tips from the owner.

As they pulled up to the stop sign in Deckers, Aaron looked over at Flies & Lies and could see it had not yet opened so they made a right turn on County Road 126 and drove another three miles to the trailhead of the Gill Trail.

A few minutes later Aaron pulled off on the shoulder and cruised onto a small dirt pullout along the road. They had finally arrived at the Gill Trail. Blake jumped out of the cab and propped open the hatchback. Aaron walked over to the passenger side and faced away from the road and shouted, "Holy cow! I have to piss! Remind me to go before we leave next time." Blake didn't respond and pulled out his chest-high waterproof fishing waders that were wadded up into a wrinkled ball. He tried to shake them back into their original shape. "Not gonna wait for me?" Aaron asked as he zipped up his fly.

"I always wait for you. That's the problem. Can you imagine how much more fishing I'd get in, if I wasn't always waitin' on your slow ass?" Blake said with heavy sarcasm and a smile.

Aaron laughed. "Get over yourself, drama queen! I'll have my gear on and ready to go before you even lace up your boots."

They joked back and forth while getting ready for their trek to the canyon. In no time, they had slipped on their waders and boots, pieced together their fly rods, threw their backpacks on, and headed down the Gill Trail.

The ambient glow of the approaching dawn provided enough light to navigate the small dirt footpath. As rays of sunshine broke through from the East, Blake and Aaron's suspicions were confirmed that today was going to be a great day for fishing. The high was in the low seventies with the sun dominating a sparsely clouded sky. The aspen leaves that had just begun to change from the light green of summer to the bright yellow of fall, flickered in the light morning breeze against the dark green backdrop of the ponderosa pine forest.

Blake and Aaron spent little time enjoying the beauty of the morning as they had witnessed the grandeur many times before. They hiked at a fast pace south on the trail with one goal in mind—to catch the early morning hatch at one of their favorite stretches of the canyon. With these favorable weather conditions, the aquatic bug population would be hatching in full force, no doubt creating a smorgasbord of mayflies and midges for the trout to feast on. Their fervent hope was that the fish would be eating bugs off the surface of the water, generating an opportunity to throw dry flies to rising trout.

In no time, Blake and Aaron were looking down the trail at their intended destination; a 90-degree turn to the east of the South Platte River known as Cow's Crossing. The hundred-yard stretch of river was a mixture of deep pockets of clear swirling pools that surged against large jagged boulders and expansive shallow riffles of ankle-deep water.

The challenging obstacles of the area were often enough to keep most anglers looking for easier water to fish, which added to the area's appeal. Although difficult to master, Blake and Aaron learned that if an angler could throw pinpoint casts followed up by smooth technical mends, Cow's Crossing could produce some of the best fishing in the canyon.

They split up in an attempt to cover more water in search of feeding trout. Blake almost immediately identified a rising trout about 15 feet off the bank. The trout was sipping floating white specks from the surface. Blake began studying the water to see what the trout was feeding on. Angled beams of sunlight shined over the tops of the ponderosa pines illuminating the hundreds of white-winged bugs that hovered over the river.

Blake reached down into the water just off the shore where he saw one of the flies floating along and cupped his hand underneath the bug. He allowed the water to sift through his fingers until the small black-bodied, six-legged creature was trapped in the light film of wet residue still left in his hand. He recognized the bug's brilliant white wings and translucent three-pronged tail. The bug was no bigger than a fingernail shaving.

"Tricos!" Blake yelled.

"What?"

"Little black tricos! Tiny ones! Size 18 or 20!" The numbers represented the length and gauge of the wire of the hook that the fly was tied to. The higher the number assigned to the hook, the smaller it was.

Blake and Aaron were used to fishing small flies in Cheesman Canyon. Most of the aquatic bug life in the tail water stretches of the South Platte didn't reach the larger sizes of the big freestone rivers of the Northwest. The rows in their fly boxes were lined with hundreds of tiny hooks decorated with wraps of thread and thin wire to represent the larva and pupa that inhabited the waterway. The dry fly patterns that represented the fully developed stage of a trico were not much bigger and nearly impossible to see if they were floating on the water more than six feet away. This reality didn't deter Blake from attaching the lightest tippet he had to his leader and tying on a small black-bodied dry fly that closely resembled the hatching bugs.

Blake maneuvered along the bank of the river until he was perpendicular to the rising fish. He made two quick false casts that sailed six feet above the river before committing his fly to the water. The fly gently touched down on the surface of the water and floated just over the trout's head. The trout swam up within an inch of the surface before diving back down rejecting Blake's offering. Undaunted, Blake picked up his line and pulled the fly from the water. He allowed the fly to glide in the air behind him only once before casting it to the same spot for another try. On the second pass the trout rose to the drifting fly, and with the tip of its nose, barely pushed through the top of the water and opened its jaw allowing the fly to float into its mouth. The trout then sank nose first.

Blake sharply snapped back on the rod driving the fly deep into the top corner of the trout's mouth. The water, just above where the fish took the fly, began to boil as the fish tossed from side to side trying to dislodge the hook. The rod bent forward as the trout made an instinctive run upstream away from Blake. Blake walked along the bank trying to match the trout's run. He waded into the river just off the bank as the trout began to flail, splashing near the surface. Blake kept the rod tip high over the trout's head, which kept solid pressure on the fish, making it difficult for the trout to attempt another run. He pulled out his long-handled wood-framed landing net that he always kept tucked into the small of his back, secured by the belt of his waders. With one swift lunge, he netted the pan-size trout.

Although not huge, the brown trout was colorful. The top of the fish was a caramel that blended into a deep butterscotch yellow near the midsection and continued down to its belly. The fish was peppered with dark brown spots from head to tail fin. The spots were all thinly outlined in a light yellowish tan color. Among the camouflaged spots of brown were circular dots that glowed blood red.

Blake admired the trout without pulling it from the nylon mesh of the net. He took out a pair of stainless steel hemostats and reached toward the trout's mouth. He clamped onto an exposed area of the hook and plucked out the fly. He dipped the net into the water and submerged the fish in a light current just off shore. The trout swam free of the net and darted off into the riffles.

Blake looked upstream about 30 yards and could see that Aaron's rod was bent over; he had also hooked his first fish of the day.

"Big one?" Blake yelled.

"He's no monster, but he's putting up a good fight."

"Did you get him on a dry?"

"Nah, I was fishing a dry and dropped a tiny bead-head thread midge off it, just below the surface. He took the thread midge."

"Nice! You need any help?"

"No. I'm good."

Blake gave a thumbs-up and began to search for another fish.

Soon after, Aaron brought his fish to the net. It was a nice 16-inch rainbow trout. The rainbow, with its dark olive green and black-spotted back and rose-colored red stripe that ran from its gill plate down the center of its body, was the South Platte's most dominate fish species. Aaron quickly pulled out the fly that was fused to the top of the rainbow's mouth and held it gently in the current giving the fish time to revive from the battle it had lost. A minute of oxygenated water flowing through the gills of this wild beast was enough for it to snap back to life and swim off to be caught another day.

Even though Aaron and Blake were able to catch a couple fish relatively quickly, the trico hatch soon died off as fast as it had begun and so did the blemishes on the water's surface caused by feeding fish. Since the majority of a trout's diet came from insect larva and pupa, the two adapted a new strategy of fishing subsurface nymph patterns until another dry fly hatch came off. Aaron decided to go to one of his favorite patterns, a small mayfly nymph pattern called a Pheasant Tail. The name of the pattern derived from the material used to tie this fly that was harvested from pheasant feathers.

Aaron tied the pheasant tail to the end of his tippet and added another piece to the bend of the hook. He attached another nymph pattern about 15 inches below the pheasant tail, thus increasing his odds of tricking a picky trout. Just above the surgeon's knot that married his leader to his tippet, Aaron attached a bead of lead split shot to help the nymphs sink quickly in the swift current. Aaron then took a three-inch-long piece of tan macramé yarn out of his vest pocket. The yarn had been folded in half and wrapped and tied with thread just above the bend to hold it together. This frayed piece of yarn was known as a strike indicator. He attached the rudimentary device to his leader about two feet above the split shot. Aaron often used a strike indicator when fishing nymphs. The indicator would float on top of the water while his flies would drift beneath the surface. If the indicator would pause, twist, sink, or do something unnatural, it meant that a trout might have eaten the nymphs.

Blake followed the same procedure, which was customary when fishing nymphs, and the two went back to work drifting their flies through various riffles, pockets, and seams in hopes of making a solid connection with another trout.

Although they had hoped for a fast-pace morning, the fishing was quite slow. Both Aaron and Blake were still catching fish, but the hookups were few and far between. They were constantly changing flies as the finicky trout continued to reject their offerings. But they weren't deterred because they could remember times when they had been completely skunked while fishing in the canyon, so they continued to throw casts in hopes of landing one more trout.

The morning soon turned into late afternoon. Blake and Aaron decided to cut their losses and move downstream, fishing along the way until they ran out of sunlight and were forced to hike back to the Jeep.

CHAPTER FOUR

The Road Trip

Blake and Aaron worked their way downstream from Cow's Crossing, walking along an elevated point of the Gill Trail that contoured along a hillside of the canyon, overlooking the river. Aaron was walking about 10 feet behind Blake. He was scanning the river when he stopped and said, "Holy shit, Blake! Holy…flipping…crap! Is that…is that a trout or a log?"

Blake squinted at the river. "I don't see it, dude."

Aaron shook his head in disbelief. "Seriously? Holy crap, man, that fish is huge!"

"Walk me into it; I still can't see it," Blake said.

"How can you not see that thing?" Aaron grabbed Blake by the shoulder in frustration and pulled him a few feet down the trail. "Do you see that big boulder across the river with that sapling growing out of it?"

"Yep."

"Come off the boulder about eight feet toward the center of the river, and then go upstream about—"

"I've got him now," Blake said. "Whoa! You're right. That's a monster 'bow."

The rainbow trout was one of the biggest they had ever seen in the canyon. The long dark figure of the fish was suspended in the center column of a deep trough that was surrounded by giant bus-sized boulders that lined the shore on either side. The behemoth trout was swimming back and forth against the current like a great white patrolling an ocean shoreline. The trout was feeding furiously on subsurface insects drifting in the water. Aaron studied the fish as the white color from the inside of its mouth flashed every few seconds as the predator devoured the helpless pupa caught in the current.

Aaron wanted that trout. He surveyed the area in search of the perfect spot to cast and drift his flies toward the trophy. But the elusive fish was swimming in a horrible spot. The boulders choked out the shoreline, and the water was far too deep to wade. There might have been a chance to throw a long cast from a small piece of exposed sand-covered shore about 40 feet downstream from the trout, if it weren't for a boulder the size of a small house on the West side of the river. The boulder had an oblong edge that hung over the river and obscured any chance of a decent cast.

Aaron studied the situation for a minute, playing out possible scenarios in his mind before saying, "All right, here's the plan. I'm gonna stand on that big boulder and make my cast." Aaron, pointing at the small piece of exposed shoreline downstream from the boulder, continued, "You go down to that sand-covered landing. When I hook that bad boy, I'll fight him from the top of the boulder and walk him over to you. Then you net him."

Blake laughed. "Are you for real? The top of that rock is at least 15 feet up! You're gonna hook that fish and fall off."

Aaron rolled his eyes. "Ah, ye of little faith. Just watch the master at work."

"I'm in, if you think you can do it; just be careful. I'm gonna be pissed if you crack your skull open, and I have to carry you out of here on my back."

"Relax. You just focus on netting the 'bow. I'll focus on not falling off the boulder."

Blake shrugged his shoulders and started walking down the hill toward the landing. Aaron, with a look of determination, headed toward the boulder.

The boulder butted up against a hillside made of small loosely compressed pebble-sized granite. Aaron was able to effortlessly walk down the hill and onto the top of the boulder. He was surprised at the amount of gravel that, over time, must have eroded from the hillside and now layered the top of the rock. Aaron walked toward the edge of the boulder and slipped slightly on the loose gravel, but he was able to widen his stance and catch himself. He peered over the edge and into the water, spotting the rainbow below.

Blake, who had made it to the landing, called out to Aaron, "Is he still there?"

"Yep. Same exact spot."

Aaron stripped a healthy amount of line from his reel and pulled the slack through the eyelets of his rod. He tied on a size 20 flashback pheasant tail nymph pattern that was producing well for him earlier that morning. Then he attached an 18-inch length of tippet to the hook shank of the pheasant tail pattern. He tied a size 22 black thread midge to the tippet that dangled below the pheasant tail. He wanted the two flies to sink to the middle column of the trough. Aaron removed the heavier split shot he had on the line and replaced it with a lighter weight. He removed the strike indicator from his line for fear that it might frighten off the massive fish. With a deep breath he let loose of the flies while pulling back on the rod and began his cast.

Although the trout was feeding ferociously, Aaron suspected it would take several casts before he found the perfect drift that would coax the trout into taking the flies. On the first drift Aaron put the flies about five feet in front of the trout. As the flies drifted downstream, he wondered if that was far enough ahead of the trout to give the flies enough time to sink down to the middle column before the current carried them past the feeding lane. Believing the flies had already passed the trout, Aaron pulled up on the rod to make his second cast. As he raised his arm, his line went tight, and the tip of his rod bent sharply over the water. Aaron screamed out in disbelief, "I got him! Blake, I got him!" The giant trout's mouth and jaw breached the surface of the river. It shook its head splashing water in every direction.

Aaron's upper body was pulled toward the water as the monster rainbow made a hard run upriver. The squeal of the spinning reel told the story of the trout's strength, as it ripped line away. Aaron took a step back with his right foot in an attempt to recover his balance. As he transferred his weight, he slipped on the loose gravel and tried to place his weight back onto his left foot, but it was too late; Aaron was going down hard.

Panic set in, and Aaron yelled, "Oh shit! Oh shit! Oh shit!" His feet slid out from under him, and his body slammed against the edge of the boulder as he heard the sound of a snap echo through the granite-lined canyon. The wind had been knocked out of his lungs. He slid over the edge of the boulder and fell head first to the river below. With a deep-sounding *kursplunk*, Aaron sank to the rocky bottom. His head and left shoulder bounced off the river bottom, and his first reaction was to try to immediately stand up and try to get his fly rod tip up in hopes that, by some miracle, the trout was still hooked on the end of his line.

Aaron popped out of the water and thrust his fly rod high in the air. He couldn't feel any tension against the line or rod. He tried to take a gasp of air but struggled to inflate his lungs. He could hear Blake calling, "Aaron! You all right, man?"

Wheezing with every failed breath attempt, Aaron eked out a horsed and labored response. "I—I'mmmm…gooooood!"

Blake, trying to hold back his laughter, asked, "Do you still have him hooked?"

Aaron reached up with his left hand searching for his fly line but quickly realized that his graphite rod had snapped above the cork handle. He looked frantically for the broken end before feeling the river current pull a couple inches of line from the bottom of his reel that was still securely attached to the butt end. He tucked the remaining piece of his rod under his left armpit and held it tight between his arm and upper body. Aaron pulled the line, which was still dangling from his reel, from the depths of the river with a hand-over-hand movement until he reached the leader.

Blake waded toward the middle of the river, trying to see upstream around the edge of the boulder to catch a glimpse of what was going on. He was able to lean over enough to see most of Aaron but not enough to fall into the depths of the river. Blake saw Aaron standing in a calm chest-deep pocket of water holding the end piece of the curled and frayed leader that had snapped from his tippet and flies.

"Where's your rod?" Blake asked.

Aaron grabbed the handle and reel that was tucked under his arm and held it up. Blake burst into laughter and said, "No way! Are you kidding me?" Aaron just stood there soaking in the river with a look of disgust on his face. "That's the *master* at work all right! You didn't break anything, did you?"

"Bones? No! Pride and one of my favorite rods? Yes!"

"You're killing me, man! That's too funny! I can't believe you fell off that rock! You're gonna make me piss myself!"

Aaron, overcome with the ridiculousness of the situation, succumbed to uncontrollable laughter along with Blake.

Blake motioned to the shore and said, "Swim over here, and get out of those wet clothes. I have a pair of long underwear and a fleece in my pack."

Aaron smirked at Blake, let out a sigh, and shook his head in defeat. He slowly waded over to the shoreline and stepped onto the riverbank with fat, heavy waders full of icy cold South Platte water.

The sun was starting to set, but the two friends were experienced outdoorsman, and hiking out of the canyon after dark was something they had done many times. Instead of hiking out wet and in discomfort, Aaron changed into Blake's spare long johns and fleece, while Blake searched the forest for fallen branches and bits of tinder to start a small fire. As Blake built the fire, Aaron rang as much of the water still trapped in the fibers of his soaked clothing out onto the ground and draped the damp garments on a small boulder near a makeshift fire pit that Blake had made using a few rocks. Aaron then turned his waders inside out and hung them from the low-hanging branch of a small aspen, hoping the inside would dry out a little.

Blake used a cheap plastic lighter, that he religiously carried in his pack, to light a small tinder bundle he had made using pine needles and dry grass.

Once the tinder caught fire, Blake stacked a teepee of small dry twigs around the flame. The fire grew quickly as Blake continued to feed the crackling flames with larger pieces of dry wood. Aaron sat down next to the fire and watched the embers pop off the tips of the flames. He held his palms out until the heat from the fire warmed his water-wrinkled fingers.

"Man, that feels good," Aaron said as he rubbed his hands together. "Thanks for the fire."

"No problem. Let's hang out for a while and get you dried off, then we'll hike out."

There was a moment of silence as Blake and Aaron enjoyed the fire along with the quiet ambience of the red and orange sky at dusk. It had been a fishing adventure for the books. They were going to walk away with a great story involving a cliff-diving incident that resulted in a broken fly rod. They had only seen two or three anglers the entire day, which was rare in this world-famous stretch of river. The weather had been great, they caught a few trout, and now, they were sitting in the great outdoors huddled around a warm fire listening to the sounds of the river rushing by.

Aaron broke the silence. "You know what we need?"

"What's that?"

"We need to go on a road trip this summer."

"That sounds good. I think it's about time we went back to Gunnison."

Aaron smirked. "Come on, man, we need to get out of Colorado. Let's go to Wyoming."

"I'm up for that. Where are you thinking?"

"I always hear guys talking about how great Grey Reef and the Miracle Mile of the North Platte River are. I was thinking we could drive out there."

"I like it. When we're done we could drive up to Jackson Hole and fish the Snake River."

Aaron grinned. "I like where your head's at. And after that, we could drive up into Yellowstone. We could camp out and fish the Fire Hole River like we've always wanted."

Blake shrugged his shoulders. "Well, if we're already that far north, we should go fish in Montana as well."

"Now you're talkin'," Aaron said. "But let's not stop there. Let's go for the gusto and finish the trip in Alaska."

"Oh, I like it," Blake said. "I'd give anything to throw a line in Alaska. Let's go for it!"

Aaron asked, "Hey, do you have a pen and something to write on?"

"I have my journal in my pack. Why?"

"We should write this down. Let's not just talk about it this time. We have a few months to plan the trip out but right now…tonight…let's commit to making this happen."

"I like it. Hold on. I'll get my journal." Blake opened his pack and took out a small wire-bound notebook that he used to keep track of the water temperature and insect life on the river during each trip. He opened the notebook and wrote *Road Trip* and underlined it. Underneath he started writing out the plans for the trip with a list of places they wanted to fish in Wyoming, Montana, and Alaska. The plan wasn't perfect, and there was quite a bit of fine tuning that needed to be worked out, but at least they were seriously working toward a long out-of-state summer fishing trip.

Blake and Aaron tossed around ideas for a few more minutes before packing up for the hike back to the Jeep. Aaron was still a little damp, but he was far better off than he had been. Blake took an empty plastic water bottle and filled it with river water to extinguish the fire. Once the fire was out, he pulled out a small flashlight from his pack, and they hiked out of Cheesman Canyon and headed back to the Jeep.

Exiting the Gill trailhead, Blake and Aaron could see dim lights at the pull off where they parked that morning. There was a man in a red Chevy pickup who had obviously been fishing Cheesman Canyon. He was parked next to the Jeep. The man was putting away his fishing gear in the bed of the truck. He had his radio turned up, and it sounded like he was listening to the news.

Blake walked up to the man and said, "How'd you do today?"

The man replied, "A lot better than the people out in New York."

"What happened in New York?" Blake asked.

"I'm just hearing of it now, and I don't have all the information, but it sounds like two commercial airliners were flown into the World Trade Center this morning."

"What? How could that happen?" Aaron asked.

"The news is reporting that it was a terrorist attack. Sounds like both towers collapsed, and thousands of people are presumed dead."

"Dear God!" Blake said.

"The radio in my Jeep doesn't work. Can we hang out while you put your stuff away and listen to the report?" Aaron asked.

"Sure, but I'm only going to be here a few more minutes. I've got to get home. I can't believe this happened this morning, and I had no idea."

Blake and Aaron huddled around the front driver's side door of the pickup trying to get as many updates as they could before they were forced into an information blackout during the long drive home. They were in disbelief as they listened to the report. Their seemingly innocent and fun-loving view of the world had now been turned completely upside down.

CHAPTER FIVE

Day of the Zeke

Over the next several days the world would learn of a Saudi Arabian-born Islamic radical named Osama Bin Laden. Bin Laden, along with his nefarious terrorist organization known as Al Qaeda, were the culprits responsible for the 9/11 attacks. Televisions in living rooms across America were tuned into 24-hour cable news outlets that documented the recovery efforts of the victims in New York City, the Pentagon, and the wreckage of Flight 93 that crashed in a remote field in Pennsylvania. The news aired live commentary and debates from military experts and politicians who gave their opinions concerning what America's response to these attacks should be. Fear and helplessness consumed many as they watched the coverage of emergency crews, National Guardsman, and civilian volunteers pour over the mounds of debris from the collapsed Twin Towers in search of survivors. Many in the United States braced themselves, as they believed this style of mass casualty attack was only the first of many. Some Americans chose to pray at candlelit church services in an attempt to cope with the tragedy. Other patriots attended uplifting concerts intended to raise money for the families of the fallen, while many young men and women raced to military recruiting offices for a chance to avenge the murders of 2,996 souls.

As for Blake and Aaron, they didn't know what to do. They had been so disconnected from anything going on in the world that they felt like they were getting a master's degree worth of foreign affairs education in just a few days. It was hard for them to piece together what was actually happening and why. They wondered if this was just a small band of outlaws that could easily be destroyed by the military might of the United States or if the perpetrators were soldiers sent from some obscure country they had never heard of and that, most likely, America would be at war with in the next few months.

Over the next couple weeks, news reports claimed that it was suspected that the Taliban, made up of extremist tribesman in Afghanistan, were assisting Bin Laden and Al Qaeda by hosting terrorist training camps and allowing the terrorist group to organize bases in their homeland. But the most significant transgression of the Taliban was the harboring of Bin Laden and his top officials in the rigorous caverns of the Tora Bora Mountains. With the Taliban unwilling to turn Bin Laden over to the United States, military action in Afghanistan seemed inevitable.

When they weren't at work or sleeping, the boys sat in the living room at Aaron's house watching the news and hoping to get the latest developments. Blake and Aaron had several discussions about what they might do if the nation went to war. Blake was eager to enlist in the military and fight while Aaron was more reserved and wanted more facts before jumping into such a life-changing decision. Mr. Grady, seeing the boys' anxiety, stress, and frustration, pointed out that there was nothing the two could do in the immediate future. He suggested that Aaron and Blake take a break from the torment they had been putting themselves through over the past couple weeks and go fishing.

Aaron felt like a day trip to the South Platte might be beneficial, and after a little coaxing, he persuaded Blake to go with him. The two decided to fish a stretch of the South Platte River known to anglers as the Dream Stream.

The Dream Stream was a three-and-a-half-mile section of the South Platte River that flowed out of Spinney Mountain Reservoir and emptied into another reservoir called Eleven Mile. This medium-sized stretch of gold-medal water was surrounded by distant mountains in a vast grass-covered valley that was divest of any trees or tall vegetation to interfere with the long casts and impressive loops that so many anglers loved to throw. The true nature of the river's nickname was earned from the large trout species that inhabited the depths of the nearby Eleven Mile Reservoir and migrated into the river throughout the year, giving anglers a chance at some of the best trout fishing in the state.

The next morning Blake and Aaron set out on the hour-and-a-half drive to the Dream Stream. Still craving the latest information about America's possible response to the attacks, not much was said between the two as they intently listened to Aaron's newly repaired car radio. While approaching a small rural gas station, Aaron looked down at his fuel gauge and said, "I better get a few gallons while I still can." Aaron pulled into the gas station and parked next to one of the pumps.

Blake pulled his wallet out of his back pocket to get some gas money. He handed a 20-dollar bill to Aaron and said, "Enjoy it, buddy. You won't be getting gas money from me for a while."

"Oh yeah? Why's that?" Aaron asked.

"I decided to join the military."

Aaron rolled his eyes. "I'll believe it when I see it. You can hardly go a week without fishing, let alone a year or however long it'll be before you're allowed to go on leave."

"Well, I don't know how to convince you, but I'm serious. I'm going to enlist next week."

Aaron, looking a little stunned, said, "OK, if you say so."

"Come with me," Blake pleaded. "We can enlist together, maybe serve in the same unit." Aaron stared out the window without answering. "Look, I can't turn my back on this. I need to help. I can't sit here and do nothing, while others are out there fighting."

"But what about our lives? Our plans? Did you forget about our trip to Alaska?"

"We'll still be able to do that when we get back. Please come with me. This might be the only chance we have to serve together. Just think about it."

There was a short uncomfortable silence until Aaron opened his door, and said, "Well, I guess I'd better gas it up so we can get out of here."

Aaron fueled up the Jeep, and they continued to drive west down the highway toward the river. The discussion about Blake's potential enlistment was not brought up again during the remainder of their drive. They traveled about 15 more miles until they made a turn onto a little backcountry dirt road.

Kicking up a cloud of dust and gravel behind them, they followed the road that cut through the wind-tormented golden blades of grass that covered the wild open prairie. The road eventually led them to a small dirt parking lot that was only a few yards from the famed stream.

Aaron pulled into the parking lot and stopped the Jeep. He stepped out of the car, stretched, and took a deep breath. "I think I'll throw steamers to start the day."

Blake said, "Go for it. I'm not messin' around. I'm going to nymph and catch me a big boy."

"Don't knock my streamers. Some of the biggest trout ever caught were hooked on a streamer."

A streamer was a fly that was tied to resemble a small baitfish. The pattern was fished on a large hook, attached to strong thick tippet, and stripped through the water to mimic a sick or wounded minnow. The goal was for the angler to strip the streamer through the water in hopes that it would trigger the carnivorous predatory instinct of a large trout, causing it to chase and eat the fly. Though not as productive as nymphing was on the Dream Stream, streamer fishing was Aaron's favorite form of fly fishing. There was just something so incredibly thrilling about the ferociousness of the take, that it gave Aaron a huge adrenaline rush every time he set the hook.

Aaron tied on a small brown-and-white streamer that was made with thin strips of dyed rabbit fur, while Blake set up a nymph rig using his typical two-fly method. When they were finished, they headed out to the river. Aaron wasted no time as he began slowly moving up river and casting across the water without spending any time sight fishing. Aaron's theory on streamer fishing was to always stay on the move, working as much water as he could until he came across the right trout at the right time that was willing to take the fly.

His technique was flawless as he cast across the river and allowed his streamer to sink near the middle column of various slots, channels, and seams in the current. As the fly would slowly drift downstream, the line would start to straighten as the current pulled it away. The streamer would begin to pivot back toward the middle of the river as it tethered around the tip of the fly road. This was known as the *swing* in streamer fishing vernacular. Aaron would retrieve the streamer by pointing the tip of the rod downstream, and then he'd strip the line through the water in short rhythmic bursts, which caused the fly to bounce and jig as it moved up the current. This action was designed to convince a large hungry trout that an easy meal was limping along just waiting to be devoured.

Aaron continued to cast the streamer and strip it back in this fashion as he slowly worked upstream. He looked across to the far side of the river and could see a long undercut beneath an overhanging bank that ran about 15 feet long. The bank had long burnt-yellow blades of grass that hung over the side like hay from a barn loft. The grass covered the gap between the bank and the surface of the water, which effectively camouflaged a deep seam under the water. Aaron cast straight across the river toward the front end of the deep slot. His streamer drifted for a couple yards near the edge of the bank before the tension from the current pulled the fly into a swing. As the streamer began to veer away from the bank, a long dark shadow began to emerge from underneath the grass. Aaron's heart pounded as it became obvious that the shadow was a large trout, and this large trout was following his streamer.

As the fly completed its swing, Aaron grabbed the fly line tight between his left thumb and index finger and began to strip two quick six-inch bursts followed by a full second pause. He kept a silent cadence as he repeated the stripping pattern, *Strip, strip, pause...strip, strip, pause.* With every strip of the line the fish would thrust its tail to keep pace with the streamer. Aaron began to breathe heavily as the trout shot up at the fly bumping its snout against it but not committing to a strike. The fish kept swimming closer to Aaron as he continued to strip the fly in an attempt to provoke the aggressive trout. Finally, with a snap of the trout's tail fin, it charged the streamer one last time. The trout drew closer. The massive back and dorsal fin of the fish breached the surface of the water like a rising submarine causing the water to form a smooth *V* in its wake. The trout opened its jaws, engulfed the streamer, and clamped down. The fish turned back toward the bank, and Aaron stripped the line firmly through the eyelets of the fly rod, which sunk the hook of the streamer deep into the trout's bottom jaw. Aaron lifted his rod tip high and could feel the sturdy pull from the solid hookup. The trout ripped line from Aaron with a strong run back toward the deep slot, but the heavy pound strength of the tippet coupled with the solid hold of the hook all but guaranteed that Aaron would land this trophy-class trout.

Blake could see Aaron fighting the fish and ran upstream to help. When he arrived, he could see Aaron reach down into the water and net a nice 22-inch metallic gold-brown trout. Blake yelled, "Nice one, man! Where'd you find him?"

"He was under the bank on the opposite side!"

"You want me to take a photo?"

"Nah, I'm good. I'm just gonna take a quick one of him in the net," Aaron said.

Blake was excited about the potential for catching a big brown trout so he set off to make a claim on his own fish. He walked upstream peering across the river in search of long dark shadows lurking under the canopy of the grassy undercut bank. He paralleled the river methodically studying every square foot of water that lined the opposite side. Blake took a half step and froze. He could see the tail fin of a large trout waving from under the bank. As his eyes adjusted to the shadow, he could see the unmistakable hooked kype from the lower jaw of a massive male brown trout. Blake slowly stepped up to the edge of the river and made a cast toward the dark rim where the ghostly shape of the trophy brown hovered. His first cast fell short by about a foot, but Blake let it drift by the brown anyway knowing that picking up his line prematurely might spook the monster. His second cast was right on the mark as his nymphs passed through the target zone perfectly. The strike indicator paused triggering Blake to instinctively set the hook. The line snapped tight, and Blake's heart rejoiced. He could feel that something wasn't right. The fish had not flinched, and the line was stationary. "Damn it! Hung up."

Aaron was just upstream and could see the bend in Blake's rod. He called out, "Got one?" Blake shook his head, and Aaron could tell by Blake's posture that he had snagged his flies on the bottom of the river.

Blake tried to figure out how to get his flies unstuck without spooking the trout. He began to make short tugs on the rod in hopes of unseating the flies. When that failed he began to escalate the length and force of the tugs. Suddenly, the river bottom released its hold on the flies, and they sprung violently out of the water, straight at Blake's face. He quickly ducked to avoid getting impaled by the airborne hooks, and the abrupt movement spooked the trout in the process.

Blake watched as the brown darted up river about 20 yards and settled in a deep pool at a river bend. Aaron was standing just above it. Blake said, "I just spooked a massive brown up toward you!"

Aaron searched the front end of the river bend expecting to see the trout swim out from the pool. Aaron called back, "I think he's still in this deep pocket. He never swam past me."

Blake jogged up to the bend and asked, "Can you see him in there?"

"No. It's too deep, but he must be in there."

They stood over the deep run searching for the elusive fish. After about a minute of gazing into the depths, Blake said, "That's pretty deep. The water's too murky to see the bottom."

"I'd just fish it deep and dredge that thing blind. Who knows? You might get lucky."

Blake moved his indicator up high on his leader and put an additional bead of split shot on his tippet. He went to work throwing short casts upstream of the bend and sinking his nymphs deep through the narrow channel of water where he believed the trout was hiding. The drift itself was not very long and did not require a complicated cast. Blake could simply lift the tip of his rod at the end of the drift and short stroke the rod tip to launch his flies back to the beginning of the run.

As Blake began the monotonous task of working his nymphs through the short pool, Aaron asked, "So, you're really going to join the military?"

"Yes, I am," Blake said with conviction. "I'm going to enlist in the Marine Corps on Wednesday."

Aaron nodded and stared blankly at Blake's strike indicator and fly line as they floated on the surface of the river. The boys remained silent as Blake made a couple more unsuccessful drifts through the channel. Aaron turned and started walking downstream.

Blake asked, "You OK?"

"I'm good. I'm gonna fish downstream a bit."

"Don't go too far. I might need your help netting this beast when I hook him," Blake joked.

Aaron laughed. "I won't hold my breath."

Aaron walked about 30 yards down river and suddenly heard Blake yelling, "Aaron, I got him! I got him!"

Aaron turned around to see Blake's rod bent over into the deep channel. He ran back up to the hole to assist. When he got there, he asked, "Is it that big brown?"

"I think so. When I set the hook I could see a bright yellow flash as he turned." Blake said as he continued to fight the fish. The fish seemed heavy and was using its weight to anchor itself on the bottom of the pocket. Blake said, "This thing is stubborn as hell. He won't come up at all. He keeps bullying me to the bottom."

"Walk downstream a little, and see if that brings his head up."

Blake walked down stream to try to put more pressure on the fish. The tactic began to work as the presumed brown turned and made a run downstream out of the deep pocket and into the shallow riffles. Blake began walking at a face pace alongside the river trying to keep up with the brown as Aaron ran down the river to get in front of the fish. The trout was making a strong run, and Blake could not get it to turn and come back. Aaron waded into the river about 20 feet from the fish and placed himself in perfect position to intercept the trout. He waited patiently so he could make a solid netting attempt.

The sun was shining in Blake's face, and he was having a hard time seeing where the fish had taken his line. He saw Aaron lunge toward the center of the river with his net in hand. Aaron scooped the basket into the river and raised it about a foot above water. All Blake could see was the dark silhouette of a large fish in the light nylon mess of the net. Blake raised both hands up in victory and yelled, "Yes! Nice net job!"

Aaron was quiet for a few seconds as he knelt down over the net examining the fish. Then he laughed. "Don't thank me yet!"

Blake, anticipating bad news, asked, "Why? What's wrong?"

"Nothing's wrong. If your intension was to catch this prize-winning *Zeke!*"

Aaron hoisted a large freshwater suckerfish up over his head. The brown and yellowish colored bottom dwelling slough was about 20 inches long with a broad width and bulging eyeballs. It had pink fleshy lips shaped like a suction cup that dangled about a half inch underneath its snout. The sucker would use its wrinkly oval mouth to suck the algae from the river bottom. If an angler was drifting his flies on the bottom of the river, it wasn't uncommon to accidentally hook into one of these slime eaters. Nicknamed a Zeke by Aaron and Blake, the sucker was considered a trash fish by most anglers and was a disappointing sight to Blake.

The story of how the sucker got the nickname *Zeke* went back a few years when Blake and Aaron were fishing the South Platte River near Deckers. There was another angler who had brought his black Labrador retriever to the river that day. It wasn't uncommon for anglers to bring their dogs to the river, but this particular lab was young and undisciplined. The lab would constantly get into mischief causing its owner to yell, "Zeke, come! Zeke, no! Zeke, drop it! Zeke, get out of there!" The owner repeated the obnoxious commands over and over until Blake and Aaron moved on to another spot.

Later that day, Aaron hooked into a small sucker. As he was reeling it in, he mockingly started giving it commands, "Zeke, come! Zeke, over here! Zeke, drop the flies!"

Blake got in on the action by calling out, "Don't listen to him, Zeke! Come over here, Zeke! Good boy, Zeke!" The banter continued until the release of the sucker back into the water.

Still holding the 20-inch sucker above his head and grinning from ear to ear, Aaron announced, "Ladies and gentlemen, I present to you the last trophy fish ever caught by Blake Jacobs as a *civilian*...behold, the mighty Zeke!"

"I'm not leaving for boot camp tomorrow, you jerk!" Blake said, shaking his head. "Besides, there's still plenty of daylight left to redeem myself. Now put that nasty thing back in the water, and let's get back to work."

Aaron held onto the sucker with one hand and gave Blake a sarcastic salute with the other. "Yes, sir! Right away, sir!" He gently tossed the suckerfish back into the river and began wading to shore.

Blake walked downstream to meet up with Aaron. Aaron stood in the river facing the tall grassy bank. Blake offered his hand to Aaron. Aaron grabbed onto Blake's wrist, and the two locked arms in a sturdy grip. Blake leaned back as Aaron stepped onto the grass and pulled himself up onto the riverbank. With their hands still clasped on each other's wrists, Blake asked, "How are you going to get by without me here to help you?"

Aaron looked Blake in the eyes and said, "I won't...that's why I'm coming with you."

"Are you serious?"

"Yep. The second you told me you were going...I knew I was, too. We've been friends for far too long for me to let you go by yourself." Aaron put his arm around Blake's shoulder. Blake did the same, and they embraced for a moment before Aaron said, "OK. Enough of this mushy crap, we've got some fish to catch."

They continued to fish for the rest of the day and well into the evening. With the certainty of their enlistments on the horizon, they cherished each cast they made and savored the thrill of every fish they caught as they gradually closed out a truly superb chapter of their young lives.

CHAPTER SIX

An Early Christmas

Four weeks after enlisting in the United States Marine Corps, Blake and Aaron reported for duty at the Marine Corps Recruit Depot in San Diego, California, for 12 weeks of Marine recruit training, more commonly known as *boot camp*. During their time in boot camp, Blake and Aaron had the Marine Corps values of honor, courage, and commitment drummed into them morning, noon, and night. They were tested physically and mentally by the constant onslaught of pressure and bedevilment of their drill instructors, who were tasked with purging the ideals of individualism from the minds of their recruits and replacing it with the belief that obedience, sacrifice, and love for God, country, and the Corps came before all else. The training was arduous and fatiguing but for two fit young men who had feasted on physical outdoor activity in their former lives, they excelled in the challenging environment.

Once they finished boot camp, they entered into the School of Infantry (SOI) at Camp Pendleton in Southern California. For aspiring infantryman, this is where the rubber met the road. This 59-day training course force fed Marines a steady diet of marksmanship, land navigation, open-field battle tactics, urban close-quarter combat techniques, and amphibious-assault maneuvers. Blake and Aaron were in heaven. They had never experienced anything like it in their lives. The two were enthralled by the inspiring stories they were told of legendary Marine engagements of past conflicts and humbled that they were being handed the torch of Marine Corps honor, sacrifice, and courage to carry with them during their time of service. Blake and Aaron were bursting with motivation and pride; they were truly infatuated with the Corps. They could not believe they were not only being entrusted to throw grenades, shoot belt-fed machine guns, and carry around rifles, but they were also getting paid to do it. For the first time in their lives, they felt like men.

After SOI Blake and Aaron were assigned to Second Battalion, Fourth Marine Regiment out of Camp Pendleton. Also known as the 2/4, this hard-charging, meat-eating battalion of Marines had a long and proud reputation of being among the best infantry battalions in the business. So much so, that they were nicknamed the *Magnificent Bastards*. Blake and Aaron were honored by the assignment and worked tirelessly to live up to the battalion's battle-tested reputation by keeping in excellent physical condition and training as hard as they could to improve their combat readiness.

Over the course of the next year, Blake and Aaron's hard work and dedication to the Corps resulted in promotions. Blake was promoted to Lance Corporal and Aaron earned the rank of Corporal. As satisfying as it was to be recognized for their hard work, Blake and Aaron thirsted for the chance to put their infantry skills to the test and be deployed to Afghanistan. Unfortunately for them, the 2/4 was not called up to join the fight against the Taliban.

In March of 2003 the United States lead a multinational military coalition and invaded Iraq with the goal of removing the country's dictator, Saddam Hussein, from power. Hussein was accused of being a supporter of Islamic terrorist organizations and also possessing weapons of mass destruction, which violated international law. The buildup of military forces was the largest organized since World War II with allies ranging from Great Britain to Poland. But despite the grand size of the invasion force, the 2/4 was not called into action, and the Magnificent Bastards would be forced to sit on the sidelines during this historic military engagement. Over the course of the next several months the 2/4 was stationed stateside at Pendleton, with orders to respond to any homeland terrorist attack or crisis that might arise in the U.S. For Blake and Aaron it was a disappointment as they watched, what seemed like, the rest of the world fight terrorism.

Although the invasion of Iraq was an overwhelming victory for the allied forces, the occupation was anything but. Slowly the local populace turned from being grateful for the liberation of their country, to frustrated and angry with the lack of basic services, like electricity and water, which were knocked out by the coalition's bombs during the invasion. A sectarian power struggle between the ethnic tribes of the region started to form as Sunni and Shias began fighting each other for control of the country. It didn't take long for the violence between the tribes to bleed over into insurgent attacks on coalition forces who were patrolling the Iraqi neighborhoods in an attempt to keep the peace.

A region that was becoming increasingly volatile and hostile toward the American occupation was an area of the Al Anbar Province near the city of Ramadi. For the Magnificent Bastards, this Sunni-controlled area of Iraq would be the calling they had been waiting for.

In December of 2003 the 2/4 was given notice that the battalion would be deployed to Iraq. The deployment was scheduled for February of 2004. With less than two months before they would be shipped off to Ramadi, Blake and Aaron were given nine days of leave. They immediately booked a flight to Colorado to spend those precious days with their family.

Three days after they arrived in Littleton, Blake and his mother spent the day over at the Grady house for an early Christmas celebration. The morning started out with Mr. Grady reading the story of Christ's birth from scripture. When he finished, Mr. Grady had everyone gather around and hold hands as he said a prayer of thanks for the blessings they had received in their lives and also prayed for God to watch over Blake and Aaron during their time in Iraq.

The Grady home was filled with happiness. Contagious sounds of laughter and cheer echoed through the rooms and halls of the house. With holiday music playing in the background, gifts were exchanged and humorous stories of past events were remembered. Mrs. Jacobs and Mrs. Grady teamed up in the kitchen to create a spectacular feast of prime rib, mashed potatoes and gravy, green bean casserole, buttered dinner rolls, and leafy garden salad. For desert they prepared hot homemade cinnamon apple pie to be served with a scoop of vanilla ice cream. The intoxicating aroma of the feast added to the joyful ambiance of the holiday gathering.

While Mrs. Jacobs and Mrs. Grady worked away in the kitchen preparing the meal, Blake, Aaron, and Mr. Grady talked in the living room near the Christmas Tree. Mr. Grady poured three glasses of whiskey. He raised his glass and made a toast, "To the greatest blessings in my life…the two of you. May God return you home safe to me and your mothers." Blake and Aaron raised their glasses, and they all sipped in unison.

Mr. Grady, looking a little choked up, cleared his throat and changed the conversation. "You guys should go fishing tomorrow."

"Blake and I were talking about that earlier," Aaron said. "We can't go anywhere too far…it would have to be a day trip somewhere."

"How about the Blue River?" Blake suggested. "It's close, and we could grab a beer and a bite to eat in Silverthorne afterward."

"That works for me. I haven't fished the Blue in ages," Aaron said.

The stretch of the Blue River that Blake was referring to, was a section that flowed out of Dillon Reservoir through Silverthorne, a little Rocky Mountain town about an hour and a half from Littleton. Although the fishing on the Blue was well renowned in angling circles, the town itself was not known as a fishing town but instead focused on catering to the thousands of skiers who visited the snow-covered mountain ski resorts.

The reason for the Blue's celebrity among anglers was due to a tiny fresh-water shrimp know as a *Mysis*. The Mysis Shrimp was only about the size of a grain of rice, but millions of them inhabited the depths of Dillon Reservoir. As the dam released water out of the tail end of the reservoir, thousands of these protein-packed shrimp were swept from the bottom of Dillion and dumped into the swift current of the Blue River. Trout were known to line up in the channels of the river allowing these white little crustaceans to flow right into their mouths. The fish would gorge themselves day and night on these calorie-filled morsels, and the result was some of the biggest and most colorful trout anywhere in the country.

As Blake and Aaron made hasty plans for their fishing trip, something caught Blake's eye. It was his mother. She was lovingly gazing at him from the kitchen. He could see that she was looking at him, not as a man, but as the once infant child that she use to hold in her arms. Her disquiet face told the story of her worry. A worry any mother would have. Blake walked into the kitchen and set his glass down on the counter. She faced him and he stood there looking adoringly at her. Her hair was greying. The crow's feet splintering from the sides of her eyes and the age spots on her cheeks, were the scaring remnants of a hard life of sacrifice. A sacrifice that Blake all too often took for granted but today, truly appreciated.

"Hi mom," Blake said as he held her hand, gently caressing it with his thumb.

"Hi sweetheart. Are you getting nervous?"

"A little, but everything's going to be OK. I promise you."

"I know it will. I trust that God will watch over you and Aaron."

"He will, I have no doubt," Blake said.

"No matter how hard things get, never lose your faith in Him."

"I won't," Blake said. "Mom? I'm feeling ashamed right now."

"Why?"

"Because I never took the time to tell you how much I appreciate everything you've done for me in my life."

"You don't have to, Blake."

"No Mom, I do. You've given up so much, working so hard so I could have a good life. You've never let me down. No matter how tired you were, you always made time for me. You hardly ever had the chance to enjoy your own life, because you were so busy making sure I could enjoy mine. And now, here I am going to war, and I realize…that I'm asking you to sacrifice even more, and that's not fair to you."

"Maybe so sweetheart, but life is rarely fair. Besides, you're my whole life. Everything I've done since the day you were born, I did for you. So when you say I didn't enjoy my life, you're wrong. I lived my life the only way I knew how and now I see you standing here and I'm so proud…so very proud Because of you, my life is a success and I wouldn't change it for anything."

"I love you Mom," Blake said as he wrapped his arms around her in a warm embrace.

"I love you too, sweetheart," she said, kissing him on the cheek.

"Hey everyone, dinner's ready," Mr. Grady called out.

They sat down at the Grady's dining room table with the rest of the family and enjoyed a delicious Christmas dinner. It was going to be the last time they were all together for a while, so the talk of politics, terrorism, and deployment were left out from the conversation. The family instead focused only on carefree topics and stories of pleasant memories, because despite the worries of the world and the stress of things to come, the family was together. For that moment...that perfect moment...their world was complete.

CHAPTER SEVEN

Last Cast Before Iraq

The next morning Blake and Aaron drove to the Blue River for one last chance to throw a line before they deployed to Iraq. They followed their usual routine of leaving before sunrise in hopes of arriving at the river at first light. Nothing put a damper on a fishing trip like fighting for pole position with a bunch of teenage snowboarders in a traffic jam, so it was important to get a jump on the early-morning ski traffic that would congest I-70 west of Denver.

The forecast called for light snow and temperatures in the low thirties. As far as Blake and Aaron were concerned, those weather conditions were perfect. It was going to be warm enough to get some decent action from the trout but cold enough to discourage lesser anglers from venturing out on the water.

As they drove along the interstate toward the river, they talked about fishing strategies and tried to ignore the anxiety that had been nagging at them ever since they received their orders to Ramadi. In seemingly no time, they arrived in Silverthorne.

A small mountain village tucked away in a spruce pine forest that was sheltered by the backdrop of large snow-covered peaks, Silverthorne was a home base for many ski adventurers in the winter and bikers, runners, campers, and equestrian sports enthusiasts in the summer. Blake and Aaron had only one interest in this outdoor recreation epicenter, and that was the Blue River.

The Blue River flowed north out of Dillon Reservoir and divided the small mountain town. Shops, restaurants, and concrete walkways lined both sides of the river for the first few miles. Although clean, rustic, and wholesome, one could often hear the sounds of a lively bustling town from the banks of the river. Not exactly a secluded stretch of water by any means, but if an angler wanted to lay claim to trophy-size trout, Silverthorne was the place.

Blake and Aaron pulled up to the river within sight of the dam and parked. They took a few minutes to stretch their cramped muscles from the long drive and to allow their lungs to adjust to the thin mountain air.

Blake surveyed the Blue before gearing up for the day. Just above the surface of the river floated a thin mist caused by the warmer water from the reservoir colliding with the frigid air. The crystal-clear mountain water of the Blue was flowing at a steady pace and looked to be averaging about ankle to waist deep in most places; the perfect flow for wading just about anywhere in the river.

Blake stood on a service road that ran along an embankment on the South side of the river. He diligently looked down over the gin-clear water in search of the red stripe of a rainbow trout. Almost immediately Blake found a bright red line swimming through the riffles. He looked over at Aaron who was tying a leader onto his line and said, "I already see a nice one. I have a feeling we're gonna have one hell of a good day."

Aaron, who had just finished cinching the tag end of a knot by pulling it with his teeth, said, "Don't just stand there, it's not like we'll have a chance to come back tomorrow. Get your ass in gear!" Blake clapped his hands with excitement and ran back to the Jeep to gear up.

The two spent most of the day fishing, never leaving each other's sight, just in case one was to stumble across one of the famed trophy trout. As the day wore on, the two had yet to spot any trophies, but they enjoyed themselves nonetheless, catching several large rainbows painted with the brilliant telltale colors of jade and crimson from the brush of the abundant nutrients that flowed through the currents.

As Blake walked the shoreline searching for a fish, the clouds broke for a brief moment exposing the light blue sky and allowed a beam of sunlight to cast itself onto the water. Aaron walked up behind Blake and said, "There's a nice one right there off the far shore."

"Where?"

Aaron pointed. "Just a foot off those willows. He was invisible until the sun hit him."

Blake looked over toward the willows and could see an orange metallic reflection holding in a shallow channel. "Looks like a brown. Haven't seen many of those today," Blake said.

"Well, go get 'em, turbo," Aaron said, as he turned and started walking away from the river.

"Where you goin'?"

"I'm gonna take a break. I'll watch you for a while."

Blake made a few casts to the far side of the river, but the brown trout rejected his offerings. He pulled his line in to change nymphs and studied the trout's movements before selecting a new fly pattern from his box. The trout slowly rose from the center column of the channel and poked his nose just above the surface. Blake looked through the ray of sunlight and could see that the sudden change in atmospheric temperature, brought on by the clearing sky, triggered a small midge hatch. "He's hitting the surface," Blake said.

"Yeah, looks like a little midge hatch just started."

Blake quickly rerigged his line to accommodate a small dry fly pattern that closely resembled the hatch. He made a smooth cast, and the fly gently touched down on the calm water. As the fly floated over the channel, the brown swam up underneath it and sipped the fly from the surface film. Blake set the hook. "There he is! First drift!" Blake said with a huge grin.

"Nice, man!" Aaron said.

Blake fought the brown trout for a couple minutes before cleanly netting it. He popped the hook from the trout's mouth, dipped his hand into the basket, and held the brown up with one hand for Aaron to inspect.

"That's not a bad fish," Aaron said.

"He's not long, but he's got a little girth to him," Blake said, while turning his hand, admiring his catch. Blake knelt down and gently released the trout back into the current. He stood up and shook the water from his hands. Then he walked over to Aaron, who was leaning on a large rock near the bank, and sat down next to him. Blake asked, "Ready for beers yet?"

"I'm gettin' there," Aaron said, as he stared at the river.

"You nervous?"

Aaron, knowing what Blake was referring to, said, "Ever since we got our orders."

"Me too. I've been thinking a lot about what our lives would have been like, if none of this ever happened."

"None of what?" Aaron asked.

"No 9/11…no Marine Corps…no Iraq."

"We'd probably be dead broke working some crappy minimum wage job and fishing every chance we got."

Blake laughed. "So what's wrong with that?"

"Who said there's anything wrong with it? Sounds like bliss, if you ask me."

Blake took a deep breath as he peered into the cold, crisp riffles. "It sure does."

The two sat in silence as the thought occurred to Blake that they may never fish a Colorado stream or river again. Who knew what was ahead? Neither had ventured outside Colorado before they joined the Corps, let alone a foreign country 7,000 miles away.

A deep anxiety fell over Blake's heart as he began to wonder if he may have put too much pressure on Aaron to join the military. What if something happened to him? Could he ever forgive himself? Blake gave a silent prayer: *God, please watch over us...please. Keep us safe. I'd give anything to have Aaron and me make it back home unharmed. Please, Lord...please.*

While Blake prayed, Aaron stood up. He cupped his hands over his eyes to shade the glare of light.

"See something?" Blake asked.

"It's hard to tell," Aaron said, as he squinted while he studied the water. "These fish blend in so well with this damn river rock I can't be sure."

Aaron picked up his rod and made a cast out toward the far bank. As his strike indicator and line floated down the river, Aaron lifted his rod tip high to pick up the slack in the line that was being pulled downstream faster than the indicator and smoothly rolled it back upstream into a perfect mend. The yarn indicator floated past a boulder that was poking about a foot out of the water and drifted across a fairly deep pocket. The indicator was swiftly sucked under the water, and Aaron thrust his rod tip up to set the hook. The line went straight as the sudden tension from the hookup snapped the droplets of water on the line into a fine mist. A long tubular rainbow trout shot out of the river and crashed back to the water.

"Whoa! Did you see that?" Aaron yelled.

Blake stood up with his jaw hanging open. "Are you kidding me? That thing's a monster!"

The enormous trout made a strong run upstream. Aaron's reel screamed as the line was ripped away. Aaron ran along the bank trying to keep up with the fish. He stumbled over the smooth river rock that lined the shore as he began making ground on the beast. Blake made a mad dash upstream to get into position.

Blake suddenly heard Aaron yell, "Shit!" Blake turned around and looked back downstream to see Aaron lying face first in an ankle-deep riffle. Aaron rolled over onto his side and held his arm and rod straight up in the air as the fish bullied more line from his reel.

"Get up! She's gonna break off!" Blake yelled, as Aaron struggled to get to his feet.

"I'm trying! It's slick as hell!" Aaron slid on the slick river bottom desperately trying to get back to his feet.

"Come on! Come on! Hurry!" Blake yelled, as he watched from the shore.

"Shut the hell up! You're not helping!" Aaron said, as he clumsily scampered back to his feet and ran down the river bank, reeling in as much slack line as he could in a wild attempt to catch up with the fish.

"Cross the river! Cross the river!" Blake yelled.

"What?!" Aaron yelled, as he could barely hear Blake over the rushing water.

"Cross! The! River! She's gonna break you off on this rock!" Blake pointed to a large boulder on the same side of the river.

Aaron looked up at the large rock directly in front of him. He was horrified to see that the trout had swum along the outside of the rock and crossed in front of it. His fly line was being pulled tight against the right side of the boulder. He could feel the vibration from the tension as his line scraped against the gritty granite surface while the trout continued to pull. Aaron knew, much more of this and the line would snap. He made a mad dash toward the center of the river, but with every step the river got deeper. He wasn't even halfway across, and the water was almost up to his chest. One more step and the water would be over the top of his waders. Aaron stopped for a second in search of another option.

"What are you waiting for! Go! She's gonna snap the line!" Blake yelled.

"There's a deep hole here! I can't cross without going under!"

"Just go for it! Trust me, she's worth it!"

Aaron stepped forward and sank several more inches. The arctic river water began to spill over the top of his waders and rushed down the inside. The sudden contact from the frigid water felt like a thousand tiny needles stabbing Aaron as the water went from his armpits to his feet. "Whoa! Holy shit! That's cold!" Aaron said, as he hopped forward through the deep hole on his tiptoes attempting to get over to the other side.

"Don't be a puss! You're already wet! Just get across already!" Blake yelled.

"Easy for you to say!" Aaron said, as he finally reached the far bank. Aaron ran bowlegged upstream as the water inside the bottom of his waders sloshed around.

The strategy of crossing the river worked, and Aaron was able to angle his line away from the rock, saving the leader and tippet from snapping. With the rock no longer protecting the fish, the trout swam upstream into a shallower stretch of river. The fish was tired. It stopped running for a moment and held steady in a soft current trying to recover. Aaron slowed down as well trying to reel in slack line and take a quick breather.

"Dude! You've gotta get pressure back on her, or she's gonna make another run on you!"

Aaron started wading back into the river trying to get close enough to the rainbow so he could get his rod tip and line directly over the trout's head. He knew he had to win this battle soon, or his frayed and tattered leader would finally break under the pressure. The water boiled just above the trout's head as she began to shake her head back and forth in a final effort to throw the hook. "I think she's almost ready, man! Get over here!" Aaron said.

Blake ran back downstream just enough to escape the trout's peripheral vision and then carefully walked to the river's edge. He pulled out his landing net and slowly waded up behind the trout, trying not to spook her. "Ready?" Blake asked.

Aaron nodded and brought his rod tip back toward Blake. The fish rolled over in the water and drifted downstream. Blake was in the perfect position to net this behemoth, but as soon as the trout spotted him, she thrust her tail and swam between his legs before he could get his net in the water. The trout began ripping line from Aaron's reel as she bolted downriver. Blake was now standing between Aaron and the panicked fish with the fly line between his legs. "Ahh!" Blake yelled. He lifted a leg as high as possible and threw his body to the side to clear the fly line and get out of Aaron's way. Blake, unable to catch himself, splashed facedown into the knee-high water. His waders began filling with the biting-cold river water. "Sweet mother of all that's good! It's freezing!"

Aaron laughed. "Serves you right, dickhead! Now, if you don't mind, a little help would be nice!"

"I'm up!" Blake called out, as he jumped to his feet and hustled down the shoreline to intercept the fish. He rushed as fast as he could to catch up with Aaron who was in hot pursuit of the out-of-control trout as it continued to strong-arm its way downstream.

"Hurry, Blake! Hurry!" Aaron yelled. "This line's gonna break any second, I can feel it!" Suddenly the trout turned back on Aaron and made a hard run upstream. The fly line went slack. Aaron began frantically stripping line through the eyelets of the rod to try to reestablish pressure on the trout. "Oh shit!" Aaron's line was whipping around like a wet noodle. The trout was swimming directly at Blake. With no time to get out of the path, Blake plunged his net between his legs and into the water. Aaron stripped the last inches of slack from the line just as the fish was about to maneuver around Blake's legs. The line went tight. The rod tip bent toward the water. The trout's snout was thrust up to the surface and suddenly...*snap!* The rod tip swished back toward Aaron; the fly line recoiled from the water, slapping him in the face. "Nooo!" Aaron yelled as he realized the leader had finally broken.

"Waaahooo! Yes! Hell yes!" Blake screamed. "I got 'er, dude!" Blake, barely able to lift the net from the water, showed a huge rainbow trout. With its head in the basket and Blake holding onto its tail, the trout was so big that only half of its monstrous body fit in the net.

"Yes! Yes! I fuckin' love you, man!" Aaron yelled with his arms raised over his head.

"I can't believe it! He swam right into the net just as the line snapped!" Blake said, as he made his way to the riverbank.

Aaron reeled in the remainder of his line while he waded upstream to meet up with Blake. Blake kept the fish trapped in the net under the water just off shore.

"Oh, my heart's racing. Let me see that beast," Aaron said, as he walked up to Blake. The trout was magnificent. A 30-inch hen with a near 20-inch girth. Her colors were so crisp, she looked like a painting. A work of art, airbrushed by nature and a trout that would make any other angler green with envy.

"That's a fish of a lifetime, right there," Blake said.

"I know it. I could live to be a thousand and never catch one better," Aaron said, as he huddled over the fish admiring her grandeur. He looked up at Blake and said, "Although, I never would've got her in, without your help. Damn, you're a good friend."

"Correction, I'm the greatest friend ever," Blake said with a smirk.

Aaron threw an arm around Blake's shoulder and said, "My best friend…my brother."

Suddenly a voice rang out. "Holy shit! That's the biggest damn fish I've ever seen!"

Blake and Aaron looked up to see an angler standing up on the service road. "What'd you hook that thing with?"

"If you come down here and take a photo of us with her, I'll tell you," Aaron said.

"Deal!" The man called out as he slid on his backside down the snowy embankment.

Aaron handed the man his camera and stepped back into the river beside Blake. "Hold her under her head, and I'll hold the tail," Aaron said.

Blake reached under the water and placed his hand gently under the rainbow. He looked over at Aaron and said, "On three. One, two, three." The two lifted the trout from the water, and the angler snapped a few shots of them. They put the trout back into the river and helped nurse her back to normal. She swam off unharmed, and Blake and Aaron sat on the bank, laughing and reminiscing about the crazy events that led up to them landing that unbelievable rainbow trout.

Their worries and anxiety over deploying to Ramadi were numbed for a brief moment as they forgot about the stress and tribulations of the war-torn world and took time to simply enjoy life.

CHAPTER EIGHT

The Ambush

The incoming rounds from small arms fire kicked up bits of dirt and pavement as they impacted the ground around the convoy. The high-pitch sound of zipping twangs caused by the unstable ricochets of copper-coated lead tumbling end over end after first skipping off of the street and against the light armor plating of the Humvee, flew past Blake's head. He ducked down behind the left front corner of the vehicle until there seemed to be a slowing of rounds impacting his position. He leaned out in front of the Humvee and targeted a window from a building on the right side of the street where he had just seen the muzzle flash from an insurgent's rifle. He took quick aim and raked a volley of rounds starting on the wall to the left side of the window, across the opening, and finished by punching the last few rounds through the wall on the right side of the window. Blake took cover just as the insurgents answered his shots with a blistering array of suppressive fire.

Doc Wells, who was closely hovering over the two injured Marines, yelled to Sgt. Tomlin, "We're sitting ducks out here! We need to move these two wounded inside that building while we wait for extract!" The building Doc Wells was referring to was a small single-level residence on the left side of the street only about 20 feet from the convoy. Although not bulletproof, the small house would provide some level of concealment while also getting the wounded Marines off the ambush point and out of the street.

Sgt. Tomlin took a quick look at the structure to size up its potential before yelling to Blake, "Jacobs! On me!"

Blake ran over to Tomlin who was kneeling near Doc Wells. Tomlin looked at Blake and said, "We need to take that building. You and I are gonna clear that thing, and then we're gonna set up a CCP for the wounded and defend it until the QRF gets here." A CCP was an acronym for Casualty Collection Point. CCPs were often set up when the amount and severity of the wounded would immobilize a small unit.

Blake nodded and said, "I'll take point, Sarge!"

"Roger that! I'm right behind you!" Tomlin said.

Blake crouched low and raised his rifle. He moved toward the front door of the building at a fast pace, and Tomlin followed about two feet behind him. As he approached the entrance Blake gave a swift kick to the closed front door of the house. The door flew open and slammed against the inside wall. Blake stepped into the opening and pivoted on his left foot making a hard turn as he entered and then pointed his muzzle at the hard corner that ran along the same wall as the entryway. Blake could see that there was nothing in the corner and immediately started to collapse his field of fire along the left sidewall all the way to the center of the back wall. Blake walked the path along the walls and visually cleared the adjacent space behind any piece of furniture that was capable of concealing a threat. Then he yelled out, "Clear left!"

Sgt. Tomlin, who had performed the same clearing procedure on the other side of the room, answered back, "Clear right!" They quickly moved through the house, systematically searching any area that could pose a threat to the Marines. Once the house was clear, Tomlin yelled to Blake, "Get back out there, and help Doc move the wounded!"

"Roger that!" Blake said, as he turned and ran for the entrance.

Blake ran past the opening of the front door as several enemy rounds hit the door frame, kicking loose pieces of wood and dry plaster. Blake looked up to see an insurgent running at a full sprint from the other side of the street toward the CCP. The combatant was holding an AK-47 and firing from his hip as he advanced on Blake. Blake quickly knelt down on his knee, raised his rifle to his shoulder, and hastily shot at the enemy with a burst of automatic fire. Several of the rounds thumped against the insurgent's chest pounding free small clouds of dust that were caught in the fabric of his shirt, causing him to collapse facedown. For good measure, Blake followed up by shooting another volley of rounds into the enemy as he lay on the ground. He took a deep breath and scanned the surrounding area for more threats before he ran out to Doc Wells. "Doc! We're ready to move the wounded!"

"OK, let's move Petting first! Grab a shoulder strap and his belt!"

Blake grabbed on to Petting's belt, then grabbed the right shoulder strap of his tactical vest. Doc Wells gripped the other side of Petting's belt and vest and said, "On three we lift him up and run him over to the CCP! We don't put him down until we're inside! Got it?"

"Got it!"

Doc Wells started the countdown, "Ready? One, two, three, up!" Blake and Doc Wells stood up from a kneeling position and lifted Petting off the ground. They rushed Petting through the doorway of the building and placed him deep into the front room.

Blake and Doc Wells ran back out to recover the second wounded Marine, as the other three surviving Marines laid down a wall of suppressive fire to support the movement. Huddled behind the armor of the Humvee, Private First Class Tyler Mayes engaged the insurgents with his belt-fed, fully automatic 240B machine gun, while the other two, Private Omar Holcomb and PFC Josh Garcia, used their M4 rifles to repel any enemy advance. The enemy attack intensified as more and more insurgent fighters showed up to take part. The right side of the street was rich with muzzle flashes.

After getting the last wounded Marine into the CCP, Blake went back out onto the street to support the other three Marines that were defending against the insurgent attack. Blake again crouched behind the cover of the damaged Humvee, but this time he stationed himself to the rear of the vehicle since Tomlin was covering the front of the motorcade from a window in the CCP.

Blake scanned his new sector of fire and could see a flash of rapid movement coming from down the street toward the rear of the motorcade. It was a vehicle. Initially Blake thought it might be the QRF, but as the vehicle got closer he could see that it was a small white Deawoo sedan. These sedans could be spotted nearly everywhere in Iraq, and one thing was for sure, this was not the QRF. The vehicle was driving at a high rate of speed right toward the Marines. Blake new this was a suicide bomber driving a VBIED right into them. Blake yelled, "Contact rear! Veebid! Veebid! White car! Six o-clock! 75 meters!"

Mayes quickly turned his attention from the right side of the street and targeted the sedan with his machine gun. The sedan's tires squealed as it made sharp serpentine turns to navigate around the debris from the battle. Once through the apex of each turn, the engine of the sedan would rev furiously building up the RPMs as the driver fanatically tried to close the distance and get close enough to deliver the payload of deadly ordinance. Mayes unleashed a volley of automatic fire, targeting the engine block of the sedan and then walked the rounds up and through the windshield, which shattered and splintered as the rounds ripped through the glass and cut through the thin aluminum skin of the sedan.

Without warning, the sedan exploded with a thunderous *kaboom* as the rounds hitting the vehicle prematurely detonated the explosives, sending a fiery cloud of dirt and debris over a hundred feet in the air. A vicious concussion from the blast's shockwave ran over Blake like a freight train, knocking him onto his back. Another cloud of dust engulfed the motorcade. Blake closed his eyes tight, ground his teeth, and shook his head attempting to fight off the sting of the blast. He choked from the rancid dirt in the air as he struggled to recover. Blake was exhausted, demoralized. He wondered if any of them would survive this relentless attack. Blake caught himself in this brief moment of weakness. He began to talk to himself, "Come on! You're a Marine! Get back in the fight! Get back in the fucking fight!" Blake snapped out of his daze. He got up on a knee and began calling to the other Marines, "Who's up? Sound off! Who's up?"

"Holcomb's up!"

"Garcia's up!"

"What about Mayes?" Blake yelled. "Mayes! You up?" Mayes didn't reply.

"He's over here...he's over here, Jacobs!" Garcia yelled out. "He's OK, just a little shook up!"

Blake, realizing the Marines were in serious danger of being overrun, yelled, "Well, get him up, and pick up a sector! They'll be coming again any second!" Just then the sharp hiss of an RPG warhead cut through the dust, forming a spiraling funnel in its wake and impacted the back end of the operable Humvee with a deafening explosion. The concussion from the blast threw Blake back to the ground. "Son of a bitch!" he yelled.

"Medic! Medic!" a voice called out.

"Who's hit?" Blake asked.

"Holcomb's down! He needs a medic!" Garcia answered.

Blake forced himself to his feet and ran through the cloud of dust toward the sound of Garcia's voice. When he arrived he saw Garcia and Mayes huddled over Holcomb, who was laying facedown, unconscious, and had a piece of metal shrapnel about the size of an axe blade sticking out of his back near his right shoulder. "Grab him, and fall back to the CCP! I'll cover!" Blake ordered. "Come on! Move!" Blake yelled as he raised his rifle and fired toward the right side of the street.

Garcia and Mayes each grabbed one of Holcomb's shoulder straps and dragged him toward the CCP. Blake fired until he ran his rifle magazine dry. Just as the bolt of his rifle locked to the rear, the curtain of dust lingering in the atmosphere settled back to the ground, exposing a clear view of the right side of the road. Blake could see the insurgent who had just fired the RPG at them. The combatant was down on one knee desperately trying to reload another warhead into the launcher. Blake pressed the magazine release on his M4, which dropped the empty aluminum magazine from the well of his rifle. He reached across his chest and pulled a fresh magazine from his vest just as the insurgent locked the warhead in place. Blake had to hurry. The insurgent raised the RPG and pointed it at Blake. Blake struggled as he hurried to place the magazine in the rifle. He fumbled with the magazine as it clanked against the well. Then it slipped. He watched the magazine tumble and fall end over end until it crashed to the dirt. Defenseless, Blake looked up at the insurgent who was peering at him through the scope of the RPG. With Blake solidly in his sights, the terrorist was a trigger pull away from ending Blake's life.

Blake stared with defiance as the insurgent pressed back on the trigger. *Boom! Boom! Boom! Boom!* A series of loud bangs reverberated from down the street as the insurgent holding the RPG practically disintegrated in a red mist. Blake quickly turned and looked down the street. It was the QRF; they had finally arrived. The turret on the lead Humvee was armed with a .50-caliber machine gun that was pummeling the right side of the street with heavy armor-piercing rounds. The fierce ordinance ripped through the exterior walls of the buildings that the insurgents were hiding behind, and the thunderous report of the machine gun suppressed the enemy's attack to almost a standstill. Blake had never seen anything so beautiful. He screamed out, "Oorah!" and then yelled back to the CCP, "The QRFs here!" He immediately took cover behind the downed Humvee, reloaded his M4, and watched as the Marine reinforcements dominated the battlefield.

Due to the devastation caused by the VBIED, the QRF's Humvees were blocked from driving up to Blake and the other Marines. The vehicles were forced to stop about 50 meters short of the CCP. A group of five infantrymen dismounted the Humvees and ran across the scarred combat zone to link up with Blake.

"Glad to see you saved a few for us," a familiar voice said.

Blake looked up. It was Aaron. "Damn it's good to see you, brother!" Blake said as he locked hands with Aaron and pulled him in for a hug.

"Well, as much as I'd like to hear all about what went on here, I think we'd best load up the wounded and get them the hell out of Dodge while we still can."

"Agreed," Blake said.

Sgt. Tomlin ran out from the CCP and approached Aaron. "Grady, it's good to see you."

"Likewise, Sarge. What's your situation?" Aaron asked.

"We've got a total of seven KIA. Four in the burned-up Humvee and three from this one. We've also got three critically wounded in that house.

I've got four Marines including myself to help with the extract and one corpsman who can accompany the wounded."

"Roger that, Sarge. We've got fire teams coming from all over to help with the recovery of the downed vehicles and the KIA, but they won't be here for a while. My lieutenant wants all the wounded evacuated immediately. The rest of us can stage with the remaining QRF vehicles and defend the motorcade until reinforcements arrive," Aaron advised.

"Sounds good, Grady," Tomlin said, as he turned to his Marines who were now crouched nearby waiting to receive instructions. "My guys, listen up! Me and Jacobs are gonna set security here and cover this flank, while the rest of you move the wounded to the QRF vehicles. Corporal Grady and his crew will provide overwatch while you carry the wounded. Stay alert, Marines, and keep your heads on a swivel…this thing ain't over yet!"

CHAPTER NINE

Hell Out of Dodge

The movement of the wounded across the gap was complete. Sgt. Tomlin and Blake were the only ones yet to be evacuated to the QRF vehicles. The insurgents' attack had subsided from the blistering engagement they had experienced earlier, but intermittent enemy rifle fire was still plaguing the battlefield. Blake waited for Tomlin's command to move to the QRF vehicles. Before Sgt. Tomlin gave the order, he took one more look across the street in search of enemy threats. He spotted movement. Something was crawling along the rooftop of a building on the right side of the street. It was a sniper moving into position. Tomlin called to Blake, "Jacobs! Hold!"

Blake, unsure why Tomlin didn't want to take advantage of the lull, said, "Say again, Sarge?"

"Just hold for right now!"

"Roger that!"

Tomlin could now only see the end of the sniper's barrel. The sniper himself, was concealed behind a short thick brick wall. The rifle was trained on the gap between the downed motorcade vehicles and the QRF. It was obvious that he was set up to ambush any Marine that tried to make the crossing. Tomlin maneuvered around the downed Humvee to get a good enough angle to take the sniper out.

The gunfire had all but stopped, and Blake looked across the gap toward the rescue vehicles. Everything was at a standstill. Blake could see Aaron looking toward him as the Marines took up defensive positions in anticipation of another attack. Blake thought, *What's taking Tomlin so long? Dammit! I could have run there and back about 10 times already.*

Tomlin continued to methodically cut down every conceivable angle, but he still could not maneuver enough to get a clean shot on the sniper.

Blake grew increasingly apprehensive. He was nearly out of ammunition. Could the two of them survive another assault? He couldn't believe Sgt. Tomlin hadn't given him the order to move. Blake thought it was unthinkable that they weren't using this precious time to evacuate. Anticipating that Tomlin would give the order for him to move any second, Blake got down in a crouched position and set his feet in preparation for the sprint across the gap. Seconds seemed like hours as Blake took long deep breaths waiting for the order. Then he anxiously checked back with Tomlin. "Sarge? We ready or what?"

Tomlin, who was about to call the QRF team on the radio to inform them of the sniper's location, yelled back, "Stand by! There's a sniper!"

Blake flinched and jerked forward. He felt his heart nearly burst from his chest as he had to catch himself from almost beginning his run across the gap.

Tomlin made radio contact with the QRF team and was describing the location of the sniper so they could put heavy fire on his position. The QRF opened fire with a thunderous roar from their .50-caliber machine gun. The impacts from the rounds were far off the target building, so Tomlin got on the radio and began calling for the QRF to adjust their fire. Blake could hear Sgt. Tomlin yelling, but he couldn't hear what he was saying over the noise of the QRF's gunfire. Blake wondered if he wanted him to start his run.

Tomlin shouted, "Jacobs! Wait!"

Blake turned and looked toward Tomlin, who was now focused on firing rounds near the sniper's position to help the QRF identify the location. All Blake could make out from Tomlin's command was his name. Blake yelled toward Tomlin, "Move? Sarge! Move now?" No response came from Sgt. Tomlin as he focused on shooting his rifle across the street. Precious time was being wasted. Blake needed to make a decision. He yelled out, "Moving!"

Blake's feet slid in the dirt as the bottoms of his boots fought to establish grip against the sand-covered blacktop. The weight from his helmet and tactical vest pulled his body forward as his tired legs struggled to keep pace. He took one pounding step after another. Blake felt like he couldn't run fast enough as each step felt like it took an eternity as the uncertainty of his decision to move still lingered. But Blake was nearly there.

The QRF's machine gun suddenly went quiet as the Marines reloaded the spent ammo drum. The sounds of war had ceased, and the battlefield was silent. Only about 20 meters to go. Blake's labored breaths wheezed as he pushed his exhausted body to the limits. *Crack!* An echoed shot rang out from across the street. Blake felt a deep pummel to his left thigh. The strike was so powerful that it knocked him to the ground in midstride. Blake tried to stand back up, but his left leg refused to move. He couldn't bend it or make it work at all. He watched in horror as the camouflage pattern on his brown and tan uniform pants began to soak and stain with bright-red blood.

Blake had been shot. He knew it was bad. The bright color of the blood meant his femoral artery had been cut. He had to stop the bleeding, or he'd be dead in a matter of minutes. He reached into his medical kit that was hanging from the front of his tactical vest and pulled out a tourniquet. Blake winced as a sharp burning pain ran down his leg like someone had poured molten lead into the wound. He ran the tourniquet over his foot, but as he pulled the tourniquet up toward his knee, he could see a large exit wound where the bullet had blown its way out of his calf. Strips of exposed muscle dangled from the bloody hole. He stared at the devastation of the wound. He couldn't believe what he was looking at. Blake couldn't recognize his own leg. He began to hyperventilate as he took shallow, rapid breaths. Blake was in danger of going into shock.

He heard a voice calling to him, "Come on, Blake! Snap out of it! Put the tourniquet on!" He looked up towards the QRF; it was Aaron. "We're coming to get you, buddy! But we've got to take this sniper out first!"

The QRF unloaded a barrage of gunfire and launched grenades onto the rooftop where the sniper was hiding. The display of firepower was awesome, nearly leveling the building. No doubt, the sharp shooter was killed in the bombardment. The show of force inspired Blake. He found a rebirth of energy and focus and pulled the tourniquet high into his crotch and upper leg. He pulled the nylon strap tight and cranked down on the windlass in an attempt to cut off blood that was pouring from his wound. Blake angrily yelled out in agony as the crushing pinch from the tourniquet was nearly as painful as the gunshot, but the application of the life-saving device seemed to be working. The blood loss was slowing.

After the Marine's counterattack, the insurgents mounted a counteroffensive of their own, and soon both sides were back to being fully engaged in a large-scale battle. Enemy rounds were being lobbed at Blake as he lay in the open street. Aaron yelled, "Hold on, Blake! I'm coming to get you!" Aaron looked over at PFC Garcia, who was closely nestled up beside him using the limited space behind the QRF Humvee as a sanctuary from the rapid gunfire, and said, "Cover me while I go get him!"

"Roger that, Grady!"

Aaron slung his rifle around his shoulder to free up both hands in preparation for the rescue attempt. Aaron made solid eye contact with Blake and said, "Here I come, Blake! You're gonna be OK!" Aaron's words echoed inside Blake's head. Aaron then yelled to Garcia, "I'm set!"

Garcia popped up over the hood of the Humvee just enough to see over the edge and also to get the barrel of his rifle in a good position to lay down suppressive fire. Garcia shot a continuous volley of rounds across the road to deter the insurgent's fire, then yelled to Aaron, "Move!" Aaron crouched down as much as he could and raced toward Blake.

Blake watched as Aaron ran over. He bladed his hands and swung his arms in a short slicing up-and-down motion like an Olympic sprinter as he completely committed to the rescue of his brother. It seemed like Blake was watching the event unfold in slow motion as rounds of ammunition struck the ground and kicked up small puffs of dust behind Aaron's feet as the insurgents tried desperately to get a bead on him. As Aaron drew closer, Blake could see the sunlight reflect a bright sheen of light off the layer of sweat that coated his focused and determined face. Aaron was nearly there, only a few more yards to go, when suddenly a bright-red mist burst out from the back of Aaron's neck near the base of his skull as an enemy's bullet finally found its mark. Aaron's arms went limp, and his legs collapsed. The momentum from his run carried his body forward as his limbs dangled lifelessly from his torso. Aaron crashed to the street in a chest-first slide with his arms draped at his side and his legs curled up near his waist.

The sight of Aaron being shot and falling to the ground horrified Blake. He yelled out to his lifelong friend, "Aaron! Aaron!" Aaron lay in the street completely still. Not a single twitch came from his body. His face was turned toward Blake. His eyes were still open, but his large black pupils, which seemed to stare right through Blake, did not tremble or move. Dirt and small pebbles of asphalt peppered his pale lifeless face. A dark red stream of Aaron's blood began to creep out of the wound, gently flowing around his neck until it settled in a large crimson pool that steadily expanded on the street beneath his throat and shoulders.

Blake began to slowly crawl toward Aaron yelling at him in a desperate attempt to get any kind of a response that might confirm that he was still alive. Blake's forearms slid against the slippery puddle of bright red blood that had flowed from his leg wound as he frantically tried to find enough traction to carry him closer to his friend.

As Blake crawled along the ground, he suddenly heard a series of thumps slapping against the street behind him. Alarmed, he turned his head enough to see that the sound was being caused by the flatfooted stomps from Sgt. Tomlin's feet as he ran toward Blake. Tomlin grabbed Blake by the shoulder straps of his tactical vest and rolled him over on his back. With Tomlin's back turned toward the QRF, he held onto Blake's shoulder straps and leaned back as he pulled with all his might until Blake's body began to slide against the street. With a bowlegged stride Tomlin began walking backward, slowly at first until he built up enough momentum where he could waddle at a fast pace and pull Blake to the cover of the QRF vehicles.

Tomlin, exhausted by the rescue, fell backward onto the ground as soon as the two had safely reached the security of the armored vehicles. "Medic! Medic!" Doc Wells ran over to Blake. "He's shot in the left leg, Doc. He lost a lot of blood out there," Sgt. Tomlin said before he quickly turned and ran back out into the street to retrieve Aaron.

When Tomlin reached Aaron he didn't even try to talk to him or check his injury as the insurgent gunfire escalated and began impacting all around him. With what little strength he could muster, he squatted down and grabbed Aaron's shoulder straps. With one last burst of energy, Tomlin roared out in pain as he straightened his exhausted legs and pulled Aaron up enough to drag him from the battlefield. With each strained step closer to safety, the smoldering pain from the lactic acid burned more intensely in his muscles. Unwilling to quit, Tomlin forced his legs to endure the suffering until he reached the vehicles.

Tomlin again fell to the ground after reaching safety. He crawled over to Aaron to examine his wound and could see that the gunshot that pierced the back of his neck was fatal. The base of Aaron's skull had been severed from his spine, and only Aaron's skin and the muscle tissue from his neck held his head to his shoulders.

Doc Wells, who was working on Blake's leg, took a quick pause and looked over at Tomlin for an update on Aaron's condition. Tomlin made eye contact with Doc Wells and simply shook his head to indicate that Aaron was gone.

After Blake saw that Aaron had been pulled to safety, he insisted that Doc Wells care for Aaron before attending to his injury. "Doc, I'm OK. Aaron needs help bad. Help Aaron first! Please Doc…he's hurt bad!"

Doc Wells ignored Blake's appeal and continued to put pressure on Blake's wound. Blake began rolling from side to side to discourage Doc Wells's treatment. Blake screamed out in frustration, "Aaron first! Doc, you've got to help Aaron first!"

Doc Wells forcefully grabbed Blake by the shoulder straps of his tactical vest and violently shook him. "Jacobs! Listen to me!" Blake, stunned by the by the abrupt jolt, locked eyes with Doc Wells. "He's gone! Aaron's gone! And if I don't get this bleeding under control you're gonna be gone, too!"

Blake felt numb. He dropped his head back, and his body went limp. He stared up at the sky as if he was in a trance. The news of Aaron's death sapped the remainder of his physical strength and crushed his soul.

As Blake lay in the dirt, despair fell over his heart. He began to shiver as he felt a sudden chill race through his body. It was as if he was lying naked on the cold concrete floor of a subzero meat locker. His lips started to quiver uncontrollably. He looked up at Doc Wells and said, "I'm freezing cold, Doc."

"You've lost a lot of blood…too much blood. Try not to speak, and just hold still."

CHAPTER TEN

Blake's Darkness

Shortly after Aaron was killed, Marine reinforcements arrived on the scene and repelled the insurgent attack. Blake was evacuated from the battlefield and flown via helicopter to a military hospital in Ramadi where his serious condition was stabilized. He was then flown by medical transport to a U.S. military base in Germany where he spent two weeks undergoing emergency surgery on his tattered leg. From Germany he was flown to the Walter Reed Army Medical Center in Washington, DC, where he had several more surgeries to repair the damage caused by the sniper's bullet that entered his left thigh and spiraled down ripping muscle, severing nerves, and slicing veins until it violently exited his calf.

Aaron's funeral took place three days after his body was returned to the United States. He was buried with full military honors in a national cemetery in Lakewood, Colorado. After the funeral, Mr. and Mrs. Grady were eager to visit Blake at the medical center while he recovered. Blake, still suffering from the grief of Aaron's death, refused to see visitors or talk with anyone by phone other than his mother. Even though Blake kept in regular communication with his mother, he was very elusive about the details surrounding his injury and Aaron's death. He mainly updated her about his progress and asked her to relay his thanks to all the well-wishers back in Colorado.

After the final reconstructive surgery, Blake spent three months at Walter Reed conducting physical therapy and learning to walk again. While in recovery, Blake received a letter from Mr. Grady. Blake kept the letter on his nightstand, not wanting to read it, but unwilling to throw it out.

Every evening as Blake laid in his bed, the hospital clergyman, Chaplain McKinnon, would make his rounds, checking on the wounded. Although each day Blake respectfully refused to speak to Chaplain McKinnon, each day he would return to offer his ear if Blake wished to talk.

One evening, Chaplain McKinnon stopped by. "How are you doing, Blake?"

"I'm fine Chaplain, thank you," Blake said.

"Mind if I sit?" Chaplain McKinnon asked already sitting down in a chair next to Blake's bed.

"Actually, yes. I'm about ready to turn in."

"I'm sure a couple minutes of your time won't hurt. You know, I've been watching you for a while."

"Oh, really?" Blake asked.

"You don't talk to anyone, you rarely make any phone calls and that unopened letter has been sitting on your nightstand for a couple weeks now."

"So?"

"So, I read your file, and most people in your position would be having a tough time. I thought you could use some company."

"Thanks Chaplain, but I'm getting along just fine," Blake said.

"Well, at least allow me to say a prayer for you."

Blake rolled his eyes and sneered. "That's OK, Chaplain. God's done enough, thanks."

"Do you blame God for what happened to you?"

"Yes! Is that so surprising?"

"A little. Why?"

"I'll tell you why. I've been a believer my whole life, so was my friend. We went to church regularly, we led good lives, and where did it get us. He's dead and I'm crippled. Do you know that I would get on my knees every

70

night before a mission and pray to Him. Not that He make me a hero, or that I'd be rich someday; I only asked for His protection and protection for my friend. Was that too much to ask?" The Chaplain remained silent. "Well, apparently it was."

"I'm glad to hear your friend was a believer."

"Don't give me that whole, *he's in a better place* speech, Chaplain. His life was cut short. He'll never have the life that he deserved. And his parents? How do you think they feel about him *being in a better place?*"

"I don't know. I haven't spoken with them. Have you?" Blake didn't answer. "Well, maybe you should." Blake looked at the envelope on the night stand. "God has a plan for all of us, Blake. Most of the time we don't understand His plan, especially when bad things happen to us, but turning your back on Him isn't the answer."

"I didn't turn my back on Him, He turned His back on me."

"I realize it might feel that way, but believe me, God loves you. And although He didn't answer your prayer the way you wanted, He was with you during that ambush."

"Well, a lot of good it did. Now, if you don't mind, I'd like to get some rest. Tomorrow I've got a big day of learning how walk again."

"Of course," Chaplain McKinnon said standing up from the chair. "I'll say that prayer for you tonight, and hopefully, when you're ready, you'll say one of your own."

Chaplain McKinnon walked off while Blake stared at Mr. Grady's letter. He picked it up and opened the envelope under the light of a small reading lamp he had attached to his hospital bed. Inside was a note from Mr. Grady and an old photograph. The letter was handwritten directions to Aaron's grave at the national cemetery with a note that simply read:

Dear Blake,

When you're ready, we'll be here for you.

We love you,

The Grady's

Over time, Blake's wounds slowly began to heal. The physical therapy helped to strengthen his leg, but the damage had been so great that it would be a few more months before Blake could walk without the assistance of a cane.

On the day of his release from Walter Reed, Blake quietly booked a flight from Washington, DC, to Denver. When he arrived, Blake rented a car at the airport and set off to the national cemetery in Lakewood.

Blake stopped by a liquor store on his way to buy a bottle of Jonnie Walker Red Label whiskey, a drink he and Aaron were allowed to sample during special family occasions as teenagers and a drink that the two shared from time to time as young adults. He bought two clear shot glasses along with the whiskey, in preparation for a ritualistic last drink at the grave of his fallen brother.

Blake pulled through the gated entrance to the national cemetery where Aaron had been laid to rest. He parked off to the side of the blacktop roadway that weaved through the cemetery. He pulled his cane from the passenger side seat as he stepped out of the car. Blake reached back into the front cab to retrieve a small brown paper bag that contained the bottle of whiskey and the shot glasses. He gazed across the field of ivory-white tombstones that lined the cemetery in perfect rows. He looked down at Mr. Grady's handwritten directions and scanned the names on the tombstones until he found the final resting place of his beloved friend.

Aaron's tombstone was made of a white and gray marble. It was a traditionally shaped slab that was about 18 inches across and two-and-a-half feet tall. It was about four inches thick with an arching top. A Christian-style cross was etched near the top of the marker. Below the cross, was an inscription:

Cpl. Aaron Grady
US Marine Corps
Iraq
March 7 1983
April 19 2004
Purple Heart
Psalms 104:10

Blake recognized the Bible verse scribed on Aaron's tombstone. It was Mr. Grady's favorite scripture verse. Blake had heard Mr. Grady recite the passage several times over the years. It read:

He makes the springs pour water into the ravines; it flows between the mountains. (Psalms 104:10)

The thought of the verse prompted Blake to reminisce about the outdoor adventures they had gone on as children. Blake reached into his back pants pocket and pulled out the worn three-by-five-inch photo that had accompanied Mr. Grady's letter. The partially faded picture was of two ten-year-old boys standing on top of the world with their arms draped over each other's shoulders, with the beauty and grandeur of the Continental Divide in the background. This photo was taken on a day that Blake would never forget, the day he and Aaron first hiked to Silver Dollar Lake; the day they were introduced to fly fishing.

Using his upper body strength to compensate for his weakened left leg, Blake braced himself against his cane and slowly knelt down on his right knee. He leaned the photo up against the base of Aaron's tombstone and stabilized it by slotting the bottom edge of the picture between the short blades of freshly mowed grass. He gently sat down on the grass and placed his cane down on the ground. Blake reached into the paper bag and pulled out the bottle of whiskey along with the two glasses. He poured the liquor in each glass. Then he rested one on the ground next to the photo and held the other in his right hand. Blake sat in silence just staring at the photo and holding the shot glass.

Blake tried to remember the details of all their fishing adventures from the day they hiked up to Silver Dollar Lake to the last cast at the Blue River before they deployed. One hour turned into two, and in seemingly no time, four hours had passed. Oblivious to the passage of time, Blake just sat there with a stoic look on his face. Soon the sun began to set, and a caretaker for the grounds walked up to Blake and said, "Sir? Sir? Excuse me, sir, but the cemetery's closing for the day."

Blake looked up for the first time in hours and said, "OK. Thank you. Do you mind if I take just one more minute?"

"Not at all," the caretaker said, as he turned and walked away.

Blake raised his glass of whiskey and drank the shot in one swift gulp. The whiskey burned as it flowed down his throat, but Blake did not wince from the coarse taste as he had every other time. He left the photo next to the grave but picked up the bottle and his cane. He stood up, using the cane to support his frail body, and slowly hobbled back to the car.

He started to pull away but stopped to take one more look. He took a deep breath and then took his foot off of the brake and slowly drove toward the cemetery exit.

Blake drove south down the highway heading in the direction of his home. He drove past vast open fields that backed up to the Colorado foothills. He felt an abrupt feeling of anxiety come over him. His leg began to ache forcing him to jostle in his seat for a more comfortable position. Blake thought that listening to the radio might calm his nerves. His hands started to quiver as he tried to turn the knobs on the stereo. He took a deep breath and ran a hand across his face from his forehead down to his chin to help relax his anxiousness. A loud and sudden honk came from the left side of the car. Startled, Blake sat straight up in his seat and yanked the steering wheel hard to the right as he realized he had slowly veered into the next lane nearly striking another vehicle. Blake yelled out in frustration, "Damn it! That's it!" He pulled the car over on the shoulder of the highway. He exhaled and rested his head on the steering wheel.

He stayed in that position for a minute before he picked his head up and looked out at an open field of grass. Blake stared at the bottle of whiskey sitting on the front passenger seat as he pondered what he might do next. He grabbed the bottle and his cane and slowly got out of the car. Blake staggered into the field in the direction of the foothills, until he lost sight of the highway. He found a flat area among the grass and carefully sat down, placing his cane and the bottle beside him.

The sun had fallen. A still light blue glow silhouetted the mountains of the Front Range. The dim light that remained to the West was quickly swallowed up by the cool blackness of night to the East. The flickering brilliance of light emanating from the countless stars, dominated the moon-deprived sky. The calm hush of the night tamed the wild sounds of the field; only the defiance of a light breeze blowing against the grass broke the silence.

The breeze brought with it a brisk chill that swirled in the thin air. Blake folded his arms across his body and rubbed his hands against his torso as the cold crept up his spine causing him to shrug his shoulders to insulate his neck. His leg throbbed as the damaged nerve endings registered messages of sharp pain throughout his impaired limb. Blake was immediately reminded of the cold and pain he felt when he was lying, near death, on that battle-scarred street in Iraq.

Trying to blot out the memory of that day, Blake forced his eyelids shut. This only made things worse as his mind conjured up the vivid image of Aaron's pale lifeless face staring at him. Sounds from the battle now haunted him as yelling, gunshots, and explosions echoed in his mind. The more Blake tried to stop the overpowering recall of that day, the more intense it became. Soon Blake was reliving the moments right before Aaron's death, playing out possible scenarios where he could have done something different that might have saved his friend's life. Blake processed the information over and over. The only possible synopsis that resulted in Aaron surviving the battle was if Blake would not have gotten himself shot. Then there would have been no rescue attempt by Aaron, which meant that Aaron would still be alive; it was that simple. Blake kept internalizing the emotional results of his conclusion. He was the one to blame. His eagerness to retreat prematurely from his position got him shot, causing Aaron to leave the safety of cover to rescue him. Aaron died trying to rescue him. Aaron died young and alone in a foreign land because of *his* decision…his stupidity…his cowardice.

Blake buried his face in his hands. He began to sob uncontrollably at the realization that his recklessness killed his only brother. Blake's audible cry carried across the field as the emotions of pent-up guilt, that he had been carrying since Aaron's death, poured out of him. "Why didn't I wait? Why couldn't I have just waited?" Blake yelled out.

The pain Blake felt in his heart was unlike anything he had ever experienced. He was filled with an emptiness and torment that was unbearable. He had never felt so alone and didn't want to face another minute, let alone another day. He questioned how he could possibly live with what he had done. Blake needed to stop this feeling of anguish that was spreading through him like a wildfire.

He could feel the fresh aftertaste of whiskey still stinging his tongue and throat. He looked down at the bottle lying in the grass. Blake picked up the bottle and unscrewed the cap. He took a mouthful-sized swig. Blake held the liquid in his mouth for a brief moment as he realized that drinking it was an acknowledgment that he lacked the strength to face his guilt. He lowered his head and looked to the ground in defeat as tears flowed from his eyes. He slowly shut his eyes as he swallowed the whiskey. Blake could feel the harsh warm liquid cascade down his throat. With his hands shaking uncontrollably, he immediately placed the bottle back to his lips and took another drink.

Blake guzzled the whiskey, and it slowly began to cover up the pain in his heart. His senses were dulled and his ability to focus was severely altered. Blake's drunkenness did not make him feel good, but it made him feel different, and anything different was better than what he was feeling before. Blake kept drinking. The more inebriated he became the more he wanted to drink.

Finally, the bottle was more than half empty. The world seemed to be spinning out of control. The stars streaked across the sky together in one long circular motion as though he was lying on his back on top of a carousel. Blake felt dizzy, his head started to pound, and his breathing accelerated as he could feel the earth beneath him tumble like a rough sea. Blake spun and collapsed facedown. He pushed himself up slightly just before heaving the contents in his gut onto the dirt.

Blake vomited over and over as his body rejected the brutal treatment he had put it through. After the last purge, he gasped for air. Mentally and physically exhausted, Blake rolled over onto his back. Breathing heavily, he looked up at the night sky and began to succumb to the depressant effects of the alcohol. He could feel himself passing out. His vision blurred, and his eyelids became heavy before Blake went unconscious.

Blake woke up the next morning around 10:00 am. He was still lying in the field. He was severely dehydrated, and his lips were dry and chapped. His throat stung when he tried to swallow, like his gullet was lined with scales. His eyes and cheeks were crusted over with a thin arid saline film, left over from his dried tears. His head was pulsating with a deep pounding headache that was being inflamed by the blinding sunlight beating down on him. Blake struggled to sit up. He felt weak and disoriented. He held his hand up and squinted to blot out the piercing rays of the sun.

Once his eyes adjusted, he looked around for his cane. Blake found it lying just out of reach in the nearby grass. He leaned over and struggled as he pulled the cane toward him and placed the base of it on the ground. Blake, already feeling completely fatigued, pulled himself up to his knees. From there, he took a small pause to give his body time to search for a little more energy. Once he felt his strength was recharged enough to attempt to stand, Blake moaned as he forced himself onto his feet.

Blake labored as he lurched back across the field toward his car. When he arrived, he was greeted by a red colored *Abandoned Vehicle* warning placard which was tied to the radio antenna, courtesy of the Colorado State Patrol. The placard said that Blake had 48 hours to remove his car from the side of the road or it would be towed. Blake thought, *Well, at least they didn't tow it. That'd been one hell of a walk home.*

He removed the placard and threw it onto the floorboard. Blake started the car and pulled onto the highway and started to head home. His leg began to ache. It had been over 24 hours since he had taken any pain medication. The agony of his leg wound brought back the emotional pain he was feeling the night before. Blake's throat was dry from dehydration, but he didn't thirst for a drink of water. He longed for the quenching distraction from his emotional suffering and guilt that he could only get from alcohol.

Blake made a detour and pulled into the parking lot of the first liquor store he saw. He walked into the store to buy more whiskey. Filthy and still reeking of booze, Blake walked through the store. His only care was to rid himself of the cold brutal darkness that festered in his heart.

Over the next several months Blake fell into a deep depression, in which he could not recover. The more alcohol he drank, the less effective it became. He was afraid to fall asleep, as the nightmares of his self-imposed failure on the battlefield tormented his dreams. His guilt and loneliness soon turned into hate and rage. His drunken anger pushed away well-meaning friends and relatives who wanted nothing more than to help him conquer his despair. He became recluse, not wanting to talk or visit with anyone. Still living with his mother, Blake spent most of his time locked in his room unwilling to leave the house except to resupply his ever-dwindling inventory of prescription drugs and alcohol. His disability checks from the military funded his drinking addiction, and the abuse of the prescription numbing agents that were supposed to relieve the physical pain of his wound, were instead used to supplement the effects of the whiskey. With no purpose left in life, Blake wanted to die.

On the one-year anniversary of Aaron's death, while his mother was at work, Blake walked into the living room. He opened a drawer of a wooden hutch and stared down at a stainless steel short-barrel snub-nose .38 caliber revolver that Blake's mother kept in the house for protection. He picked up the pistol and opened the cylinder to confirm the weapon was loaded. Blake tipped the gun back and let the hollow-point bullets slide from the cylinder and drop into his hand. He inspected the rounds by rolling them around in his palm. Satisfied, he slowly placed each round back into the cylinder. He closed the cylinder until it locked shut. Blake stood in the living room for a brief moment as he felt the weight of the pistol balance in the palm of his open hand.

Blake walked back to his room where he had pieces of memorabilia from his past scattered all over. His floor was littered with pictures of him and Aaron as young boys to their adventures as young men. A pile of fly boxes, journals, military patches, coins, and photos from their time in the Marine Corps were spread across the floor. Blake sat down on his bed and placed the pistol beside him on the mattress. He picked up a half-empty bottle of whiskey and took a large gulp as he scanned the mounds of memories that chronicled the story of their life, a happy life…a life before this miserable darkness. He reached down to the floor and picked up a photo of him and Aaron holding a beautiful 30-inch rainbow trout that Aaron hooked and Blake netted on the Blue River right before their deployment to Iraq. That was the last fish Aaron ever caught, the last fishing trip they had ever taken, and the last time Blake could remember truly being happy.

A tear escaped the corner of Blake's eye and rolled down his cheek as the immeasurable pain and loneliness in his heart finally smothered the last dim flame of life from his spirit. The teardrop dripped off the edge of his chin and landed like a raindrop on the photo. Blake opened his fingers and let the photo gently parachute to the floor until it settled among the other scattered photos and documents.

Blake picked the pistol off of the mattress. He cocked the hammer back with his thumb and listened to the cylinder twist in the frame as a chambered round aligned with the barrel when the hammer locked back in place with a *click*. He pressed the cold end of the barrel against his right temple. Then he slowly placed his right index finger inside the trigger guard of the revolver and touched the top pad of his finger against the polished steel trigger. His hand began to shake as he searched for the courage to permanently end his pain. Blake squeezed his palm and fingers around the handle of the gun as a stream of tears flowed from his eyes. He began to put pressure on the trigger anticipating that at any moment the concussion from the blast of the bullet would silence the screams that haunted his mind. His finger molded around the thin strip of steel as the trigger began to give way. Without warning…a crack rang out. *Bang!*

CHAPTER ELEVEN

A Moment of Redemption

*B*ang! *Bang! Bang!* Blake shuddered when he heard the loud sound and took a deep breath. He frantically looked around the room. He was still alive. The gun had not gone off yet. *Bang! Bang! Bang!* Blake heard a voice coming from outside the house. "Blake, you in there?" It was Mr. Grady knocking at the front door. "Blake, I'm going to the cemetery later today to visit Aaron. You're welcome to come with me if you'd like." With his face still drenched in tears, Blake sat in silence hoping that Mr. Grady would just leave. "Blake, I know you're in there. Please talk to me."

Afraid to respond, Blake lowered his head in shame and looked at the floor. As he looked down, something caught his attention. It was an opened notebook, his old fishing journal. On the top inside cover there were two familiar words scribbled in pen, *Road Trip.* Below those words was the list of fishing destinations that he and Aaron came up with during their trip to Cheesman Canyon on September 11, 2001. Blake reached down and picked up the journal. He stared at the list of places that he and Aaron had planned on fishing but now would never visit. He gently rubbed his thumb over the words, hoping that the contact would somehow reconnect him with that lost moment in time.

Mr. Grady called out, "Blake, if you can hear me...just know that I love you, son." Mr. Grady slowly turned and walked back toward his home.

Blake took a deep, quaking breath, as the loving words of Mr. Grady shot through him like an electric current, reviving a shallow pulse in his otherwise lifeless heart. Mr. Grady deserved to know the truth. He needed to know that Blake was the reason his son died. Blake abruptly stood up. He ignored the pain in his leg and ran out to the lawn. He yelled out to Mr. Grady, "I'm sorry! I'm so sorry!" Mr. Grady turned to see a frail, dirty, malnourished shell of a once strong, proud, and confident young man standing before him. "It's my fault! It was all my fault," Blake said as he lowered his chin to his chest and began to cry.

Mr. Grady walked up to Blake and placed his hand behind Blake's neck and pulled him into his shoulder. He gently placed his other arm around Blake. Mr. Grady tried to soothe Blake by softly stroking the back of his head. Blake, choking on his own emotion, whispered, "I killed Aaron. I killed your son."

Mr. Grady said, "Oh Blake, I've read the official report of what happened. I've talked to Sgt. Tomlin. Let's get one thing straight…you didn't kill Aaron; the war killed Aaron. Aaron gave his life trying to save you, and for that I am *so* very proud of him. Don't let his sacrifice be in vain. Don't allow his courageous act to become meaningless." Mr. Grady took a deep breath. "And if you care about me at all…don't make me suffer through the loss of another child."

Blake pulled away from Mr. Grady and looked at him with swollen eyes. "What do you mean?"

With warmheartedness, Mr. Grady explained. "I've helped raise you since you could first talk. You've been a part of my life for as long as I can remember. You're not my blood, but you're just as much my son as Aaron is…and I would die if I lost you too."

Mr. Grady pulled Blake back into him and hugged him tight. Blake lost all restraint on his emotions and sobbed uncontrollably against Mr. Grady's shoulder. "I can't make the pain stop. It's too much. Why wasn't it me who died? It should've been me."

Mr. Grady pulled away from Blake and said, "I doubt the pain will ever go away, but you *must* face the pain if you ever want to get on with your life."

"I don't think I can," Blake said.

"What if your roles were reversed? What if Aaron lived and you had died? Would you want him suffering the way you are?"

"Of course not. I'd want him to be happy."

"Do you think Aaron would want you to live this life of suffering?"

Blake hung his head and said, "No."

"What do you think Aaron would say if he saw you like this?"

Blake looked up and gave a half smile. "He'd probably say, 'Hey, drama queen! Get over yourself and go fishing.'"

Mr. Grady laughed and said, "That sounds exactly like something Aaron would say." Mr. Grady reached up and placed his hand on Blake's shoulder. "The way you face the pain is to live a good life despite it. Live a life that Aaron would want for you, a life that would make him proud." Mr. Grady looked Blake in the eyes and said, "Now, go get yourself cleaned up…and let's go pay our respects to your brother."

Blake nodded. "Yes sir."

Blake walked back inside the house and stood at the doorway of his bedroom. He looked at the revolver sitting on his bed. Next to it lay the road trip list. Blake stared at the two items as though he was standing at a crossroad. He needed to decide his path. Blake walked up to the bed, reached down, and picked up his journal. He held it close to his chest and said, "I'm so sorry, Aaron. I won't let you down…never again."

Mr. Grady's words helped Blake turn a crucial corner in his life. Although the sadness and guilt of Aaron's loss still gnawed at his soul, he felt, for the first time in what seemed to be an eternity, that he wanted to live and that there was still purpose in life.

Later that afternoon, Blake and Mr. Grady drove out to the national cemetery to visit Aaron. Blake told Mr. Grady about the road trip that he and Aaron had planned and how he intended on making the trip from Colorado to Alaska starting in July. Mr. Grady loved the idea and felt that this pilgrimage could help heal Blake's heart. Mr. Grady promised to do what he could to help Blake with his quest.

Over the next several weeks Blake worked diligently to prepare for his trip. He started off by religiously exercising twice a day, once in the morning and once in the evening to strengthen his leg for the long journey. He spent a lot of time researching popular fly patterns for the areas he planned on fishing and then spent several hours a day tying flies and filling fly boxes with an assortment of fly patterns to get him through the two months of fishing. Mr. Grady also spent a fair amount of time researching routes from river to river and finding campgrounds where Blake could stay. He estimated the cost of fuel and food and found unique ways that Blake could travel on a tight budget but still comfortably finish his journey. The only thing left for Blake was to find a mode of transportation.

Although Blake had sent the majority of his earnings from the military home to support his mother, he did put a small portion of it away in a bank account. He used the money to buy a used red 2002 Toyota Tacoma extended cab pickup with a camper shell. The truck had over 100,000 miles on it but was in good condition. It was perfect. The truck would get decent mileage, and would still be big enough to transport everything Blake would need to take along.

The night before Blake was to set out on the road trip, there was a knock at the front door. Mr. Grady was standing there holding one of Aaron's favorite fly rods. Attached to the rod was the same reel that Aaron had used during his plunge off of the boulder in Cheesman Canyon, the same day they had planned the trip. Mr. Grady looked sad. The skin around his eyes had a rose color, and his eyes were bloodshot, like he'd been crying. He stood in the doorway with his head cocked to the side and gave a tender smile.

"Mr. Grady, how are you? Come in."

Mr. Grady said, "No I—I just wanted to stop by and give you a couple things for your trip." Mr. Grady handed Blake the fly rod and reel. "I'm sure you already know this, but these were Aaron's." Mr. Grady took a deep breath and pulled out a fly box from his back pocket and handed it to Blake. His voice cracked. "These are a few of the flies he tied over the years." Mr. Grady paused as though he was struggling to keep himself from crying and asked, "Would you mind fishing with his rod and reel and maybe try catching a fish or two with his flies? It would mean a lot."

Blake's eyes began to well up with tears. He opened the fly box and gently ran his fingers over the rows of hand-tied flies that lined the interior. "I will. I promise…and I'll bring them back to you safe and sound."

"You just worry about bringing yourself back safe and sound. OK?"

"I will. I promise," Blake said.

Mr. Grady said, "Thank you, Blake." Then he turned, and walked back toward home. Blake stood in the doorway holding Aaron's fly rod and watched Mr. Grady until he disappeared from sight.

CHAPTER TWELVE

Fire on the Interstate

I t was early on a Tuesday morning in July. Blake was standing outside his pickup that was packed from the bottom of the bed to the ceiling of the topper shell with all of the things needed for his three-month trip across Wyoming, Montana, and Alaska.

Blake's mother walked out of the house with a cup of coffee in an aluminum lined traveler's mug. She handed it to Blake and said, "For the road, sweetheart."

"I'm sorry Mom," Blake said as he took the mug. "It's like we're doing this all over again."

"Doing what?"

"Saying goodbye. I mean, I've only been home for a short time, and now I'm leaving again."

Blake's mom reached up and rubbed her open hand against his cheek. "Blake, you never came home from Iraq in the first place." She pinched her lips together trying to hold back the tears. "I barely recognize you. I know you're hurting inside, but did you ever consider that you're hurting me too?"

Blake hung his head and said, "I guess not."

"I know the little boy I love is trapped in there somewhere, but I don't know how to get through to him. If you think this trip is going to heal your heart, then by all means, go. I'm your mother, and I'll always be there for you, but please…I beg you, sweetheart, please don't come back only to shut me out again. I don't think I could bear that."

Blake stood there speechless. It was painful for him to hear this declaration from his mother. Deep down he knew his drinking and self-destructive behavior hurt her, but the sting of hearing her say it forced him to confront his actions.

Blake finally looked up at her and said, "I'm so sorry, Mom."

"I know…and I forgive you. Now get going…go find my son and bring him home to me."

The two held each other in a tight embrace before Blake got into his truck and headed off down the road.

The first two destinations on the *Road Trip* list would be the Grey Reef stretch of the North Platte River followed by the Miracle Mile stretch of the North Platte River. Both destinations were famous trout waters and were located just outside of Casper, Wyoming. Blake had a four-and-a-half-hour drive to the Grey Reef. Most of the trip would be spent driving the 275 miles of no-man's land on I-25 between Denver and Casper.

The drive north was scenic with views of open Colorado farmland that backed up against the rugged backdrop of the Rocky Mountains. Further north into Wyoming the view would gradually change to small rolling hills and flat open prairies covered in green grass as far as the eye could see. Some days the openness of the plains invited powerful winds that would blow across the highway antagonizing motorists. Today was one of those days.

As Blake made his way across Wyoming, he was sure to keep both hands on the wheel. He was in disbelief at the strength of the gale force winds that blew across the highway continuously pushing his truck to the right.

Later on, Blake saw a mid-sized sedan pulled over on the right shoulder several hundred feet ahead. As he drove closer he could see an elderly woman standing behind the car waving her hands in the air. Blake figured she had a flat or some other minor issue, so he pulled in behind her to see if he could help. He could see a rising stack of black smoke, and the elderly woman looked frantic. Whatever was going on, it certainly wasn't a flat. Blake stepped out of his car and the woman ran up to him. She was completely panicked. "Help them! Please, help them!"

Blake looked down the shoulder of the interstate that sloped down a small hill toward the smoke. He could see a four-door sedan that had rolled sideways down the hill. Blake could see an old man, presumably the elderly woman's husband, standing outside the sedan looking through the driver's side windows. Small flames were peeking through the gap from under the hood. Blake hastily stumbled down to the car, grinding his teeth in agony each time his left foot took a hard stride. He grabbed the old man by the arm. He turned to Blake and said, "They're trapped inside! I can't get any of the doors open!"

Blake looked through the windows, which were still intact, and could see a small child sitting on the back seat on the right side of the vehicle; a woman was sitting in the driver's seat. Blake looked around for something to break the rear passenger window as the flames grew larger and more intense. He found a half-buried rock, about the size of a baseball. He dug his fingers into the dry soil and clawed the rock free. Blake looked at the old man and said, "Stand back! I'm gonna break the glass!" He smashed the rock against the window. To Blake's amazement, the rock skipped off the surface leaving a scratch but failing to break the glass. The flames had now grown so big that they were creeping over the roof.

Undaunted, Blake pulled his arm back for a second try. He yelled out as he put double the force in his throw, and the rock again crashed against the window. The glass shattered into pebble-sized shards. Blake leaned into the window frame. He could see the small boy in the backseat screaming and crying. Blake yelled to the child, "Give me your hand! Come to me!"

The small boy said, "My Mommy! What about my Mommy?"

Blake said, "I'll get your mom, I promise! First, I need to get you out of there!" The boy crawled across the seat and reached out. Blake grabbed onto the boy's arms and pulled him through the window. Blake looked at the old man and said, "Take the boy, and get him far away from here! I'll get her out!" The old man grabbed the boy by the arm and started walking him up the hill toward the interstate.

The flames had now fully engulfed the front of the car, and a dark plume of smoke billowed from the burning engine. Blake poked his head back through the broken window and yelled, "Miss! Miss!" The woman looked to be conscious but was frozen with fear as the fire from the engine blasted against the windshield. Blake climbed through the open window and crawled into the backseat of the sedan. He grabbed the woman's shoulder in an attempt to snap her out of her trance and said, "Miss! We've got to get out of here! Climb into the backseat!"

The woman looked at Blake and said, "I can't move! My seatbelt's stuck!" Blake looked down at the center console and could see that the seatbelt release was crushed deep underneath the seat and center console. Blake tried to push his bladed hand between the cramped space in an attempt to trigger the seatbelt release, but he couldn't get his fingers close enough to the seatbelt lock.

Blake remembered he was carrying his collapsible knife and reached into his pocket. He struggled to grip the thin blade and pull it from the handle as the intensity of the situation diminished the dexterity in his fingertips. After several attempts the blade finally broke free of the handle, and Blake locked the steel back in place. He reached across the woman's chest and pulled the belt away from her body as much as he could. Once he had enough room, Blake sawed the heavy nylon strap.

The woman yelled, "It's hot! I can feel the heat on my legs! Hurry!" Blake finally cut through the belt and dropped the knife onto the front passenger seat. He grabbed the woman and pulled with all his might as he tried to yank her into the backseat. The woman screamed in pain, "Wait! Wait! Stop! My legs are stuck!" Blake looked down at the woman's legs. He could see that the bottom of the plastic dashboard assembly was crushed against her, pinning her knees. The flames began to melt the top of the dashboard as the plastic near the windshield began to blister and bubble. Beads of sweat dripped off Blake's nose and chin as the heat from the fire turned the inside of the sedan into a raging oven. The woman began to panic. "I'm gonna die! I'm gonna die!"

Blake yelled, "Listen to me! You're not gonna die! I'm gonna get you out of here!"

Fighting through the throbbing pain in his leg, Blake swung his legs around the passenger seat and settled into the space between the two front seats. He braced his left leg against the back of the center console and began kicking with his right leg as hard as he could at the bottom of the dash board near the woman's legs. Initially the plastic cover simply caved in and popped back into place. Blake looked down at the front passenger side floor board and could see flames creeping into the cab. Blake kicked harder and with more frequency as he knew they didn't have much time left. The woman screamed out in pain with every one of Blake's kicks as it drove the hardened plastic deeper against her legs. The woman cried out as she saw the flames begin to breach into the interior. "It's too hot! It's not gonna work! You have to get out of here! Just go!"

"I'm not leaving! You're gonna be OK!"

Blake's right leg went numb as he had lost all strength in the limb and was running on pure adrenaline. The heat from the fire was nearly unbearable as the windshield began to collapse. Blake hauled back and kicked the dashboard with every ounce of energy he had left. Finally the dashboard cracked at the bottom. Blake lunged forward and gripped underneath the dashboard with both hands. He pulled with all his might. He could feel the plastic slowly start to give way as the dashboard began to tear along the seam of the crack. The bottom of the dashboard began to lift from the woman's legs. Blake yelled, "Push your legs towards me!" The woman leaned to her left to leverage her knees toward the hole that Blake had made for her. Blake held onto the dashboard with his right hand and quickly scooped both the woman's knees with his left. He pulled her legs free and crawled into the backseat. He grabbed her from behind and pulled her into the backseat just as the flames cut into the front interior of the cab. Blake dove headfirst out of the backseat window and collided with the ground outside of the car. He jumped to his feet, reached into the cab, grabbed the woman by her arms, and fell backward pulling her free.

Blake fell onto his back and the woman fell on top of him. Blake asked, "Can you stand? We've got to get away from here!"

"I think so. Help me up." Blake stood up and grabbed the woman by the arm; he pulled her to her feet as she draped her arm around his shoulder.

They staggered away from the burning car until Blake felt they were a safe distance from the blaze. Still holding the woman's arm, Blake gently lowered her to the ground. As soon as she was safely lying down, Blake crashed down beside her.

Blake looked up and stared at the sedan that was now completely engulfed in fire. The sound of sirens could be heard in the distance as emergency fire crews and police arrived. The woman rested her head on Blake's chest and said, "Thank you. Thank you." Breathless, Blake couldn't say a word and simply placed his hand on the back of her head and held her.

An ambulance drove down the hill. Two paramedics got out and checked on them. One of the medics asked, "Ma'am. What's your name?"

The woman said, "Allison Grace." The medic asked her what had happened. Still crying, she explained to the medic that the wind had blown her off the side of the road causing her car to roll off of the highway. She went into the hair-raising tale about how Blake had saved her and her son from the burning car. She suddenly stopped midsentence and franticly asked, "Where's my son? Where's Trevor?"

"He's up at the highway getting checked out. We found him with an older couple. Are those your parents?"

"No," Allison said. "I'm not sure who they are. They must have just stopped to help."

"Well, don't worry, he's safe with another ambulance crew. We're going to take the two of you to the hospital. OK?"

A paramedic came over to Blake to check on him. Blake's hands and forearms were cut up and bloodied. The medic cleaned off the excess blood and found that none of the cuts were deep enough to require stitches. After getting bandaged up, Blake declined the medic's advice for a precautionary trip to the hospital, and the medic again focused on helping Allison.

Blake was contacted by a Wyoming Highway Patrolman who asked for his account of what had happened and his contact information. As the

90

trooper talked with Blake, he watched the paramedics prepare to load Allison into the ambulance. She had been placed on a rolling gurney to help stabilize her for the trip to the hospital in Casper. He locked eyes one last time with Allison as they wheeled the gurney into the ambulance. She smiled at Blake as she raised her right hand, gently waved, and mothed the words, *thank you.* Blake waved back to her as the doors of the ambulance were slowly closed.

When Blake was finished giving the patrolman his information, he walked back up to the interstate and got in his truck. He went to insert the key into the ignition, but his hand was shaking. Blake took a deep breath to calm his nerves and sat in silence. Once he settled down, he put the key in the ignition, started the truck, and continued north toward Grey Reef Reservoir.

CHAPTER THIRTEEN

An Unlikely Fishing Buddy

Blake's mind raced. He couldn't believe what had just happened. He replayed the events over and over in his mind. Everything happened so fast that he didn't have a chance to talk with Allison or Trevor before they were taken away. Blake wondered if they would be OK…he wondered if he would ever see them again.

When Blake crossed into Casper he turned onto the highway that would take him to the body of water that fed that famous stretch of the North Platte River, the Grey Reef Reservoir. He drove down the county highway across the vast open prairie for several miles before seeing the turn to the Grey Reef. Blake drove along an old dirt road searching for a riverside campground close to the dam. Eager to finally reach his destination, Blake sped down the road that paralleled the river. Suddenly an animal ran out into the middle of the road.

Blake slammed on the brakes to try to avoid hitting the small creature. The wheels of the truck locked in place and slid along the dirt and gravel bringing the truck to a steady halt. Blake jolted forward in his seat as the truck came to an abrupt stop. The pickup settled back on its axles as the cloud of dust that was chasing the tail end of the truck quickly caught up and rolled over top of the vehicle surrounding it like a thick mist. Blake peered through the cloud as it gradually settled, slowly revealing the animal.

It was a dog. A young mutt no more than 30 pounds. Unalarmed by the near collision, the dog stood in the middle of the road facing Blake's truck. It had a face full of dirty matted hair with a curtain of long knotted-up bangs that draped over its eyes. Its mouth hung wide open with a bright-red tongue that dangled from the left side of its face as it panted to cool itself from the heat of the sun. Its thin torso was covered by long curly dark gray hair and was supported by four raggedy, lanky legs that were peppered with burrs from the weeds of the open field. The mutt looked to have a little mix of Schnauzer in him. The dog was a mess. No collar meant that he was probably unwanted and abandoned. Whatever had happened to this poor pup, he seemed in good spirits.

Blake leaned out of the window and called to the dog, "Here, buddy…here, boy," as he slapped his left hand against the outside of the door. The dog jogged over to the window and jumped up against the door. Blake patted the dog on the top of his head and said, "You don't have a mean bone in your body, do you, buddy?"

Blake stepped out of his truck and raided the cooler that he had stored in the bed of the pickup. He pulled out a few slices of lunch meat, held them up, and told the dog to sit. The pup immediately sat its hind legs and butt down on the ground in obedience. "That's a good boy. Here you go," Blake said as he tossed the meat to the dog. The dog caught the slice in midair and inhaled it in one monstrous chomp. "Man! You're a hungry guy," Blake said. The dog just licked its mouth and snout and looked back at Blake with wide-eyed anticipation. "OK. OK. Here ya go," Blake said as he threw another piece of lunch meat to the mutt.

Blake allowed the dog to finish off the package of meat and then got into his truck and drove toward the campground. Looking in his rearview mirror, Blake could see the dog jogging behind his truck trying to keep up. Blake shook his head and thought, *Great, I should've never given that mutt any food. Now I'll never get rid of him.*

When Blake arrived at the campsite he got out of his truck. He looked down the road and couldn't see the dog anywhere. Somewhat relieved, Blake walked around to the back of his truck to start unpacking his camping gear. As he turned the corner he was startled by the dog, who was sitting patiently. "Seriously? Where did you come from?" The goofy looking mongrel just sat on the ground panting, its tail sweeping the dirt as it wagged. "No more food! That food's for me. Understand? I'll get you some water, but after that you've got to go."

Blake took out a bowl and poured some water in it. The dog walked over to the dish and began slurping down the water with its tongue. Blake unpacked his truck and began to set up camp. He set up his tent and then made a small fire. Blake propped up a lawn chair and sat down next to the fire pit. The dog walked over next to Blake, laid down on the ground, and rested its head on its front paws. "Make yourself at home," he said sarcastically. Blake watched as the dog closed its eyes as the warmth of the fire comforted its grizzly face. "I bet that fire feels good. I wonder how many nights you've spent out here on your own." Blake reached down and petted the dog on his head. His hair was grungy and stiff like hay. "Whoa…you need a bath, buddy. Well, you're not getting in my tent smelling like that. I can tell you that much." Blake looked around, then stood up and walked over to his truck. He pulled out an old wool blanket and shook it out. He laid it on the ground next to the fire pit and patted his hand several times on the blanket. "Here boy. Come lay down over here. I'll put some more wood on the fire before I turn in, and if you're still hanging around tomorrow, maybe I'll give you a bath."

The dog walked over to the makeshift bed and laid down. Blake stood back up and walked over to a small woodpile that he had comprised earlier and picked up a large branch and walked back over to the fire. The dog looked fearfully up at Blake as he carried the large stick. As Blake walked closer, the dog's ears fell back as it tried to tuck its hind legs under its torso. The pup began to cower and shake. With a tender voice Blake said, "Hey, buddy, what's the matter? I'm not gonna hurt ya. This is for the fire." Blake sighed. "Poor guy. You've probably been beaten a few times. Well, don't worry, that's not what I'm about." Blake gently put the stick in the fire and petted the dog one last time as an act of reassurance before he turned in for the night.

The next morning Blake woke to the sound of rushing water from the North Platte River and the smell of fresh air. He opened the tent flap and looked up to see a clear crisp blue Wyoming sky. When he looked down, he found that mangy homeless mutt laying in the dirt just outside the door. Blake shook his head. "Why am I not surprised?" The pup jumped up with excitement with his ears pointed up and his tail wagging wildly. He stood up on his hind legs with his paws retracted like a miniature tyrannosaurus rex and jumped in place. "OK. OK. I know what you want." Blake walked over to the cooler. "I didn't factor you into my food rationing, pal. I'm gonna need to go into town and get you some dog food later. I can't keep givin' you a package of lunch meat for every meal." Blake tore open a fresh package of sliced ham.

He ripped the meat into small bite-sized pieces and placed them into a bowl. He cracked a few raw eggs over the ham and stirred it with a fork. The dog did his best to sit still while Blake prepared the meal, but it looked like the pup was sitting on a spring the way his butt popped up off the ground a few inches and then settled back down every time Blake made a complete rotation of the fork around the inside of the bowl. Blake smiled as he watched the dog's torment, "OK, buddy, you've been a good boy. Here ya go." Blake sat the bowl on the ground and left it. To his amazement the dog sat still just staring at the bowl. Blake said, "Now that's a good boy. OK, get it!" The dog lunged at the bowl and devoured the meal. Blake ate a bite of breakfast himself before suiting up in his fishing gear and heading out to the river to make the first cast of his journey.

Blake spent the morning wade fishing the Reef near the dam while that dirty battered mutt sat on the river bank and watched him fish the entire day. Every time Blake would hook into a trout, the dog would prance back and forth along the shoreline wagging his tail with delight as Blake would fight the fish. Eventually Blake brought a netted rainbow over to the dog. Blake let him sniff the trout. He placed the trout back in the water while the pup looked on. The trout quickly swam off with a splash of its tail fin, and the dog jumped into the river and gave a pouncing chase for a couple of feet before giving up.

An older gray-haired man who was fishing within earshot of Blake, asked, "Is that your dog?"

"You'd think so the way he's been following me around," Blake said.

"What's his name?"

"I've just been calling him Buddy. He seems to answer to it."

The older man smiled. "Buddy. I like that. The name's Emmanuel Tibbins, but most everyone calls me Tibbs."

"Blake Jacobs. Nice to meet you Tibbs. You live around here?"

"Nope, from Montana. Just out here on vacation. I think we're camped in the same campground. Mine's the white motorhome."

"Red Toyota with the camper shell," Blake responded.

"You a vet?" Tibbs asked.

Blake, caught off guard by the question, asked, "What makes you say that?"

"Yeah, you're a vet," Tibbs said. "Marine I'm guessin'. I can always spot a fellow *jarhead*. Infantry or air wing?"

"Infantry—I was in Ramadi with the 2/4." Blake admitted reluctantly. "How about you?"

"*Nam*…or—*Vietnam* as you kids like to call it. I was with the 1/9," Tibbs said. "You fishin' here long?"

"A couple days, then I'm headed to the Miracle Mile," Blake said.

"You gonna float this beast or just wade it?"

"I'm on a tight budget, so I'll do the best I can on foot."

"Well, I've hired a guide to take me out on a drift boat tomorrow if you're interested. It'd be my treat."

"Seriously?"

"Sure. I'd welcome the company. Meet me at my motorhome at o'seven-hundred. I'll make us breakfast and coffee before we head out," Tibbs said, as he turned and headed back toward the river bank.

"Thanks. I'll be there. Anything I can bring?" Blake asked.

Tibbs turned and chuckled. "Yeah, some flies that'll catch me a huge trout. See you tomorrow. *Semper Fi,* Marine."

Blake grinned. "Oorah, *devil dog.*"

Blake could see thunderstorms developing on the horizon to the West. He looked at Buddy and said, "Well, if you're gonna sleep in my tent tonight we've got to get you cleaned up."

The two headed back to camp where Blake used the camp's water faucet to wet down Buddy and lather him with shampoo and conditioner. "I know this stuff isn't for dogs, but it'll have to do for tonight," Blake said as he scrubbed the dirt and mange from Buddy's coat. After rinsing Buddy off and drying him the best he could with a small towel, they sat by the fire hoping the turbulent storm would pass them by.

The night sky to the West gradually turned pitch black with not even a mild contrast to depict the prairie from the heavens. Then suddenly, the sky would flicker with brilliant jagged streaks of white lightning that would split and spider as the bolts raced to the ground, instantly revealing the identity of the landscape and the ominous storm clouds in the atmosphere; then, in the blink of an eye, it would stop, returning the world to a black abyss.

With every flash of lightning and every rumble of thunder, Buddy became increasingly nervous. He panted as he paced around the fire. Light rain drops began to fall. Blake looked at Buddy. "Well, so much for it missing us. Looks like we're in for a long night, Buddy." Blake walked over to the tent and held the flap open. "Come on." Buddy looked skeptical as he stood up and cocked his head sideways attempting to understand what Blake wanted. "It's OK, boy, come on," Blake said. Buddy hesitantly jogged over to the tent, slowly stepped through the opening, and once inside, immediately plopped down in the middle of Blake's sleeping bag. Blake shook his head and said, "Again…why am I not surprised?"

Kaboom! The deafening thunder suddenly cracked as a bolt of lightning crashed against the ground near the campground. Blake was startled from his light slumber and sat straight up. His forehead was speckled with beads of sweat as he took short panicked breaths. The rain pounded the tent as the thunderstorm punished the thin nylon fabric of the flimsy shelter. *Boom!* The strike of another bolt caused Blake to clench his teeth and squeeze his fists closed as his body jolted from the surprise of the unpredicted wallop of electricity. The sound of the roaring thunder caused by the vicious lightning that tore through the atmosphere was relentless. Blake, who had never been frightened by thunder before, found himself trembling. With every sudden impact, he was reminded of the battle that had changed his life forever. Blake's mind raced, and anxiety slowly began to consume him.

Buddy pushed his nose underneath Blake's arm and nestled close beside him. Blake could feel Buddy shaking uncontrollably. Buddy's fear helped distract Blake from his own angst as he held the pup close and began petting him. "It's OK, Buddy…it's OK. I'm right here. Nothing bad's gonna happen. Calm down, boy. We're gonna ride this storm out together."

CHAPTER FOURTEEN

Always Faithful

The next morning Blake and Buddy showed up at Tibbs's motorhome. There was a small folding table with two lawn chairs set up outside. The door of the motorhome was propped open and the aroma of freshly brewed coffee was wafting through the air. Tibbs popped his head out of the open door and said, "Ah, you made it. How'd you sleep last night?"

"Like a baby," Blake said rolling his eyes.

"Yeah, you look it," Tibbs said with a grin. "Don't sweat it, I've got coffee brewin'."

"I know, it smells great."

Tibbs asked, "How do ya take it?"

"Black with sugar, please."

"You got it," Tibbs said.

Tibbs disappeared back into the motorhome, and Blake sat down at the table. Blake took a look around the campsite for a second and then called out, "So what's on the agenda?"

"Well, first off, you're gonna taste one of the greatest ham and cheese omelets ever made. Second, I've hired a guide named Chris Oarsman to float us down the river. He comes highly recommended by the fellas at the fly shop in town. They say he knows every inch of the North Platte," Tibbs said as he continued to work in the kitchen.

"Seriously? His name is Oarsman?"

"I know. How can we go wrong? It must be a good omen."

"Well, however the day turns out, I'd just like to say thanks for everything," Blake said.

Tibbs walked out holding a cup of coffee and a plate with a massive omelet. "No need to thank me, Marine…I should be thanking you for all you've done for this country." Tibbs placed the plate on the table in front of Blake and sat the cup of coffee beside it.

Blake lowered his head and quietly responded, "Thanks…I appreciate it."

Tibbs walked back into the motorhome and returned moments later with a plate of scrambled eggs. He set the plate on the ground and called for Buddy. "Here ya go, boy."

Blake shook his head, "Spoiled mutt. Enjoy it while you can, Buddy. After today it's gonna be dried dog food for you."

Tibbs sat down at the table with his own plate and said, "Well, dig in."

Blake cut into the omelet with the side of his fork and took a bite. "How is it?" Tibbs asked.

"It's really good. Thanks again."

"My pleasure."

"So let me ask you something. How'd you know I was a vet?" Blake asked.

"Just an educated guess. You've got that look."

"What look is that?"

"That look of unease. Like the weight of the world is bearing down on you. You're pretty young to be carrying around that kinda load, unless you've lived through some pretty rough shit," Tibbs said as he took a bite of food and sipped his coffee. "And when I saw that hitch in your step, I just knew."

Blake was stunned by Tibbs's intuition. He sat in silence with a dumbfounded look on his face, before asking, "Is it really that obvious?"

"Not to those who haven't been through what you're goin' through. But I see that look every morning when I stare in the mirror. It's invisible to most, but for me, it's as recognizable as daylight."

Blake didn't know what to say. He just sat there staring at Tibbs while he nonchalantly went back to eating his breakfast. Tibbs stopped eating for a moment, looked at his watch and said, "Ah shoot! All my rambling is gonna make us late. We've got to meet Chris in about 15 minutes. Eat up Marine, we've got some fishin' to do."

Blake and Tibbs finished eating and geared up for the float trip. Tibbs said, "What do think about letting Buddy hang out in the motorhome today? I can keep the air conditioner on."

"Honestly Tibbs, he's a stray I picked up a couple days ago. I don't know if he's house broken or what. For all I know he'll destroy the inside before we get back."

"I'm not worried about it," Tibbs said. "I take it he didn't piss in your tent last night?"

Blake just shrugged. "No, but it could've been a fluke for all I know."

"I have a feeling Buddy will be just fine. Besides, there's not much in there that he can mess up anyway."

"I'll say this about you Tibbs, you've got to be the most trusting person I've ever met."

"Trust can be a powerful ally, young Blake. You should try it on for size. You might like it," Tibbs said with a wink.

The two walked from the campground down to the boat launch a few yards away. Waiting for them was a man who looked to be in his early thirties. He was standing next to a large row boat known as a drift boat. The drift boat had a flat narrow bow. The middle of the craft was wide, giving it balance and stability so one could easily stand as it drifted down the river. The stern curved inward but was walled with a flat butt section in the back just shy of merging into a point. There were three seats mounted onto the boat one near the bow, one in the middle, and one in the stern. The seats on either end were reserved for the anglers, and the one in the middle was for the guide. Long wooden oars lay through steel horseshoe shaped oarlocks that were mounted on each side of the top rim of the hull near the guide's chair.

Tibbs walked up to the man and held out his hand out. They shook hands and Tibbs said, "Chris, it's good to see you again. I'd like you to meet my friend Blake."

Chris turned to Blake and shook his hand. "Chris Oarsman. Nice to meet you."

"Blake Jacobs."

Chris said, "Well, Tibbs tells me you know your way around a fly rod."

"A little, I don't have a lot of drift boat experience, but I can cast it anywhere you want."

"As long as you keep your casts out to the sides of the boat and you're not shootin' line over the top of my head, we're gonna be just fine," Chris said with a grin.

"I can definitely handle that," Blake said.

"Well, let's get you two rigged up and get going."

Blake and Tibbs pulled line from their reels and began to rig up their fly rods before they set out. Chris stood by and advised them on what flies had been working well on the river. Blake was going to start the day fishing streamers, and Tibbs, a stubborn old-school angler, insisted on fishing dry flies. "What type of streamer have they been keying in on?" Blake asked Chris.

"Let me see what you got," Chris said. Blake reached into his pocket and pulled out Aaron's fly box. He opened up the box and displayed the patterns to Chris.

"Oh, these are nice. Did you tie all these?" Chris asked.

"No, a friend of mine tied 'em."

"The whole box?"

"Yep. Every last one."

"There must be 300 bucks worth of flies here. That's some friend."

"He sure was," Blake said softly.

Chris, sensing that he may have touched on a sensitive topic, stopped his inquiry. He reached into the box and pulled out a black-colored streamer made of dyed pine squirrel hair and said, "This one's money. They'll definitely chase this." Blake nodded with gratitude, took the fly, and tied it to the end of his tippet.

Once they were rigged up, Tibbs and Chis got into the boat while Blake pushed them loose from the shore. Blake jumped into the back of the boat just as the current pushed the boat down river. Chris steered the bow of the boat pointed downstream and started giving instructions. "Tibbs, there are tons of grasshoppers falling off of the banks from the willows and grass into the river, that's why I had you tie that hopper pattern on your line. Cast that bad boy just off of the bank, and try to make it splash a little when it hits the surface of the water. That splash will usually induce a strike from anything swimming near the shore." Tibbs gave Chris a thumbs up and began working the edge of the bank with his fly. Chris then called back to Blake, "Blake. Same thing as I told Tibbs. Cast your fly as close to the bank as you can. Only difference, when the streamer hits the water, start stripping line fast—10 to 12-inch strips and keep your fly moving."

"You don't want me to let it dead drift a little before I strip?" Blake asked.

"Nope. Trust me, just keep that streamer moving," Chris said.

Blake made a cast toward the bank just as Chris had instructed. When his streamer hit the water he began pulling the line in short fast strips trying to keep the streamer in motion. He continued to strip the fly until he had brought it back to the boat. Chris called to Blake, "Not bad, just strip a little faster during the retrieve. Don't worry, these fish aren't shy."

Blake made another cast toward the bank. This time as soon as his streamer hit the water he began stripping the fly line in fast bursts keeping the streamer on the move and not allowing it to pause. Suddenly, from beneath the undercut bank, a dark shadow accelerated toward Blake's streamer. Blake's heart began to pump rapidly as he grasped the fly line between his thumb and index finger and ripped it through the eyelets of his fly rod at a fast pace. The shadow blasted through the current in hot pursuit of the streamer. Blake kept stripping the line as the shadow gained on his fly. With a powerful thrust, the shadow overtook his streamer. The white color from the wide-gaping mouth of the fish flashed and in an instant disappeared as the trout slammed its jaws closed over the streamer. Blake stripped one last time setting the hook in the predator's maw. The fish tossed and thrusted sideways in the water trying to break free from the hook's hold. "Fish on!" Blake yelled as his rod bent over the side of the boat.

"Good one!" Chris said. "That looks like a decent brown. When you can, bring him over to the left side here, and I'll get him." After a short but ferocious battle, Blake was able to guide the trout near Chris. Chris brought the oars in and grabbed a huge landing net with a long handle that he had stored inside the boat. "Rod tip up for me, Blake," Chris said as he leaned over the side of the boat and trapped the fish inside the nylon net. Chris handed the handle of the net to Blake and got back on the oars. Blake reached into the net and pulled out a heathy male brown trout. "You want a picture with that brown, Blake?" Chris asked.

"Nah, he's done his part. I'm gonna get him on his way," Blake said.

Blake held the brown in the water and gave it a chance to revive before he let it go and watched it swim away. He picked up his rod and said, "That was fun. Let's do that again."

Before Blake could attempt another cast he heard Tibbs call out, "Got him!" Blake looked toward the front of the boat to see Tibbs's rod tip bent over the water.

"Nice, Tibbs!" Blake called out, as Chris rowed the boat out of the current toward the shore.

Blake put his fly rod down inside the boat and grabbed the landing net. "You got it, Blake?" Chris asked as he stayed on the oars trying to keep the boat from turning.

"Yep. I think I can land it from here," Blake said.

The trout shot out from the surface of the water and splashed back down into the river. "Wow! This is a good fish!" Tibbs said with excitement. "He's givin' me one hell of a fight!"

"Keep your rod tip up Tibbs, and try to guide him over to Blake," Chris said.

Tibbs continued to fight the trout until he could feel the fish tiring. With a grimace, he turned his body toward the back of the boat and guided the trout near Blake. Blake plunged the net into the water and scooped the large trout up in the net. "Got him!"

Tibbs yelled out, "Nice job! Thanks for the assist, Marine! *Semper Fi!*"

Blake reached down into the net and pulled out a beautiful 20-inch rainbow trout and held it up for Tibbs to admire. "You want a photo, Tibbs?" Blake asked.

"That's OK, young Blake, he's done his part—send him on his way," Tibbs said as he gave Blake a wink. Blake leaned over the side of the boat and released the trout.

"Hey, Tibbs, I've heard that term used before, but I'm not a military man. If you don't mind me asking, what does Semper Fi mean?" Chris asked.

Tibbs said, "It's not a military term, Chris. It's the Marine Corps way of life." Tibbs took a shallow breath. "It's short for *Semper Fidelis*, which is Latin for *Always Faithful*. Every Marine is taught to maintain the highest level of dedication to his service, his country, but most importantly to his fellow Marines." Tibbs paused, looked over at Blake, then continued, "*Semper Fi* is a Marine's commitment to always be there for his brothers in arms; whether on or off the battlefield. Not *sometimes faithful* or *when it happens to be convenient I'll be faithful*—but *Always Faithful*. For me, it's an absolute. No matter what, I'll always be there to help a Marine in need. It's a way of honor that can be explained, but unless you served in the Corps, it can never truly be understood."

It was then that Blake realized Tibbs was talking directly to him; reminding him that he wasn't alone in his journey to find peace. He recognized Blake's pain and somehow understood it. This relative stranger, who he had only met a day ago, could relate to Blake's suffering and in his own cryptic way, was assuring him that if the time came where Blake needed his help, Tibbs would be there for him.

They continued down the river and had one of the most action-packed days of fishing Blake could remember. *The bite was on* as they say in the fishing world as every few casts seemed to produce a strike from a hungry trout. Blake hadn't enjoyed himself like this in quite some time. Laughter and yells of excitement filled the air as fish after fish were brought to the net and then released back into the river to fight another day.

Later that afternoon, after the float trip was over, Blake and Tibbs returned to the campsite to find Buddy enjoying the cool air conditioning of Tibbs's motorhome. To Blake's surprise Buddy had behaved, not even causing a dimes worth of damage. Before Blake and Buddy went back to their campsite, Tibbs invited them over for some burgers that he planned on grilling later that evening, and Blake graciously accepted.

As Blake and Buddy walked over to their campsite, Blake could hear a faint ringing coming from inside his tent. It was his cell phone. He unzipped the tent door, reached in, and grabbed his phone. He didn't recognize the number.

A female voice said, "Hi. I'm looking for Blake Jacobs."

"This is Blake. Who's this?"

"Blake, this is Allison…Allison Grace."

CHAPTER FIFTEEN

Tea Party

The sun began to set in the West as the glow from the sinking star reflected a mixture of yellow and orange against the underbellies of the scattered clouds that hung in the vast Wyoming sky. Blake and Buddy sat on the shore of the river and listened to the calming sounds of the rushing waters of the North Platte. Blake held a small black streamer in his hand. It was one of Aaron's flies. In fact, it was the same streamer that had hooked Blake's first trout that morning. Blake caressed the soft fur of the streamer with his thumb as he reminisced about past fishing trips he and Aaron had taken. He missed his friend terribly. Buddy could sense Blake's sadness. He pushed his nose under Blake's left elbow and burrowed his body between Blake's arm and torso until his head popped out from underneath Blake's hand. Blake smiled and scratched Buddy on top of his head. "Thanks, Buddy. I'll be ok. How about we go find Tibbs and get some dinner?"

Blake and Buddy walked across the campground toward Tibbs's motorhome. They found Tibbs huddled over a steel cooking grate that he had laid over a campfire pit. Tibbs had a metal spatula in hand and was tending several ground-beef patties that were sizzling over the open fire. "Just in time—hope you're hungry," Tibbs said. "How do ya like your burger cooked, Marine?"

"Medium's fine," Blake said.

"What about Buddy?"

Blake laughed. "Something tells me he's not picky."

"So…is this your last night here?" Tibbs asked.

"Yeah, I'm heading to Casper tomorrow."

"Casper? I thought you were going to the Miracle Mile after this?"

"I was but...I had to change my plans. I'm meeting someone there. It's kinda last minute."

"Meeting *someone*? You mean, a *girl*?"

"Yes, Tibbs, a girl—but it's not like that. She's just someone I helped out on the highway a few days ago, and she's taking me out for dinner to say thanks."

"Well, don't leave me in suspense *leatherneck*, what's her name?" Tibbs asked.

"Allison."

"She young?"

"What's with the grand inquisition, old man?" Blake joked.

"Answer the question recruit!" Tibbs said in his best drill instructor voice.

"I'd say she's about my age—I guess."

"Last question—I promise," Tibbs said as he raised his right hand. "She pretty?"

"Yes. She's pretty. But like I said, *It's not like that.*"

"Where ya plan on staying?"

"I'm just gonna get a hotel room for the night. I've got stuff to do in town. I need to buy food and a collar for Buddy and maybe get some laundry done. "Besides, it'd be nice to take a real shower as opposed to this flimsy portable camp shower I've been lugging around."

"No need to explain, Marine. I get it, you don't want show up to your hot date smellin' like a river turd," Tibbs said with a sinister grin.

"I told you, it's—"

"Sorry, sorry, I know, *It's not like that.*"

Blake smiled and shook his head, "You're quite the character."

"These look about ready," Tibbs said as he flipped a couple of the burgers. "Grab yourself a paper plate and a bun and let's eat."

After eating, Tibbs and Blake sat around the fire and talked fly fishing for an hour. Blake looked at his watch, and said, "I better turn in. I want to get an early start tomorrow."

"Well, I'm sorry to see ya go. I've sure enjoyed your company Marine. I'm glad our paths crossed."

"Likewise Tibbs. Thanks for the float trip and the chow. I really appreciate it. I hope we meet again."

"Well, if you ever find yourself up near Bozeman, Montana, make sure you stop by for a cup of coffee. Here's my address and number," Tibbs said as he handed Blake a folded piece of paper. Blake took the paper and held out his hand. Tibbs shook it and said, "Semper Fi Marine."

"Thanks for everything, devil dog," Blake said.

The next morning Blake packed up and he and Buddy made the half-hour drive into Casper. Blake spent the day picking up supplies for him and buddy and found a hotel. That evening Blake got cleaned up for his dinner date with Allison. Before he walked out the door he turned and looked at Buddy who was lying on the bed. "I'll be back soon, boy."

Blake drove to a small country restaurant on the outskirts of Casper called the Pronghorn Bar & Grill. The small western-themed tavern was as rustic as they come, complete with wood siding and a log-framed deck that sheltered the main entrance. A dim golden glow escaped the windows along with the muffled sound of a live country music band.

Blake walked through the front door and looked for Allison. The place was packed with the dinner rush, and Blake stood near the front entrance trying to look over the mounds of people that cluttered the foyer. A voice called out, "Blake! Over here!" Allison was in the process of standing up from a small table that she had obviously reserved. Blake recognized her immediately but took pause as if he was seeing her for the first time. She was stunning, a natural beauty. Allison was wearing a yellow full-length drawstring halter top summer dress. The soft cotton fabric of the bare-backed gown hugged the smooth curves of her hourglass body. Her light brown shoulder-length hair was sun kissed with soft highlights, and the bright yellow color of her dress accentuated her lightly tanned skin.

Allison ran up to Blake with a huge smile on her face. She sprung to the tips of her toes as she wrapped her arms around his shoulders and held him tight. "I'm so glad you came," Allison said with a sigh.

"It's no problem I was still pretty close to town when you called."

"I got us a table. Let's go sit down," Allison said. They walked over to the table and sat. A waitress walked up. "Sam, this is Blake. The one who saved me and Trevor," Allison said. "Blake, this is my friend Sam. We used to work here together."

"So you're the knight in shining armor I've heard so much about," Sam said.

"He's even more handsome than you described," Sam whispered to Allison.

"It's nice to meet you," Blake said bashfully.

"What can I get you two to drink?"

Allison said, "I'll have a draft Coors Light."

"And for you, Blake?"

"Just a water for me, please."

"Don't be silly!" Allison said. "This is my treat. Get yourself a beer, a shot, a mixed drink—" Allison paused and put her hand up to her mouth and whispered, "Just don't order a wine cooler. I'll never hear the end of it."

Blake leaned across the table and whispered back, "I kinda quit drinking recently."

"Ah! Say no more," Allison said as she turned to Sam. "Cancel the beer, Sam. Two waters, please."

"Comin' right up," Sam said.

"Thanks, Allison," Blake said with a smile.

"No problem."

"So. I've got to ask…how'd you get my number?" Blake asked.

"From the police report. Hope I wasn't out of line."

"No, I'm glad you called. I was worried about you two. I take it, you and Trevor are OK?"

"We're just fine. Thanks to you, we walked away with only a couple minor burns, few bruises and scratches—and one hell of a headache. They kept us in the hospital overnight as a precaution, but we both got a clean bill of health the next morning."

Just then a middle aged man, who was sporting an impressive beer belly and wearing a white straw cowboy hat, walked up to the table. Allison stood and gave him a hug. The man squeezed her tight and said, "I'm so glad you're OK. Sam was showing me the pictures of the crash. Thank God you and Trevor weren't killed."

"Well, thank God and also this man," Allison said as she pointed to Blake. "Ike I'd like you to meet my rescuer, Blake Jacobs. He's the one who pulled me and Trevor from the wreck."

The man held his hand out and shook Blake's hand. "Blake, it's nice to meet you. Thank you so much for saving our Allison."

"Ike's the owner of the Pronghorn," Allison said.

"I am indeed, so let me buy you a drink, Blake. What's your poison?" Ike asked.

"I appreciate it Ike, but I'm OK for now."

"Nonsense. Sam! Sam!" Ike yelled as he waved his arm motioning Sam over to the table. "Set my man Blake up with a drink of his choice and bring me a tequila."

Allison looked at Blake and said, "Ike's pretty stubborn. He won't let it go. You might as well get a drink or he'll pester us all night."

Blake sighed with frustration.

Allison turned to Sam and said, "Hey Sam, why don't you bring me and Blake two *Allison Style* bourbons."

"Two bourbons on the rocks, comin' up," Sam said before she walked over to the bar.

"I really shouldn't drink that," Blake said to Allison.

"Trust me, just one drink. Please?" Allison pleaded with Blake.

"Fine. But just the one."

Sam returned shortly after with two whiskey glasses of bourbon and a shot of tequila for Ike. Ike raised his glass and said, "To Blake...for saving Allison and little Trevor. You'll always be welcome here."

Blake nodded in gratitude and reluctantly raised the glass to his mouth. Initially he took a small sip but as the liquid poured over his taste buds, he couldn't help but lift the glass back up for a second swallow, then gulped the remainder and slammed it on the table.

"Ha! That's what I'm talkin' about!" Ike said. "Well done! How about another?"

Blake looked at Sam and said, "I'll take another just like that."

"You got it," Sam said with a tilted grin.

"Well, you two enjoy yourselves tonight. Blake, if you need anything just let me know." Ike said as he walked away.

Blake looked at Allison and said, "So that's an *Allison Style* bourbon? Iced tea? I was worried about falling off the wagon and you knew all along Sam had brought me iced tea?"

"See, you can trust me," Allison said, then giggled. "You should've seen the look on your face when you first tasted that tea. I just about spit my drink all over the table! Good job by the way, for playing it so cool. I was worried you might blow it."

Blake was impressed. Allison was like no girl he had ever met before. She was fun, smart, confident, and had a contagious carefree attitude. Blake sat there while they ate their dinner, listening to Allison's life story. She explained how she got married at 18 to her high school sweetheart and became pregnant shortly after, only to have her husband run off with another woman before Trevor was born. She told how she and Trevor lived with her parents who managed a small cattle ranch outside of town and how she was going to school part time and had aspirations to one day become a grade school teacher.

Blake was enchanted by her radiant blue eyes that seemed to have a personality all their own. He carefully studied her face. She had light dusting of freckles around her nose and one small dimple in her right cheek that only appeared when she smiled.

"So, aside from giving up alcohol and saving women and children from burning cars, what does Blake Jacobs do?" Allison asked.

"Well, up until about a year ago, I was in the Marine Corps."

"Ah! A military man. That explains the courage." Allison said.

"And now, well, I'm fishing my way across Wyoming and Montana in hopes of ending up in Alaska before September."

"That's one hell of a fishing trip. When are you leaving Casper?"

"Tomorrow morning actually. I'm gonna go camp near the Miracle Mile stretch of the North Platte for a couple days. After that, I'm headed to Jackson Hole to fish the Snake River."

"That's too bad," Allison said. "I was hoping you were gonna hang around for a while."

Allison spun around in her chair as she heard the band begin to play a slow twangy love song. Allison turned back to Blake. She looked at him with a flirty smirk and asked, "So…can you dance?"

"Not well," Blake said with a laugh.

"Come on. Dance with me."

Blake stood up and held out his hand. "I guess I owe you a dance after saving me with that iced tea."

Allison smiled, stood up, and took Blake's hand. He led her out to the dance floor. They turned and faced each other. Blake reached under Allison's left arm with his right hand and placed his open palm high on her back. Allison placed her left hand just below Blake's right shoulder along his upper arm. They clasped their free hands together, and Blake stepped forward with his left foot just as Allison took a step back with her right. At arm's length, they gazed into each other's eyes as they slowly danced their way counter clockwise around the dance floor. With every series of steps, they felt more at ease in each other's arms. Soon the stiffness in their muscles began to relax, and the inches of empty space that separated their bodies began to dissolve.

Blake released his hold on Allison's hand, slipped both his arms down around her waist and pulled her closer to him. Allison slid her hands onto Blake's shoulders and delicately wrapped both her arms around his neck. She rested the side of her head on his chest and closed her eyes, as they held each other while slowly swaying back and forth to the music.

Allison was reminded of the safety she felt after Blake had pulled her from the wreckage of the burning sedan. With the memory of the terror she experienced that day still fresh in her mind, she found herself once again comforted by the protection of Blake's warm embrace.

The song came to an end, and Allison lifted her head from Blake's chest and looked into his eyes. A tear escaped her eye and raced down her cheek. Blake wiped the tear away with a gentle swipe of his thumb.

"Are you OK?" Blake asked.

"Sorry, I don't know where that came from," Allison said.

"I—I should probably get going," Blake said.

"Yes—of course, your fishing trip. You've probably gotta get up pretty early tomorrow."

"I really had a good time tonight, Allison. Thank you so much for everything."

"No. Thank you, Blake. Thank you for what you did for me and my son," Allison said as she gave him a hug goodbye. "You have my number, so if you ever find yourself near Casper again…stop and say hi."

"I will. I promise."

Blake took a few steps toward the front door before he heard Allison call out, "Thanks for the dance, Blake Jacobs."

Blake turned around with a soft smile. "Thanks for the iced tea, Allison Grace."

CHAPTER SIXTEEN

A Moment on the Mile

Blake went back to the hotel and settled in for the night. Restless, he laid awake thinking about Allison. He was infatuated with her. He wanted to stay in Casper and see her again, but he had to face the fact that he didn't set out on this journey to find love. Even a few days' detour might throw a wrench in his plans to make it to Alaska by early autumn. He just couldn't take a chance on postponing his trip any longer, but he also couldn't stop thinking about the night he and Allison had and how good he felt when he was with her.

The next morning, he and Buddy set out on the hour-and-a-half drive from Casper to the Miracle Mile. Buddy sat in the front seat with a tilted head and an inquisitive look on his face while listening to Blake mumble to himself as he tried to work out a plausible scenario that might allow him to see Allison again before he left for Jackson Hole. Just then, Blake's cell phone rang. It was Allison. Blake answered. "Hey. I was just thinking about calling you."

"Oh yeah? You gonna hang around here for a little bit?" Allison asked.

"Unfortunately, no, I'm driving to the Miracle Mile as we speak, but I was thinking maybe you could drive out to the river tomorrow. It's not that far. I could make us lunch."

"Hmm…"

"Come on. I make a mean turkey sandwich."

"Only if I can bring Trevor," Allison said.

"Absolutely!" Blake said with delight. "That'd be great! The three of us can go for a hike along the river, fish, or whatever you want." Blake spent the next few minutes talking with Allison and working out their plans for the next day. Afterward, he drove for another hour before pulling up to a camping spot along the famed Miracle Mile.

The nickname *Miracle Mile* was deceiving because this stretch of the North Platte was about five-and-a-half-miles long. Referred to only as *The Mile* by angling aficionados, it was a wide stretch of river boasting a healthy population of large rainbow and brown trout; some even reaching the 10-pound range. The landscape was diverse, with a mixture of wind-blown prairies and tall shrub-covered hills with large rocky outcrops. The area was wild and remote with no accommodations except poorly maintained dirt roads that lent access to a few dispersed campsites along the river. As far as Blake was concerned it was the next best thing to heaven.

Blake didn't waste any time. He quickly set up camp and rigged up his fly rod. He walked to the bank of the river, took a deep breath, and scanned the grand scenery. He let out an exaggerated exhale, looked at Buddy, and said, "Let's do this." Then he and Buddy set out exploring the river.

Blake walked upstream surveying the multiple seams, pools, and channels created from the heavy current colliding with the rocky structure of the river bottom. Before too long he spotted a promising-looking trough that he wasn't about to pass up.

He had a nymphing rig ready to go with a couple of Aaron's mayfly nymphs tied to the end of his tippet. Before Blake threw his first cast he studied the channel for movement, and as soon as his eyes adjusted to the water, he was spotting dark shadows moving in the trough. "This looks good, Buddy," Blake said with a hint of excitement. Buddy stood there with his tail wagging wildly as he sensed the happiness in Blake's voice.

Blake let out a few feet of line and cast his flies near the front end of the trough. On the first drift, Blake's strike indicator flinched. He snapped his fly rod up to set the hook. Blake's rod tip bent down toward the water, and he could feel an intense tug coming from the end of his line. "Got him!" Blake yelled out as he began to fight the trout. Buddy began jumping up and down on the river bank, but as quickly as the battle began, suddenly the line snapped loose, and the end of Blake's rod straightened. "Noooo!" Blake yelled as he realized the fish had come off. Hoping that the trout had only thrown the hooks, Blake quickly stripped in his line. "Son of a bitch! He broke me off! And on the first damn drift! Those were Aaron's flies!" Blake yelled out angrily as he examined the frayed end of his tippet. "Dammit! I knew I should've used stronger tippet. What the fuck is wrong with me? I can't afford to lose any of his flies!"

Buddy laid down on the ground with his head between his front paws. After seeing Buddy cower in fear, Blake paused, took a deep breath, and said, "Sorry, Buddy. I shouldn't have lost my cool. It's OK, come here, boy." With his head down and his tail tucked, Buddy carefully walked over to Blake. Blake pet Buddy on the head and said, "Maybe I'll just fish my own flies until I get the hang of this river. Sorry for yelling, pal."

Blake stored Aaron's fly box in his backpack for safe keeping and took out one of his own fly boxes. He tied on a heavier pound-strength tippet to his leader and tied on fresh flies. Blake went back to fishing the trough. After a few more drifts, Blake's line went tight once again. Blake could feel the heavy tension of a solid hookup. The trout turned in the water, and a flash from the sunlight reflecting off the trout's scales gave Blake a glimpse of the battle that would ensue.

"Holy cow, Buddy!" Blake yelled after seeing the length and girth of the fish. "This thing's a toad!" The trout bullied its way down deep into the trough as it tossed its head from side to side trying to dislodge the hook. Blake kept steady pressure on the fish by keeping his rod tip over the trout's head. The wild trout began to swing its body and tail violently as it pulled its way down to the bottom of the river. Blake's reel made a short zipping sound with each of the trout's tail thrusts until the survival instincts of the fish fully engaged, and the trout turned and made a strong downstream run. The drag on Blake's reel whaled as the fish used the strength of the fast current to assist in its escape. Buddy barked and ran down the shoreline in hot pursuit.

Blake was forced to give chase as well, running downstream along the river bank trying to keep pace with the trophy fish. Blake held his right arm straight up, keeping the tip of his rod aimed toward the sky. In a mad dash to catch up to the trout, he brushed past willow bushes and jumped over rocks along the bank. The fish was merciless with its downstream run, relentlessly pulling line downriver. Blake ran as hard as he could, hurtling over any obstacle in his way until he caught up with the elusive trout. When he did, the fish swam toward him causing slack to form in the line. Blake knew without tension on the line the small hook would likely fall out of the trout's mouth. He frantically stripped line trying to retrieve enough to put pressure back on the trout. A stack of fly line began to pile up at Blake's feet. Then, the trout suddenly changed direction and made another downstream run toward a slew of white-capped rapids.

With the fly line at his feet, Blake had no choice but to quickly reel in as much slack line as he could before he could continue. He pinched the line between his right index finger and the cork of the rod to keep the pressure on the trout and with his left hand reeled the slack line from his feet trying to spool it back to the reel as fast as he could. The trout continued its ferocious run and Blake lightly adjusted the pressure enough to allow some slack line to feed through his finger and the cork of his rod.

Blake finally got enough slack line spooled to move again. He again ran down the river just as the trout entered the rapids. Blake knew he needed to be as delicate as possible and only keep enough tension on the trout to keep the fly from popping out of his mouth. As strong as this current was, any extra pressure was sure to snap the tippet. To accomplish this, he had to keep solid pace with the current. As Blake continued to run, he looked ahead and could see that there was a decent-size pool at the end of the rapids. This is where Blake stood his best chance at landing the fish.

Blake watched as the trout rolled out of the last rapid. He could now clearly see that it was a giant brown. Blake kept solid tension on the fish as it finally slowed trying to recover from the fight in the calmer water. He reeled the fish closer as the tired behemoth flailed still not willing to give up. The trout was now within range. He held his rod up high with his right hand and reached with his left around his back and slid his landing net from behind his wader belt. Blake reached down with the net as the brown trout tossed and belly rolled like a crocodile as it made a last-ditch attempt to free itself. He lunged forward with the net, plunging it into the water and thrusting it underneath the trout. With all his might, Blake pulled the net out of the water only to discover the trout was teetering on the back edge of the net with most of its body still outside the mouth. "Come on! Come on! Stay in!" Blake yelled as the weight of the trout's tail slowly pulled the rest of its body free.

The fish splashed back into the river and immediately made another run to get away. Blake quickly tucked the handle of the landing net under his left arm and awkwardly went back to fighting the fish. The exhausted trout didn't get far before he finally submitted to the pull of Blake's line. He reached into the water with the net for another try and scooped the trout head first into his landing net. Blake screamed out, "Yes!"

He looked down into the net to see a beautiful brown-sugar-over-butter-colored kyped jaw male brown trout that easily measured over 25 inches and weighed close to seven pounds. "Waaahooo! That's what I'm talkin' about, Buddy!" Blake yelled. Buddy spun around in circles sharing in Blake's joy.

Blake's heart suddenly felt something it hadn't experienced in quite some time—true exuberance. In that one magical moment after the grueling battle with the magnificent brown trout, Blake forgot about Iraq…about Aaron's death…about his painful darkness. It was like he was transported back to a time of innocence when all he knew was the simple life of a free young man who loved to fish.

But the moment was just that…a moment, and as suddenly as it had appeared, it was gone. Blake, still lost in the euphoria, looked up almost expecting to see Aaron waiting to take a photo of Blake's trophy but of course, he was not there. Blake's breathing began to slow, his smile dissipated, and his leg began to ache from the arduous run.

Blake turned his attention back to the trout. He admired its beauty for a moment as he gently nursed the fish back to health by holding it in a small channel just off shore. Blake was thankful for that temporary moment of peace that the fish had brought him. Even though the feeling didn't last but a few minutes, it was a moment that a year earlier Blake could never had imagined experiencing again. After a few minutes the trout's strength returned and it swiftly swam away, kicking up a splash of water as it flapped its tail fin. Some of the water splashed onto Blake's chin and cheek. He smiled and slowly wiped the droplets from his face as he watched with gratitude as the brown returned to the depths of the river.

CHAPTER SEVENTEEN

Heart of a Lion

The next morning Blake awoke to the sound of a low growl coming from Buddy who was standing at the door of the tent. "What's wrong, boy?" Blake asked. "Ya hear something?" The sound of a vehicle prompted Blake to get up and poke his head out of the tent. An old tan Ford pickup pulled up next to his truck and stopped. The driver's side door of the truck opened with a rusty squeak and out stepped Allison. "They're here already? Crap! I slept in!" Blake threw some clothes on and hurried out of the tent.

"Well, hi there Sleeping Beauty," Allison joked, as Blake emerged from his tent hopping on one foot while trying to put a shoe on. "Hope we're not too early? I must have heard you wrong when you said to meet here at nine."

"Sorry, my fault. I must have overdone it a little when I was fishing yesterday." Blake looked behind Allison to see a short little brown haired boy peeking out from behind her leg. "Hey, I know you. Remember me, Trevor?"

Trevor ducked back behind Allison's leg. "He's pretty shy," Allison said. "Trevor, tell Mr. Jacobs hi."

Trevor peeked his head back out from behind Allison's leg and said, "Hi, Mistow Jacobs."

"You can call me Blake if you want," Blake said in a kind tone.

Trevor looked at Allison for approval, and she said, "It's OK. You can call him Blake."

"OK, Bwake," Trevor said with a grin.

"He's cute. How old is he?"

"He's four. He has a little trouble with his 'L's and sometimes his 'R's," Allison said as she ruffled Trevor's hair.

"Trevor, do you like dogs?" Blake asked. Trevor smiled and nodded. "Well then, meet my dog. His name's Buddy."

Trevor walked up to Buddy and said, "Hi, Buddy." Buddy ducked his head down as Trevor pet him. Buddy seemed alarmed and overly guarded. His tail stood straight up but didn't wag as he sniffed Trevor's leg. Suddenly Buddy began to growl.

"Buddy! No!" Blake said. He pulled Buddy away from Trevor and looked at Allison. "Sorry, I've never seen him act like that. Maybe he's just not used to kids."

"It's OK. I'm sure he'll get used to us after a while."

Blake knelt down to be at eye level with Trevor. "Do you want to go down to the river and throw some rocks?"

"Yes!" Trevor said.

The three of them walked down to the river while Buddy followed at a safe distance. Buddy seemed on edge, as he paced behind them. When the group reached the river, Buddy stopped and sat on top of a small hill and watched.

Blake looked around and found a smooth flat pebble. He picked up the rock and turned to Trevor. "Watch this." He threw the pebble sidearm toward the water. The rock spun through the air and skipped off the surface of the water for a few feet, then skipped again. Trevor's jaw dropped. "You want to see that again?" Blake asked.

Trevor nodded enthusiastically, and said, "Yes!"

Blake picked up another rock and repeated the feat a few times over. Trevor soon joined in the fun, and they threw rocks together. Allison sat in the grass and watched them. Blake looked up at Allison, and they smiled at each other. Blake turned to Trevor and said, "Hey sport, keep throwing those rocks. I'm gonna go talk with your Mom for a bit."

Blake walked over to Allison and sat down beside her. "He's a pretty cool kid," Blake said.

"He sure is," Allison said as she watched Trevor toss another stone into the water.

"Can I get you and Trevor something to drink?" Blake asked.

"Sure. I'll take a water if you've got it," Allison said.

"What about Trevor? I've got soda in the cooler."

"Nah, he can share my water for now. If he's good, he can have a soda for lunch."

"Sounds good. I'll be right back."

On his way back to the camp, Blake walked up to Buddy who was whining and pacing at the top of the hill. "You need to calm down, Buddy. You didn't act like this when Tibbs was around. What's wrong?" Buddy just kept whining and making shallow woofs toward Allison and Trevor. "You better knock it off, or I'm gonna leave you in the tent," Blake said, as they arrived back at camp.

Blake walked with Buddy back down to the river with a couple bottles of water. As soon as they came within sight of Allison and Trevor, Buddy suddenly stopped and took an aggressive posture. His ears fell back and his eyebrows furrowed as he leaned forward. The hair on Buddy's mane stood up and the deep tremors from his growl rumbled as his upper lip quivered exposing his sharp fangs.

"Buddy! No!" Blake scolded. "What's gotten into you?" Buddy ignored Blake's command as his hostility increased. He crouched down. The tension in Buddy's muscles caused his legs to shiver as he prepared to lunge forward. "Buddy! Knock it off!" Blake yelled, but Buddy refused to back down. Blake reached down and grabbed Buddy's collar. Buddy snapped at Blake. Surprised, Blake released his grip on Buddy's collar, and Buddy immediately burst into a full sprint. "Buddy! No! Stop!" Blake yelled as he watched Buddy charge toward Allison and Trevor. "Allison! Look out!" Blake yelled. Allison looked up to see Buddy descending on them at a lightning pace, snarling, with a ferocious look in his eyes. She grabbed Trevor and spun him away from the savage dog, her back facing Buddy. "Stop! Buddy stop!" Blake yelled, desperately trying to snap Buddy out of his insanity. Allison closed her eyes, held onto Trevor, and braced for the worst as the vivid sound of Buddy's nails clawing and scraping at the ground while he ran, indicated the attack was only a heartbeat away.

Buddy leaped, flying just over the two and violently crashed through the side of a large willow bush. Out from the other side of the bush came a huge cougar that was now backed up onto its hind legs with its front claws swiping the air attempting to fend off Buddy's surprise onslaught. "Oh shit! A mountain lion!" Blake yelled. "Allison. Run this way!" Blake said as he ran toward Allison and Trevor. Trevor had his arms wrapped around the back of Allison's neck as she held him tight against her chest and ran toward Blake, while Buddy bravely continued to engage the cougar.

The puma was huge, easily three times the size of Buddy. It hissed at Buddy, exposing the viciousness of its pointed yellow teeth. Buddy held his ground, barking relentlessly, thus buying precious time for Allison and Trevor to escape. The lion lunged forward swiping at Buddy with its right front claw hitting the front of Buddy's left torso. Buddy let out a yelp as the lion's razor sharp nails pierced his hide and tore through the muscle in his leg and shoulder. The force of the blow knocked Buddy onto his side. The cat quickly pounced on Buddy and pinned him down with its paws. The cougar clamped down on Buddy's neck with its powerful jaws in an attempt to crush his throat and sever his jugular. Buddy tried to turn his head to bite the lion but the puma's teeth sank deeper into his neck. With a bloody froth building in his mouth, Buddy growled and snapped his teeth together trying to defend himself but the cougar would not release its hold. Buddy wiggled and squirmed on the ground desperately trying to push himself back to his feet, but the mountain lion was too big…too fast…and too strong.

Buddy's strength was quickly being sapped as the lion's strangling bite began squeezing the final breaths of life from his body. Then suddenly, *wham!* A rock flew through the air and cracked against the cougar's skull causing it to release its jaw clamp. The lion roared in anger. *Wham! Wham!* The puma bellowed as several more rocks hit its body. "Get away from him!" Blake yelled as he ran toward the lion, picking up any rock he could find along the way and hurling it at the big cat. The cougar hissed at Blake, but Blake, full of rage, picked up a large stick from the ground and charged the lion. "Get away from him you son-of-bitch!" Blake screamed as he held the stick over his head with both hands. The lion quickly retreated. Blake threw the stick as hard as he could. The stick flipped end over end through the air like a tomahawk until it crashed against the lion's back splintering into several pieces. Stunned, the mountain lion ran off and disappeared into the shrubs leaving Buddy, covered in blood, lying on the ground.

Blake ran up to Buddy and dropped to his knees. He thought for sure Buddy was dead. He sat there panicked as he searched for any sign of life. He put his hand under Buddy's head and gently lifted it a couple inches from the ground. He could sense a shallow breath still escaping Buddy's mouth, and he could feel him twitching. Blood was still slowly running from the lacerations on Buddy's left shoulder and leg. "Hold on, Buddy, I'm gonna get you outta here," Blake said as he quickly pulled off his T-shirt and laid it on the ground next to Buddy. He picked Buddy up and carefully put him down on the shirt. Buddy began to whine from the pain. "Easy, boy, I've got ya," Blake said as he tied the shirt tight around the wounds.

"Blake! Blake!" Allison yelled as she ran back down the hill.

"Allison what are you doing? Where's Trevor?"

"He's safe. He's in the truck," Allison said as she ran up to Blake short of breath. "Oh my God…Buddy! Will he be OK?"

"I don't know. I've got to get him to a vet," Blake said as he held his hand against the puncture wounds on Buddy's neck.

"Here, use this," Allison said as she pulled off a thin white blouse she had tied around her waist.

Blake took the blouse and gently wrapped it around Buddy's neck and asked, "Where's the nearest vet?"

"About an hour from here. It's the vet we use for the animals at the ranch."

"Can you get us there?"

"Yes. The vet should be in today."

"OK, I'll take buddy in my truck and follow you over there. Let's hurry before that cougar decides to come back." Blake cradled Buddy in his arms and carried him up to his truck. He placed Buddy on the passenger seat and followed Allison out of the campground and back onto the highway.

During the long drive back toward Casper, Blake had plenty of time to think about what had just happened. Buddy must have been aware of the lion's presence throughout the morning. He tried to warn Blake the only way he knew how, but Blake never picked up on it. "I'm sorry, Buddy. I should have known something was wrong. Don't worry, I'm gonna get you all fixed up." Buddy slowly closed his eyes. "Wake up, Buddy! Hang in there for me!" Blake said as he tried to keep buddy conscious. Gradually Buddy's breathing began to labor as the sound of a watery wheeze could be heard every time he exhaled. "Come on, Buddy, hang in there. We'll be there soon, I promise."

When Allison and Blake finally pulled into the parking lot of the veterinarian's office, Allison and Trevor ran inside ahead of Blake. Blake ran around to the passenger side of the truck and gently picked up Buddy. Buddy was still breathing, but he had gone limp, and his eyes were closed.

Suddenly Allison burst out of the office followed by an elderly man, and said, "He's over here, Dr. Samuels."

Dr. Samuels walked up to Blake and asked, "What do we have here?"

"It's my dog, Buddy. He was attacked by a mountain lion about an hour ago."

"Where's he hurt?" Dr. Samuels asked as he lightly pulled back on the bandage.

"He's got a pretty deep claw cut on his left shoulder, and he's got several punctures in his neck from where the lion bit him."

"Well, let's get him back into my exam room so I can take a closer look," Dr. Samuels said.

Blake rushed Buddy into the room and placed him down on a stainless steel table. Dr. Samuels cut off Buddy's rudimentary bandages with a pair of trauma sheers and looked closer at the wounds. Blake asked, "Is he gonna be OK?"

Dr. Samuels said, "He's hurt pretty bad. I need to get to work on him right away. It'd be best if you could wait out in the waiting room."

Blake and Allison walked back to the waiting room. Trevor was already there patiently sitting in a chair. Blake sat down a few seats away from Trevor. He leaned back in the chair, tilted his head back, and let out a deep breath.

Trevor stood up and walked over to Blake. He stood there for a second as tears began welling up in his eyes and said, "Bwake?"

Blake looked over at Trevor and said, "Yeah?"

With his lower lip slightly trembling, Trevor asked, "Is Buddy going to be OK?"

Blake gently put his arm around Trevor. "I sure hope so, sport. I sure hope so."

CHAPTER EIGHTEEN

The Sergeant Who Saved Me

More than four hours had passed. Allison had taken Trevor home. Blake sat in the waiting room waiting to hear about Buddy's condition. A tall thin middle-aged man, wearing a dingy-white long sleeve twill shirt and faded straight-cut Wrangler blue jeans came in. The man scanned the waiting room before saying, "Pardon me…but are you Blake?"

Blake stood up. "Yes, Blake Jacobs."

The man held out his hand and said, "I'm Emmett Grace—Allison's father."

"Mr. Grace, it's nice to meet you," Blake said as he shook hands with the man.

"Please, call me Emmett."

"OK—Emmett."

"I appreciate everything you did for my daughter and grandson the other day."

"It was no big deal. I was happy to help."

"From what I saw of that wreck it *was* a big deal, and I owe you my thanks."

"You're very welcome, sir."

"Allison speaks very highly of you. Says you're a good man."

"She's very kind, I think highly of her too."

Emmett gave a smile and asked, "How's your dog doin'?"

"I'm not sure. I'm still waiting on word from the vet."

"Well, if there's anyone who can help him it's Dr. Samuels. He's one of the best vets in Wyoming, and he's been a trusted friend for years."

Dr. Samuels walked into the waiting room, and Blake anxiously asked, "How is he, Doc?"

"Well, he's beat up pretty bad and needed quite a few stitches. The punctures in his neck caused a lot of bleeding but amazingly didn't cause any serious injuries."

"Thank God for that," Blake said.

"Buddy's most serious injuries were caused by the lacerations to his left shoulder and leg," Dr. Samuels continued. "I've got him stitched up the best I can, but the damage to the muscle tissue was severe. I have him sedated. He'll sleep through the night and probably most of the morning. I'd like to keep him here for a couple days. After that, he'll still need to take it easy for a while until the muscle can heal."

"But he's gonna be OK?" Blake asked.

"He'll have some mobility issues for a while, but yes, in time, I suspect he'll be OK."

Emmett nodded and said, "That's great news, Dr. Samuels. Now. I'd appreciate it if you'd put the bill for all this on my account."

"Sure thing, Emmett," Dr. Samuels said.

"What? No. I mean—I appreciate it, Emmett, but I have the money to pay for this."

"Nonsense. I've got this covered. The way I see it, both you and that dog have saved my little girl and grandson, you with the crash and him with that lion. This is the least I can do. I said I'm payin' for it, and that's the end of it. Now, let's get you back to the ranch. You look like you could use some food."

"I appreciate it, but I'm camped out on the North Platte," Blake said.

"I know, Allison told me. In fact, that's where I just came from. I packed up your tent and such. It's all in the back of my truck."

"Really? You drove all the way out there and picked up my stuff? I don't know what to say."

"Just say you'll come to the ranch. Besides, Allison made me promise to bring you with me."

Blake reluctantly agreed.

"Well, all right then," Emmett said with a grin. "Let's get goin'. Dinner's gonna be waitin' for us when we get there."

Blake followed Emmett back to the ranch which was only about 15 miles from Dr. Samuels's office. They turned onto a long dirt road that lead them to a beige two-story country house with white trim and a wraparound porch. Sitting outside on a wicker-weaved patio chair, waiting for them, was Allison.

Blake and Emmett walked up to the house. Allison met them at the top of the porch steps. She gave Emmet a hug and said, "Thanks, Dad."

"Sure, honey. I'll let you two talk."

Emmett walked into the house, and Allison turned and hugged Blake tight. "Are you OK?"

"Yeah, I'm fine. How are you and Trevor?"

"Trevor's a little shaken up, but I'm OK. How's Buddy?"

"The doctor says he's gonna make it. He'll need to stay at the vet's for a few nights."

"I've already talked to my dad, he said you can stay here as long as you need to."

"I appreciate it, but I don't want to impose."

"You're not imposing, I promise. We have a guest cabin. It's empty most of the time. Please stay, just for a few days," Allison said with her hands folded and a hopeful look on her face.

"OK, OK, I'll stay," Blake said. "I really appreciate you and your family's generosity."

"Don't mention it," Allison said. "Now let's go eat. I hope you like fried chicken."

Blake walked into the house. The country-style home had hardwood floors in nearly every room and was decorated with rustic but polished, Western decor. Blake walked into the dining room with Allison. Emmett was already seated at the head of the table, and Trevor was sitting in a booster chair to the right of Emmett.

"Hi Bwake!" Trevor yelled.

Blake laughed to himself. "Well, hi there, sport!"

"Have a seat Blake," Emmett said pointing to the chair at the other end of the table. Blake sat down. A woman carrying a plate of fried chicken walked into the dining room.

"Blake, this is my mom, Ruth," Allison said as Ruth placed the chicken in the center of the table among all the other side dishes.

Blake stood up and walked around the table and shook her hand. "It's a pleasure to meet you, Ruth."

"The pleasure's all mine, Blake. I hope you're hungry," Ruth said.

"I am indeed. I can't thank you enough for having me over. Everything smells so good."

"Well, everyone have a seat," Emmett said. "Allison, would you like to say the prayer?"

"Sure," Allison said. Allison sat down next to Trevor, while Ruth sat down on the other side of the table. Blake folded his hands and bowed his head. "Dear Lord, thank you for the food we're about to eat and for the countless blessings you've given this family. Thank you for watching over us during these difficult last few days, and thank you for sending Blake into our lives. In Jesus' name we pray, amen." Everyone said the amen in unison. Blake looked over at Allison, and they exchanged smiles.

"Well, don't be bashful Blake, get yourself some chicken," Emmett said.

"Don't mind if I do," Blake said and reached over and put two pieces of chicken on his plate.

"So, Blake, Allison tells me you were a military man," Emmett said as he passed a big bowl of mashed potatoes to Allison.

"Yeah, I was with the Second Battalion, Fourth Marines."

"Ah…the *Magnificent Bastards!*" Emmett said as if he was answering a trivia question on a game show.

"Emmett! Watch your language around Trevor," Ruth said.

"You don't understand, dear, that's the nickname of his outfit."

"I'm impressed, Emmett. You know, you're the only person I've met outside the 2/4 who's known that."

"My Dad's a bit of a military history nut," Allison said, as she passed the potatoes to Blake.

"I'm not a *nut*, honey, *enthusiast*…get it right…*enthusiast*," Emmett said.

"Right, Dad, *military enthusiast*," Allison said and rolled her eyes. "Anyway, there's nothing about American military history he doesn't know."

"Really? That's pretty cool. Did you serve?" Blake asked as he shook out his napkin and placed it on his lap.

"Yeah, I did a stent with the Navy back in the 80's. Nothing exciting. Nothin' even close to what you and your generation have had to deal with," Emmett said.

Blake picked up a piece of fried chicken and bit into it. The golden crispy outside crunched as his teeth sank through the flaky crust into the juicy meat. "Mmm," Blake hummed as he savored the scrumptious chicken. "Please, don't tell my mother this, Ruth, but this is the most flavorful fried chicken I've ever had," he said as he took another bite.

"Well, thank you, Blake. I'm glad you like it," Ruth said, and smiled.

"Yes, you've outdone yourself once again, my dear. So Blake, you're headed to Alaska?"

"Yes—well, that's the plan. Although, with Buddy getting hurt I'm starting to wonder if I'll make it before fall."

"It shouldn't take you more than a week to drive there from here. What's your worry?"

"Well, I'm not just driving to Alaska. I've got a list of rivers I'm trying to fish along the way, not to mention more than a few rivers to fish once I'm in Alaska. So I've got to get there before the weather turns."

"You fishn' all by yourself?" Emmett asked.

"For the most part…although I did meet a former Marine when I was fishing the Grey Reef. I fished with him most of my time there."

"Oh yeah?"

"He was a real nice guy. A Vietnam vet named Tibbs. Said he was with the 1/9."

"Oh wow," Emmett said leaning back in his chair, "one of *The Walking Dead.*"

"The Walking Dead?"

"You don't know? The Walking Dead is what the 1/9 started calling themselves during the Vietnam War," Emmett said.

"No, I'd never heard that."

"They were nicknamed that due to the high casualty rate they suffered during the war. In fact, while deployed in Vietnam, they had the highest KIA rate of any single Marine battalion in the history of the Marine Corps," Emmett said as he buttered a dinner roll.

"Sorry, what's KIA?" Allison asked.

"It's an acronym for Killed in Action," Blake said, then looked back at Emmett in disbelief and asked, "Really? The highest KIA rate in the history of the Corps?"

"It's not that unbelievable when you consider they spent 48 consecutive months conducting combat operations."

"Seriously…48 straight months?" Blake said. "That's an insane amount of time."

"I know. Can you even begin to imagine, what *that* fella must have gone through?"

"No. I—I guess I can't," Blake said in a somber tone.

"Mommy, who's dead?" Trevor asked Allison.

"You see Emmett! Look what you've done," Ruth scolded. Nobody's dead Trevor, now eat your chicken before it gets cold." Ruth turned to Emmett and slapped him on the shoulder with her napkin.

"Sorry, that wasn't exactly an appropriate dinner topic," Blake said.

"That's OK, Blake. Why don't you tell us more about this fishing trip of yours," Ruth said.

"Well, there's really not much to tell. My best friend and I planned this road trip from Colorado to Alaska a few years back. We wrote down a list of rivers we wanted to fish along the way. Before we could take the trip, 9/11 happened, and we both ended up joining the Marine Corps and deploying to Iraq. So, now that I'm out of the Corps, I thought I'd take the trip and visit all the rivers on our list."

"How come your friend didn't come with you?" Ruth asked.

Blake looked over at Trevor, then back at Ruth and discreetly answered, "He didn't make it back from Iraq."

"Oh, Blake, I'm sorry," Ruth said. "I really put my foot in my mouth didn't I?"

Blake smiled. "No, it's OK. He was a good man and a good friend."

"What was his name?" Allison asked.

"Aaron Grady. We grew up together in the same neighborhood in Colorado. Anyway, that's why I'm going on this trip…in honor of him."

"The trip's probably helping you as well—dealing with his loss, I mean," Ruth added.

"Well, besides the burning car and a cougar trying to eat my dog…the trip, so far, has been rather therapeutic," Blake joked.

Emmett laughed.

136

"Emmett!" Ruth said.

"Oh, come on, dear, you have to admit that was pretty funny."

Ruth playfully squinted her eyes at Emmett, who winked at her.

"How long before Buddy can travel?" Allison asked.

"I'm not sure, probably a while. I'm gonna go see him tomorrow morning and hopefully Dr. Samuels will have a better idea."

"Whatever the prognosis, you're welcome to stay here as long as you need," Ruth said.

"Thanks Ruth, and thanks to all of you. I really appreciate your hospitality."

While Blake and the Grace family continued eating, they talked and laughed, each trying to one-up the other by telling embarrassing stories from their past. The more Blake learned about the Graces the more he opened up about his own life by telling stories about Aaron, his mother, and the surrogate family who helped raise him. By the end of the meal, Blake almost felt like one of the family.

After spending the evening with Emmett and Ruth, Blake had no doubt where Allison's bold confidence and humor came from. Even her beauty could not compete with the allure of her kind heart and playful spirit. As he sat there, listening to her talk and laugh, he couldn't fathom how any man could ever leave a woman like her.

After dinner, Blake and Allison drove over to the guest cabin that was about a hundred yards off the main house. Allison showed him all the amenities of the cabin and helped him get settled in.

"Well, I'd better get back to the house," Allison said.

"I'll drive you back over," Blake said.

"I've got a better idea. You should walk me back over," Allison said, holding out her hand. Blake smiled and took her hand, and they slowly walked back toward the main house.

The beauty of the luminescent cobalt glow from the full moon lit the night sky and was accentuated by the light serenade of chirping crickets.

"I like your parents. They're pretty funny," Blake said.

"They definitely have their moments. I think they like you too…I know I do," Allison said.

Blake stopped walking and pulled Allison. She turned and faced him. They looked adoringly at each other. A light breeze blew several strands of Allison's hair across her face. Blake reached up and combed the strands back behind her ear, then cupped his hand behind her neck. He looked lovingly into her sapphire eyes, slowly leaned in, and softly kissed her. They held the kiss before gently disengaging. They took a moment to gaze into each other's eyes before Allison smiled and said, "Goodnight, Blake."

Blake smiled back and said, "Goodnight, Allison."

Blake woke up early the next morning to the sound of his cell phone. He rubbed the sleep from his eyes and answered.

"Good morning, Casanova. Time to get up."

Blake smiled. "Good morning, Allison. What time is it?"

"About six-thirty."

"Good grief, how early do you crazy ranch people get up?" Blake asked.

"First off, it's *ranchers*, not ranch people. Secondly, *fish boy,*" Allison joked, "are you hungry?"

"Starved actually."

"Good, I'm making us breakfast. Get cleaned up and get over to the ranch house."

"What—like now?"

"Yep, you've got 15 minutes. Let's go, fish boy! Chop, chop!" Allison said and hung up.

Blake quickly showered and headed over. Trevor was sitting at the table eating his breakfast, and Emmett was sitting next to Trevor, reading a newspaper. Ruth and Allison were cooking in the kitchen. Allison was tending a pan of scrambled eggs. Emmett folded the newspaper and asked, "How'd you sleep last night?"

"I slept well, thanks," Blake said as he sat down at the table. "I'm very comfortable in the cabin."

"Glad to hear it," Emmett said. "What'd you have planned for today?"

"I'm gonna go check on Buddy."

"Doc Samuels called this morning and said he's doing better than expected. He'd like to keep him for one more night, but after that, I think he'll be good to go."

"Really? That's great news!" Blake said.

"Here's your breakfast, Blake," Allison said with a flirty smirk as she brought over a plate of eggs and bacon and a cup of coffee.

"Thanks," Blake said, smiling back.

"Dig in, breakfast isn't as formal as dinner around here," Emmett Said. "Well, even if Buddy's ready to go, don't feel pressured to leave. We all enjoy having you around."

"Thanks, Emmett, I might just take you up on that offer," Blake said, as he shoveled a forkful of eggs into his mouth.

Ruth and Allison sat down at the table and ate as the group picked up where they left off the night before joking around and making Blake feel like a welcome part of the family.

Emmett was half-involved in the conversation as he continued to read the paper, then turned to Ruth and asked, "Remember that Marine from up in Buffalo?"

"The one the paper did that *Hometown Hero* story on?" Ruth asked.

"That's the one. Says here, he took his own life a couple days ago."

"No!" Ruth said. "He seemed like such a happy young man. Why would he do that?"

"I'm not sure, dear. It says the funeral will be held here in Casper tomorrow morning and that he'll be buried with military honors at the national cemetery."

"He was from Buffalo?" Blake asked.

"Yeah, it's a town just north of Casper," Emmett said.

"There was a Marine in my unit who lived in Buffalo. Does it give a name?"

Emmett looked back at the paper. "Sergeant Earl Tomlin."

Blake looked down at the table devastated. Allison asked, "Did you know him?"

"He was my squad leader in Ramadi. He was the sergeant who saved me."

CHAPTER NINETEEN

Call Your Mother

B lake parked across the street from the church. It was a small white building with a steeple that towered over a set of solid oak double doors that guarded the front entrance. A short concrete path paved the way to the front. Blake walked up the stairs and stepped into the foyer. The church was packed, and many of the people were wearing military uniforms. Blake slowly maneuvered through the crowd of melancholy visitors to reach the entryway of the chapel. Once there, he scanned the interior before committing to enter.

The rows of pews were completely full except for the very front. A closed chestnut-stained oak casket with a large American Flag draped over the top was on display beneath the altar. To the left and right of the casket stood a black easel with floral arrangements decorating the floor. The easel on the left displayed a large photograph of Sgt. Tomlin in full Marine Corps *dress blues* wearing a white kingform cover, standing at attention with his many ribbons of achievement and valor, pinned to his chest. To the right, was a candid outdoor portrait of a smiling Earl Tomlin, wearing a gray T-shirt and enjoying civilian life.

As more people filed into the chapel, standing room began to diminish. People lined up against the walls, filling any empty space available. Blake found a spot to stand near the right side of the chapel and settled in as the organ began to play soft comforting gospel music. The crowd near the entrance of the chapel began to part as a middle-aged couple walked down the aisle. The man was walking tall, visibly distressed but with his head held high as he held a woman's hand. The woman, face red and eyes swollen, was holding a white handkerchief that she used to dab the tears from her eyes. Behind them walked two rosy-cheeked, button-nosed, blonde-haired girls wearing matching dark blue dresses, the oldest no more than six.

And that's when Blake saw her, walking behind the girls, holding the arm of a young uniformed Marine who was escorting her...it was Sgt.

Tomlin's widow. Her name was Mindy. She was the spitting image of the two little girls. Blake had never met her but had seen plenty of pictures of her when he was in Iraq. Tomlin used to wallpaper the inside of his hooch with photos of her and his two daughters. He rarely spoke of them unless asked but when he did talk about them, it was always with great love and affection.

The group walked up to the front pew just as the organ music concluded. After they were seated, the youngest of the two girls pointed to the portrait of Tomlin and exclaimed, "Look Mommy, it's Daddy!" Mindy leaned forward, placed her right hand over her eyes to hide her face, and began to cry. The Marine sitting next to her stood up and walked over to the little girl. He knelt down and began whispering something in her ear. The confused little girl asked loudly, "But when is Daddy coming back?" The Marine hugged the little girl tight and whispered something else in her ear. He picked her up, walked back to his seat, and sat down holding the little girl on his lap.

Congested breathing and the sound of sniffling noses echoed in the otherwise silent church. A minister entered from a small door near the right side of the chapel, walked up to the altar, and lead the congregation in the *Lord's Prayer*. Blake folded his hands but never closed his eyes. He couldn't stop staring at that little girl. He felt a deep sorrow for her. He was heartbroken for the inevitable loneliness and sadness that her innocence had thus far sheltered her from, but once realized, would undoubtedly crush her tiny heart. How could she possibly comprehend why this happened? How could anyone fully explain it to her? How could Tomlin, a man who never faltered under pressure, who never gave up despite the odds, who showed unwavering courage and selflessness on the battlefield, have done this to such a precious child…to his children…to his beautiful wife?

Once the prayer was over, the minister walked to a podium and gave a short uplifting sermon. After the sermon, the minister invited the family members and close friends to the podium to give their testimonials to the life of Earl Tomlin as they knew him. One by one, childhood friends, relatives and servicemen came up to speak about their personal relationship with this great man. They recounted humorous stories, told of his courage in the Marine Corps, and talked about his adoring love for his wife and little girls.

When it looked like no one else was going to walk up to the podium, the woman with the handkerchief in the front row slowly stood up. She sedately walked behind the podium and struggled trying to adjust the microphone down closer to her mouth. The preacher popped up from his chair and hurried over to help. She wore a wistful smile on her face as the minister finally got the microphone to cooperate. She stepped up to the podium and in a broken voice, introduced herself, "I'm Catherine Tomlin, Earl's mother." She took the handkerchief and wiped her eyes before continuing, "I appreciate all the very kind things that have been said about Earl today. Many of these stories I'd never heard before. Some of them made me cry, and some of them made me laugh. It's really nice to know that he touched so many people during his time on this earth."

She stopped for a moment, cleared her throat, and took a deep breath, like she was trying to summon the courage to continue. "I love my son." She paused, looked at the Marine in the first row and smiled, "I love both my sons." She stared at the Marine with a tender look in her eye before looking back at the congregation, then said, "But the hard truth is, Earl was stubborn and proud. Two characteristics that ultimately ended up killing him."

The congregation was hushed. Catherine continued, "He always wanted to be the leader, the one that had all the answers. He wanted to be the guy everyone came to for help, but he would never ask for any; no, he was too good for that…too strong. He thought no one could understand what he went through in Iraq. He thought he was strong enough to deal with his depression. He thought he had a handle on his *post-traumatic stress.* He didn't want to burden anyone with his problems, not even his mom. He put on an act that everything was good and right in his world." She went silent for a few seconds. "Looks like he had us all fooled."

Catherine stopped, lowered her head, and wiped the tears from her eyes. Then she looked back up and said, "The last time I talked with Earl was about three weeks ago. I figured he was just busy getting things in order as he adjusted to civilian life and that's why he hadn't stopped by or called back. After a year of sleepless nights, worrying about him as he fought in the Middle East, I was finally sleeping soundly, knowing my little boy was back, safe at home. I was looking forward to seeing him again on a regular basis. I had no idea that he was suffering. I had no idea I was about to lose him. I wish I could hear his voice again, just one more time. I see a lot of uniforms in the congregation. I bet most of you big tough military men still have mothers. When was the last time you called her? When was the last time you told her you loved her? Granted, we moms will never truly know what you go through when you're off fighting overseas. You probably don't want us to know. But we're still your mothers." Catherine's mouth began to tremble as tears ran down her face, "We carried you in our wombs! We sung you to sleep when you were infants! We wiped your runny noses and held you when you were frightened! What gives YOU the right to shut US out? What gives you the right to throw away the *life*, the beautiful life, that we have spent our whole adult lives nurturing, teaching, supporting...loving?"

Catherine stopped for a moment and angrily brushed the tears from her face. She took a slow quivering breath. The tension in her shoulders began to relax as she composed herself and quietly said, "No one person on this earth knows you...like your mother knows you. Promise me...PLEASE promise me, if you ever feel like you just can't go on, like things are getting too difficult...call your mother...tell her you love her. Let her hear your voice. Listen to her voice as she tells you that she loves you too. Let that sound comfort you...like it did when you were a child. Don't rob your mother of the chance to save her little baby boy. Don't ever hurt her like that."

Blake grit his teeth and forced his eyelids open, trying to fight back the reservoir of tears that were dammed up behind his glossy eyes as the raw anger and pure truth of what Catherine had said revealed to Blake the pain he nearly inflicted on his own family...his own mother. Catherine's words ripped off the cloak of self-righteousness Blake had been hiding behind and exposed his hypocrisy. How could he stand there and pass judgment on Tomlin for what he did to his wife and girls, when just a few months ago Blake pressed the barrel of a gun against his own temple? He didn't have the strength to reach out for help. Why was he spared and not Tomlin? Blake knew he wasn't alive because he had some innate ability to fight this darkness. He was a coward—a drunken coward. He would have blown his brains out just like Tomlin if it weren't for a chance visit by Mr. Grady. How could he question the strength of this man, nay, this Marine, who risked life and limb to pull Blake off of that street in Iraq? How selfish was he to think that he was the only person suffering from Aaron's loss...from the loss of all the Marine's killed that day?

Blake began to question everything he'd done since that fateful day. Had he ever reached out to the surviving Marines in his squad? What about the ones who were wounded? What about the ones with their limbs blown off? Were they suffering? He didn't know. How could he? He never bothered to check on them. He was too busy feeling sorry for himself, for his loss. Did he ever mourn the death of the seven other brothers he lost that day? Men that, if given the chance, would have laid down their lives for him without a second thought? No! No, he did not. How could he simply assume that a man of Tomlin's caliber would somehow be impervious to the loss of his men, his mates, and to the mental torments of combat? How could he be so callous, so incredibly selfish? Sgt. Tomlin risked everything that day to save him, but he never looked back to see if Tomlin needed saving. Blake violated the one rule that was sacrosanct among all American Warriors: *Never leave a man behind.*

Blake's eyelids trembled as he strained to hold back the insurmountable sorrow that he was feeling. He looked around, searching for an escape route through the sea of people that clogged the doorway of the chapel. Unable to find a way out, he felt himself losing control of his emotions. His eyelids finally succumbed to the unrelenting urge to close. A curtain of tears flushed from his eyes. Blake dropped his head and cupped his hand over his brow to hide the tears of shame and guilt that ran down his cheeks.

Just then, as a slew of irrepressible emotions came bearing down on him, he felt a hand softly grip his left shoulder. He quickly wiped the tears from his eyes with his sleeve. He turned his head and looked up. It was Tibbs, standing next to him, fixated straight ahead on Catherine who was now leaving the podium and walking back to her seat. He gently patted Blake's shoulder to help calm him. Blake took a moment and composed himself. He looked back up and softly said, "Tibbs?"

Tibbs turned with a kind smile and said, "Semper Fi, Marine."

Blake looked around at the people in the congregation. Other than Tibbs, not a dry eye could be seen. Blake wondered how many others in that chapel had seriously contemplated suicide and were seeing, for the first time, the intense pain it would bring. How many of these people had loved ones who had taken their own lives? How many others were suffering like Tomlin? How many lives might Catherine have changed with her heartfelt plea?

The minister walked up to the podium and lead the congregation in a closing prayer. A mixture of men in suits and uniformed Marines, acting as pallbearers, picked up the casket. They walked the casket out through the front doors of the church and loaded it into the back of a black hearse. The minister explained to the congregation the order and street route the funeral procession would take to the cemetery, then dismissed the congregation. People slowly began to filter out of the church and headed to their cars.

Blake turned to Tibbs. "Tibbs, what are you doing here?"

"I was still out fishing the North Platte and came across Sgt. Tomlin's obituary in the paper. I'm here because I wanted to pay my respects to a fallen Marine."

"Always faithful."

"That's right, Marine. Always faithful. How did you know the young sergeant?"

Blake took a deep breath and said, "He was my squad leader. I—I was shot, bleeding to death in the middle of a street near Ramadi. He dragged me to safety—he saved my life. And on top of all that, he ran back out and tried to save my best friend who'd been shot."

"Brave man. I wish I could've known him. I'm sorry for your loss, Blake," Tibbs said.

Blake nodded in gratitude and asked, "Why is it that the bravest among us have the strength to save those around them…but can't seem to save themselves?"

"That there, young Blake, is the million-dollar question. I don't know if any of us are strong enough to save ourselves." Tibbs put his arm around Blake's shoulder and said, "Come on. Let's see this through to the end. You'll feel better afterword. I promise."

The two walked out of the church. "Where did you park, Marine?" Tibbs asked.

"Right here, across the street."

"I'm over in the parking lot. I'll see you at the cemetery, OK?"

"Yeah, OK," Blake said as he shook Tibbs's hand and walked to his truck.

Blake sat down in his pickup and placed his head against the steering wheel as he tried to decompress from the emotional roller coaster. He reached into his pocket and pulled out his cell phone. He stared at the phone for a few seconds before calling. Blake listened to the rings as he waited for an answer. A woman's voice came over the line.

"Mom? It's Blake."

"Hi sweetheart. You sound upset. What's wrong?"

"Nothing's wrong, I'm OK. I—I just wanted to tell you, I love you."

CHAPTER TWENTY

My One Fear

Blake and Tibbs stood near the back of the crowd that gathered around Tomlin's final resting place. The flag-draped coffin was suspended over a predug hole. The coffin was resting on a mechanical lowering apparatus used for the final committal of Tomlin's remains to the earth. The immediate family and friends stood at the front as the minister said a prayer. After the prayer, three Marine Corps Honor Guardsmen marched forward with polished circa 1965 M14 battle rifles and conducted a traditional three volley *Nine Gun Salute*, which symbolized that the fallen Marine's body had been removed from the battlefield. A bugler softly trumpeted *Taps* as the honor guard systematically folded the flag on the coffin into a ceremonially tight triangle that completely hid the red-and-white stripes, only exposing the blue cloth with white stars of the U.S. Flag. The flag was presented by the honor guard to a sobbing Mindy Tomlin who took the flag and held it tightly against her chest. As the minister said a closing prayer, the coffin was slowly lowered into the ground until it disappeared from sight.

The minister excused the congregation, and the group of people began to disperse back to their vehicles. Tibbs looked at Blake and asked, "Can I buy you a cup of coffee?"

"I'd like that," Blake said.

Tibbs and Blake found a nearby diner. They sat at a table and ordered a couple cups of coffee. Tibbs could tell that Blake wasn't in the mood to talk about the service, so he asked, "How'd your date with Allison go?"

Blake laughed. "Do you ever forget anything?"

"Nope. It's like a steel trap, Marine," Tibbs said, pointing to his forehead.

"The date was fun. She's a real nice girl. I'm actually staying at her parents' ranch for a few days."

"Really?"

"Yeah, Buddy was attacked by a mountain lion a couple days back while we were camping on the Miracle Mile. Her dad offered me one of their cabins to stay in while he heals up."

"A mountain lion? Tell me that poor pup's gonna be OK."

"The vet said he needs time to heal, but with a little rest he should be fine."

"Well, that's good news," Tibbs said.

"Speaking of Allison's dad, he's a novice military historian."

"No kiddin'?"

"Yeah, I forget how we got on the topic, but he was telling me a little about the 1/9, your outfit. He said you called yourselves *The Walking Dead*. He said your battalion was called that because it had the highest KIA rate of any Marine battalion in the history of the Corps."

"Well, the KIA part is true and The Walking Dead part is mostly true too, but there was a little more to it than just the KIA rate."

"Do you mind if I ask about it?"

"Of course I don't mind. As long as it's another *jarhead* askin' and not some liberal hippie," Tibbs said with a wink.

Tibbs took a sip of coffee. "The name first began catchin' on after Ho Chi Minh made some speech earlier in 1966. In that propagandist speech he bragged about how the Marines of the 1/9 were already dead men, they just didn't know it yet. His plan was to kill every last one of them. He called the First Battalion, Ninth Marines, *Di Bo Chet*, which roughly translated to *dead men walking*, which in turn became, *The Walking Dead*. Although Minh started the nickname, the battalion earned it, bought and paid for with the blood of its Marines."

"The battalion was first deployed to Vietnam in June of 1965, and they weren't relieved from combat operations until July of 1969. All in all, the 1/9 sustained over 600 KIA and triple that number in wounded."

"Were you there for that whole time?" Blake asked.

"No, by the time I joined up with the 1/9, they were already known as The Walking Dead. I first stepped foot in Indochina on May 7, 1967. I was 19. Flown to an airbase in South Vietnam near Da Nang, I was assigned to the 1/9 as a replacement for Charlie Company. I remember my first day in country like it was yesterday. A green replacement, walking around the camp, completely lost. It was like no place I'd ever been. I might as well have landed on the moon.

After walkin' in circles for about 20 minutes, I finally stumbled across my assigned hooch. I walked in and found it mostly empty, except for a grizzled lance corporal sitting on a cot stuffin' something in a seabag. I introduced myself and asked which rack was mine. As he pulled the draw strings tight on that duffle bag and stood up, he told me I could have his rack. Reason being, he was on his way back home. Before he left, I asked him if he had any advice for a new *boot* like me. He threw me a smirk and said that he did, actually. He asked if I was afraid. I intuitively told him I was a Marine; I told him I wasn't afraid of anything. He laughed at my arrogance and said, *Just wait, you will be.* Then he said a little fear was healthy; it kept a grunt from gettin' complacent, kept him sharp. Helped to keep his eyes and ears open and his mouth shut. He said, *Fear becomes a problem for a Marine in combat, when he allows himself to become consumed by it. When he obsesses about every conceivable thing that might go wrong in the bush, he tends to doubt himself. Doubt in combat can get you killed or worse, get someone else killed. So do yourself a favor, kid, in fact, do your company a favor, limit yourself to one healthy fear and then get the hell over it.*"

"What was his one fear?" Blake asked.

"You know, I asked him that very question, and ya know he told me?"

"None of your fuckin' business?" Blake asked.

"Oorah Marine! That's exactly what he told me." Tibbs said, laughing, as he slammed his palm on the table. Tibbs grinned and let out a sigh. Then he reached down for his coffee. The grin gradually dissipated as he drank from his cup. He looked back up at Blake and said, "When that lance corporal told me it was none of my business, what he was really saying was that it's different for each of us and it didn't matter what *his* fear was. It was a rite of passage that I would have to discover for myself and conquer."

"Did you discover your one fear?"

"Oh, yes, and it didn't take long. You see, the Viet Cong realized early on that they couldn't win a straight-up, man-to-man fight with the U.S. Marine Corps. They started using sniper fire, hit-and-run tactics, or sometimes they'd just lob mortars at us. Anything they could so they wouldn't have to fight us face to face. They adapted a strategy of placing land mines along roads, paths, rice patties…just about anywhere. Those bastards got really good at slowing us down with those things. It didn't seem to matter where we were, we'd find mines on nearly every patrol, even in areas we'd swept a few days earlier."

"So, land mines were your one fear?" Blake asked.

"Not exactly. You see, for me it wasn't the object…whether the sniper, grenade, the random bullet flying through the air, or the land mine. It was the damage they would cause and that I might survive to endure it. I first realized this during my second patrol outside the wire. Another replacement, a fella by the name of Chip Bartlett, was walking just a few meters in front of me. A Marine who was walking just a few meters to the right of him, stepped on a mine. The explosion ripped him in half, killing him instantly. Of course, when the mine went off, I hit the deck hard. When the smoke cleared, I looked up from the dirt and saw Chip still standing there. His back was facing me. He kept leaning over at the waist, reaching down, like he was trying to pick something up off the ground. I walked up to him. I could see that he was trying to pick up his rifle lying at his feet. The trouble was that both of his hands had been sheared off just above the wrist by a piece of shrapnel from the mine."

Tibbs paused, picked up his cup, and slowly took another sip of coffee before continuing. "I'd never seen anyone die before, and I certainly never saw the carnage of someone being maimed. The strange thing was, the death didn't bother me. It seemed so final, so definitive. It was over and done with, nothin' anybody could do. Of course, I was upset that I lost a brother-in-arms, but seeing that Marine die didn't make me fearful of death. It was seeing Chip standing there in shock…the life he knew, changed forever. It was the thought that he would now have to relearn how to live. This young twenty-somethin'-year-old man would now have to manage to get along without hands. The simple things that he took for granted his entire life, like signing his name with a pen, throwing a football, or holding a cup of coffee, were stripped away from him in an instant." Tibbs looked down at the cup in his hands. "Chip's new-found reality became my one fear. My haunting fear."

"So how did you deal with it? How did you keep it from consuming you?" Blake asked.

"At first, I didn't. I couldn't. I thought about it every day for the first few weeks. That image of Chip was burned into my memory. I remember I used to stare at my hands every morning and think to myself, *Is today the last day I'm able to touch anything? To hold anything in my hands? To walk? To speak? To see?* I used to get down on my knees and pray that God keep me safe, but if that wasn't in His plan, then I prayed for Him to take me from this world, rather than have me walk through this life as a cripple. I just couldn't bear the thought of ending up like Chip. But after a while, that sort of carnage happened so often, I became numb to the sight of it. Time and time again I'd seen my friends killed, my brothers ripped to shreds, the mangled bodies of the enemy after we called artillery down on them. Every time I saw a Marine lying on a stretcher being medevacked onto a Huey because a limb was blown off, or they were paralyzed from a bullet ripping through their spine, all I could see was myself laying on that litter. I convinced myself it was only a matter of time before I would be the one loaded on that chopper."

"I eventually got over my *one* fear by accepting it as my destiny. I accepted that whatever I did, no matter how careful I was, I wouldn't leave Vietnam whole. I accepted that one day, that fear would come to pass, and a piece of me would be blown off and left behind in that elephant-grass-covered hellhole. It was only after I accepted that fate, that I finally *got over it*, and I was finally able to fully function like a true infantry Marine…hard, unforgiving, lethal, and absent of any remorse. I figured I was going to take out as many VC as I could before they got me. I wanted to ensure the enemy paid a heavy price before they took me out of the fight, and they did."

"So what happened?" Blake asked.

"I finished my first tour physically unscathed, so I reupped for another."

"After all that?"

"Yep, after all that."

"Why? Why go back?"

"Because somewhere along the way, it stopped being about me and started being about the guys around me. I'd been promoted to sergeant and given my own squad to run. I felt like I was needed…like I had to be there to make sure things didn't fall apart. I needed to be there for my guys. It was my responsibility to keep them safe, to keep them alive. The only problem was, in war, no matter how hard you try, you can't keep all your men safe. You're forced to make decisions, some that save men's lives and others that cost men their lives."

Tibbs inhaled a deep breath and slowly let it out. "Anyway, by the end of my second tour, I just couldn't do it anymore. The loss of so many friends had taken its toll. So, I left the Marine Corps and came back to the states."

"That couldn't have been easy. Did you have a tough time with it?" Blake asked.

"Not at first, but pretty soon thereafter, the wheels started fallin' off."

"What happened?"

"Well, once I reentered the civilian world, things quickly started to deteriorate. I had a hard time findin' a decent job. For most employers, there didn't seem to be anything noteworthy about being a former combat Marine.

In the Corps, I was trained and experienced in some of the most sophisticated jungle warfare techniques around. Before I ended my second tour, I was a staff sergeant runnin' my own platoon. I could operate a multitude of weapon systems, and I was entrusted with the awesome responsibility of making life and death decisions nearly every day. But as far as civilian employers were concerned, I had no skills except manual labor. Most places wouldn't trust me to turn a wrench. I felt irrelevant…pretty much worthless. In the end, it turned out that I was more valuable in South Vietnam than in my own country."

"What did you do?"

"I fell into a deep depression and started to drink…heavily," Tibbs said raising his eyebrows. "For years, I'd bounce around from one crappy job to the next, making just enough to pay the rent and to buy another bottle of booze. I was an angry man, hateful really. I didn't talk to anyone I didn't have to and no one wanted to talk to me. I didn't sleep very well. I had the most disturbing nightmares. I'd wake up in the middle of the night to the sounds of Marines screaming. The *death scream* is what we grunts use to call it. When you heard a Marine let out that high-pitch scream, you just knew there wasn't anything you could do for him. You'd still try to save him. But more times than not, he'd just slowly die right in front of you. God, that's a horrible sound," Tibbs said staring out the diner window.

Tibbs remained silent for a few seconds before returning from his trance. "Anyway, one day I got a call from a Marine I served with. He invited me to a 1/9 reunion. At first I didn't want to go, but I thought maybe it would do me some good to see some of the fellas. So, I went. When I walked into the hotel ballroom where the reunion was being held, I saw a few guys from my company sitting at one of the tables. We caught up, talked about what we'd been doing, reminisced about our time in Nam and toasted the friends we'd lost. While all this was going on, somethin' caught my eye. This man walked into the room. He stood tall, he had a certain, I don't know, energy about him. I watched him from a distance work the room, introducing himself to strangers and embracing friends. He looked so familiar, but I couldn't place him. When he got closer, I watched him raise his arm to shake a man's hand and as his suit cuff slid down his wrist a prosthetic metal hook was exposed instead of a hand. The man then placed his other arm over the shoulder of the man he shook hands with, and I could see the same model prosthetic hand on his left arm. It was Chip. The same man whose wounds struck such fear in me all those years ago."

"I found myself intrigued, almost hypnotized. I watched his every move as he interacted with the roomful of Marines. I couldn't take my eyes off him. All this time I assumed Chip was living the wretched life of a miserable cripple. But the man I saw walk in that room wasn't miserable. He looked healthy, clean cut, confident. He was wearing a nice suit along with a genuine smile. He was happy. I knew he was happy 'cause those of us who are miserable can always spot true happiness in others. It's partly what makes us so miserable…wishin' we had what they have."

"Isn't that the truth," Blake said.

"Anyway, he finally made his way to my table. He told me all about his life after he was wounded. Turns out he was a successful business owner, married, and even had a couple kids. What an incredible man he became. I made it through two tours of combat in Nam without a scratch and I was the depressed, unemployed, worthless drunk. Chip didn't last but two weeks, never even had a chance to crack a shot at the enemy before he lost both his hands, and he was the happy, successful, family man. After talking with Chip I realized I hadn't escaped my fear. I didn't leave Vietnam in one piece. My premonition of losing something did, in fact, happen, but it wasn't a limb that I lost, it was far more detrimental. I'd lost my self-worth, my spirit. In that moment, I would have given anything to trade places with Chip…even my hands. I truly envied him. No amount of physical deformity is more devastating to a man than the mutilation of his soul."

Blake sat in silence, staring down at the table as he contemplated what Tibbs had said.

"So you see Marine, I didn't know Sgt. Tomlin, but I know the battle that raged within him. That same dreaded battle I fight every day. The battle, I suspect, you're fighting right now."

Blake looked up and asked, "How do you get through it?"

"It's a little different for each of us I suppose, but I guess the one common denominator is the ones who get by accept the love and support offered by others; their family, friends, other Marines," Tibbs paused and smiled, "...their wives. They don't try to fight the pain alone. Seclusion can tear you apart like no other. The ones who try to do it by themselves often end up how I did or worse...like Sgt. Tomlin."

CHAPTER TWENTY-ONE

You're Gonna Be OK.

Tibbs looked at his watch, lifted his hand, and he motioned to the waitress for the check. The waitress brought over the bill. Tibbs looked at it and pulled a 20-dollar bill from his wallet and handed it to the waitress.

"I'll be back with your change," the waitress said.

"No thanks, darlin'. That's for you," Tibbs said with a wink.

"You're a sweetheart. Thank you," the waitress said as she walked away.

"Well, Marine, I'd better get goin'. I've got a long drive back to Bozeman," Tibbs said as he put his wallet back into his pocket.

"All done with your trip?" Blake asked.

"Yup. I'm pretty worn out. Think I'll head home. Besides, I've got a few things to do before…" Tibbs caught himself.

"Before what?"

Tibbs swiped his hand through the air as though he was brushing away a cobweb, then stood up. "Ah, never mind all that. It's a long story. I'll be happy to bore you with the details if you ever come up to Bozeman."

"Hopefully I'll be driving through there after my trip through Yellowstone. I'm thinking within the next week or two."

"Sounds good, Marine. I'll have a fresh pot of coffee waitin'," Tibbs said as he shook Blake's hand. "Semper Fi, Marine."

"Semper Fi, devil dog." Blake responded.

Tibbs was at the front door of the diner when he heard Blake call to him. Tibbs turned around and looked back at Blake. "Thanks for everything."

Tibbs gave a slanted grin. "No, Blake...thank you."

As Blake sat alone in the diner, watching Tibbs drive away, his cell phone rang.

"Hey, it's me," Allison said.

"Hey."

"Is the service over?"

"Yeah, it ended an hour ago. I just finished having coffee with a friend from the funeral."

"You doing OK?"

"I'm hangin' in there."

"When are you coming home?"

"Home?" Blake asked with hint of sarcasm.

"You know what I mean."

"I'll be back soon. First, I'm gonna drive over and see how Buddy's doing."

"Oh, Doc Samuels called right after you left and said Buddy was ready to be picked up. So my dad drove over and got him."

"Really?"

"Yep. I brought him over to your cabin. He's sleeping away here on the couch next to me."

"Don't spoil that mutt too bad. I don't want him thinkin' anyone cares about him."

"You don't fool me, Blake Jacobs. You love that dog and you know it," Allison teased.

"Guilty. But that's not the only thing in that cabin I care about," Blake said softly.

"Oh really? Do tell," Allison said with a flirty tone.

"Well, let's see. My fly collection is there, my reels, oh, and of course my fly rods. I really care about them."

"Blake Jacobs! You're a stinker!" Allison said and laughed.

Blake laughed before saying, "Allison, you crack me up. I really needed a good laugh."

"Well, I'm glad I could be of service, you little snot! Now get back here. I know Buddy's dying to see you."

"OK. OK. I'll be back as soon as I can."

"Well, hurry up. Looks like a storm's coming."

Blake walked outside the diner and looked at the western horizon. Ominous black storm clouds loomed in the distance. The orange glow of the setting sun could barely cut through the curtain of raindrops that poured onto the outlying prairie like an Amazonian waterfall cascading off a cliff side.

As Blake pulled up to the cabin, light raindrops peppered his windshield as the storm drew closer. The cabin was dark. Only a faint flickering of light could be seen through the living room window. When Blake walked in the cabin he found Allison sitting on the living room couch with Trevor. There were lit candles on the coffee table and fireplace mantle. Buddy's head was on Allison's lap as she ran her fingers through his curly hair. He slept quietly along with Trevor who was lying against the armrest of the sofa.

Allison looked up at Blake and smiled. She lightly puckered her lips and softly said, "Shhh. Buddy's in a pretty deep sleep from his medication, but Trevor just nodded off."

Blake reached down and gently pet the bandaged pup on the head. "Why are the lights off?"

"The power's out. It happens every now and then. The perils of country living, I guess," Allison said as she slowly scooted out from under Buddy and laid his head on the cushion.

The trickling rain soon turned into a downpour. The sounds of drums and taps caused by the plump raindrops on the tin roof reverberated throughout the cabin with a soothing beat. The candle flames danced as the storm's cool mist was blown in through the open windows and with it the sweet refreshing smell of the freshly washed prairie.

Allison walked over to the window and watched the rain fall. She folded her arms across her chest, closed her eyes, and took a deep breath. "Mmm. I love that smell. It smells so clean, like everything's new again."

Blake walked up behind her and wrapped his arms around her waist, pulling her close. She laid her arms over his, squeezing them against her body and resting the back of her head against his chest. Blake rested his cheek against her hair. The silky strands of her tresses had a flowery fragrance. She had a warm touch. "I'm really sorry about your friend," Allison said.

"I know. I appreciate it."

"What was he like?" Allison asked as she continued to gaze at the rain.

"Sergeant Tomlin?" Blake tipped his head back, took a long deep breath, and said, "Well, for starters he was brave, fearless really. He had a toughness about him. He pushed us, made us train hard, kept us strong. He didn't allow any drama on the team. He treated us like family and expected us to treat each other the same. It was because of him, that we became such a tight-knit group."

160

Blake paused and stared out the window. "I remember he'd spend hours in his room at night pouring over intel and studying maps, preparing for the next day's patrol. He'd get up early and inspect the Humvees hours before the mission to make sure everything was in order. He was determined to get us through our deployment in one piece. He never told us how much he cared for us, he showed us. A true leader, if I ever knew one."

"Was he there when Aaron was killed?"

"Yeah, we both were."

"Does it hurt to talk about it?"

"I don't know. I've never really talked much about it. The details, I mean."

"Maybe you should. It might help," Allison said as she turned around in Blake's arms and faced him. "I hope you know you can trust me."

"I do trust you," Blake said. "I don't mind telling you if you really want to know. At least that way you'll know the truth about me, before we take this any further."

"The truth? What's the truth?" Allison asked.

"That I'm not a brave man. That I worried more about my own skin than the lives of my friends. And it was because of my actions that Aaron died."

"I don't believe that for a second. You're the bravest man I've ever met. You risked everything to help me without giving a second thought to your own life. You saved me. You saved Trevor. You charged a mountain lion to save Buddy for crying out loud."

Blake gently pulled away from Allison and said, "It wasn't intentional, but I really screwed up. I got myself shot because I lost focus…I was scared. Aaron was killed because he ran out in the middle of the battle to save me. The mistake I made that day set into motion a lot of pain and suffering for a lot of people. If I had one wish, it'd be to get a second chance to make the right call."

"How did Aaron die?"

"He was shot, killed instantly." Blake paused. "You know, it's not like it is in the movies where you get a little bit of time to say your goodbyes or whatnot. In a blink of an eye he was gone. Dead before he hit the ground. I can't even remember the last thing I said to him."

"What about the last thing he said to you?"

Blake gave a half smile and nodded. "I actually do remember that. It was right before he ran out to get me. He yelled, 'You're gonna be OK.' Those were his last words."

Allison's eyes welled up with tears. Blake rubbed the side of her arm trying to comfort her and said, "I'm sorry, Allison. I shouldn't have told you. I didn't mean to upset you."

"No. It's just…"

"What is it?"

"Don't you remember? You said that exact same thing to me."

"When?"

"In the car, when you were trying to get me out. I remember the heat of the fire against my legs. I knew I was going to die. I told you to leave me there. I didn't want you to die too. But you refused to quit. You told me you were gonna get me out of there. I remember you said, 'You're gonna be OK.' I remember the conviction in your voice when you said that. There wasn't a hint of panic. I believed you. At that moment, I just knew that you weren't gonna let me die in that car. I knew you'd figure out a way to save me…and you did."

Blake looked down recalling that moment in the fiery wreckage. Allison reached over and grabbed his hand and held it in both of hers. Blake looked back up at Allison. She had mascara-dyed tear stains on her cheeks and her lips rolled up, pressed together as if she was trying to force a soft smile. Blake reached up with his free hand and combed her stray hair behind her ears.

Allison could see the hurt in Blake's eyes. She could see his self-doubt. She could sense his guilt. Her heart ached for him. There could be only one reason that his pain caused her pain…she was in love with him. She wasn't infatuated, and this wasn't a crush. She realized then and there that she truly loved him. She sniffed, stiffened, and with a stern look on her face said, "Now you listen to me…I know I haven't seen or done the kinds of things that you have, but I've lived plenty of life in the short time I've been in this world. Mainly because of mistakes I've made. I had plans of how I wanted my life to end up, but those plans fell short. But if one thing has helped me get through my failures, it was to learn from them and move forward. I also realize that given the chance to correct those perceived *mistakes,* knowing what I know now, I wouldn't. Because it would mean that the little boy sleeping on that couch wouldn't even exist, and there's no way I could bear that."

Allison wiped the tears from her eyes. "There was no one on that highway that day who could have saved us, except you. Now, you might be right, that the decision you made in Iraq might have set into motion a lot of pain for a lot of people. I don't know for sure and I don't think you know for sure either. But one thing is for sure, that decision set into motion a lot of joy for a lot of other people. God works in mysterious ways, Blake. If you didn't get shot in Iraq, there's probably a good chance you wouldn't have been driving on that interstate on what otherwise would have been my and Trevor's last day on earth. Have you considered that?"

Allison's lips began to tremble as she looked into Blake's eyes. "I don't care about the *truth* of what happened in Iraq. I didn't know Aaron. I didn't know that world. The only world I know is the one where a brave stranger risked everything to save me and the most important person in my life, and I will love him forever for that, regardless of any of his past mistakes."

Blake looked up at Allison. He studied the pained look in her eyes. He had to admit, she was right. If not for that day in Iraq, he would probably still be in the Corps, not Wyoming. And if not wounded in that battle, maybe he would have been killed in another. Either way, he wouldn't have been there to save her. The fire department didn't arrive at the scene of the crash until Allison's vehicle was already fully engulfed in flames. She'd be dead for sure and more than likely, Trevor too. Was his sin their salvation? Did things play out the way they were meant to? But how could any good come from Aaron being killed? How could potential tragedy have been avoided on that highway if he wasn't?

These were the kind of questions that could tear a man up. Questions that tormented one's soul. Questions that couldn't be answered. Questions, that realistically meant nothing, but to Blake, meant everything.

Blake shut his eyes in frustration. He could vividly see Sgt. Tomlin's coffin, his widow, his children. His vision suddenly flashed back to the day he pressed a revolver against his own head. If he would have pulled that trigger, he would have unwittingly sealed Allison and Trevor's fate. He opened his eyes and could see the tears again running down Allison's cheeks. He threw his arms around her and pulled her to his chest. Allison began to sob. "I'm sorry, Blake. I don't know what came over me."

"No, I'm the one who should be sorry. Please, don't cry," Blake said, as he squeezed her tight, trying to comfort her. "You're so right about everything you said. I'm gonna do my best to put the past behind me. I promise."

Allison lifted her head from Blake's chest. She did her best to compose herself by wiping the tears from her face. She smiled, stood up on her toes, and gently kissed him. She slowly lowered her heels back down to the floor, looked at him with a tender face, and said, "Blake, I'm not suggesting you forget the past, just don't live in it. If you can do that, *you're gonna be OK.*"

CHAPTER TWENTY-TWO

Meet Me for Lunch

Over the next few weeks, Blake stayed on at the ranch waiting for Buddy's wounds to heal. As a gesture of gratitude for the Graces' hospitality, Blake religiously woke up early every morning to help Emmett with much of the manual labor that went along with running a cattle operation. Emmett, thankful for the assistance, taught Blake as much as he could about the ranching business, even taking time to teach him how to ride a horse. Blake was a quick study, as he was with most things, and soon the two fell into an efficient work routine. It was almost as if they had been partnered up for years. Blake enjoyed ranch work. The toughness of the job instilled in him a sense of worth that he longed for. Working outside in the vast Wyoming countryside seemed to bring out the best in him.

In the afternoons, Blake and Trevor would spend time helping Buddy recuperate from his injuries by changing his bandages and taking him for walks to strengthen his muscles. Trevor spent the most time with Buddy, hardly leaving his side. And although not 100 percent, Buddy's desire to play and run around with Trevor helped expedite his recovery. Over time, the two grew very close, nearly inseparable.

The everyday hustle and bustle of ranch life consumed most everyone's time, and although Blake and Allison saw each other often, moments alone, where it was just the two of them, were few. One evening, after the setting sun quieted the restless ranch, Blake and Allison stole a walk on the prairie. They held hands as they strolled through the wild grass.

"I love this time of night...that deep orange glow that lines the sky right before the sun disappears." Allison said.

"It is beautiful," Blake said gazing at the horizon.

"I wonder why God made deer color blind?"

"What?" Blake asked with a shallow laugh.

"Well, He made the prairie their home but denied them the ability to see the beauty of these amazing sunsets."

"Deer aren't color blind are they?" Blake asked.

"They sure are. Have you ever seen hunters wear those bright-orange vests during hunting season? That's so the hunters don't accidentally shoot each other."

"Well, I knew that."

"Did you ever wonder why the deer don't run for their lives when they see that bright orange vest? It's because they're color blind."

"Interesting. Well, did you know that trout *can* see color?" Blake asked.

"They can?"

"Yep. In fact, they can see more colors than the human eye."

"No kidding?"

"Yep, and their sense of smell rivals a bloodhound."

"Come on, are you serious?" Allison asked.

"I'm serious. That's how salmon, cousins to the trout, can be born in a river, swim out to the ocean, live for years, and then swim back upstream and find the exact spot they were born so they can spawn and start the cycle all over again."

"Wow! Absolutely fascinating!" Allison said with a stunned look. "That you're alone, with a pretty girl, looking at a beautiful sunset, and all you want to do is talk about fish nostrils."

"You started it you little shit!" Blake said playfully as he fell to the ground while pulling Allison down with him. Allison let out a laughing scream as she collapsed on his chest coming face to face with him. Blake gently reached behind her neck and slowly lifted his head from the ground to meet her lips. Her soft kiss tasted sweet. Blake closed his eyes. He never felt more at peace than when he was with her.

After a few moments, Allison gently pulled back from Blake and softly said, "That was nice."

"I've been practicing on my pillow," Blake said with a grin.

"Gross!" Allison said laughing as she rolled off of Blake onto her back.

"I was just kidding," Blake said as he reached for her.

"No way sicko! You blew it," Allison said as she poked him in his ribs.

"Stop! I'm super ticklish!" Blake laughed.

"Oh, you should have never told me that," Allison said with a wide-eyed sinister grin.

Blake quickly sat up, pointed at her, and with a serious face said, "Allison. No!"

"Oh, yes," Allison said as she crawled toward him.

"Allison, I'm warning you. I can't be held responsible for my actions if you tickle me," Blake said while slowly moving backward.

Allison simpered, moving her eyebrows up and down. "I'll take my chances."

"OK. Just calm down. Let's talk about this."

"Too late!" Allison yelled as she lunged at Blake, tackling him back to the ground and tickling him mercilessly. "Say you're sorry!"

"OK! OK! I'm sorry!"

Allison stopped tickling Blake and held him down with her hands against his shoulders. "Now that I know your weakness, you'll never be safe again."

"You—you're one crazy lady," Blake said still trying to catch his breath.

"Crazy like a fox," Allison said as she leaned in and gently kissed him. They spent the next few minutes lying in the grass, holding each other, watching the sun fall off the edge of the earth.

The next morning Blake awoke to the beeping of his alarm clock. He reached over to the nightstand and hit the snooze button. "This five in the morning stuff is startin' to wear on me Buddy," Blake said as he rubbed his eyes. Buddy stood up from the floor and let out a high-pitched yawn.

Trevor called from outside the cabin, "Buddy! Buuuddy where aaarrre yoooouuu?" Blake laughed to himself.

Buddy ran over to the front door and began whining and pacing in circles. "I know, I know," Blake said. "You want to go see Trevor. Give me half a second you crazy mutt." Blake walked to the door. Buddy could hardly contain his excitement, his body quivering. "OK, go get 'em, boy!" Blake said as he flung open the door. Buddy bolted over to Trevor and jumped up on him nearly knocking him over. "Careful, Buddy. You OK, sport?"

"I'm OK, Bwake," Trevor said with a smile as he and Buddy ran over to the ranch house.

"Tell your Grandpa I'll be over in a few," Blake called out.

"OK!" Trevor yelled back.

Blake laughed and shook his head, "Those two." Just as Blake turned to go back inside his phone rang.

"Hey, it's me," Allison said.

"What's going on? You at the house?"

"No, I had to run into town. I'm free this afternoon if you want to meet for lunch."

"Sure. Where?" Blake asked.

"Let's just do the Pronghorn again. How about one-thirty?"

"Sounds good. See ya then."

Blake got cleaned up and walked over to the ranch house for a quick bite and a cup of coffee before he and Emmett headed out to work the ranch. They spent the day mending the barbed wire fence that surrounded the ranch. They drove along the acres of fence line looking for fallen posts and weak points that needed to be reinforced or patched. Emmett hardly allowed a moment of silence, rambling on about little known military facts that he found interesting and talking at length about his personal strategy to defeat terrorism.

"Ah, there's a spot," Emmett said as they drove up to a section of fence that had blown over. Emmett got out of the truck and stood in front of the damaged stretch of fence. He took his cowboy hat off with one hand and scratched the back of his neck with the other. "Fixin' these fences is a never-ending job, Blake."

"Oh, yeah?"

"Yeah, I don't know how many times I've been out here puttin' these posts back into the ground." Emmett laughed and smiled. "I'm gonna miss it."

"Miss it?"

"Well, I got a phone call this morning from Jack Polanski. He's the owner of this ranch. Seems he's sold it to another outfit," Emmett explained.

"So wait? Does that mean you're out of job?"

"It would seem so."

"Is that what the new owner said?"

"Oh, I don't know for sure, but that's usually how it works. This new outfit will bring in their own people to run the show. Jack said the official closing won't be for a couple months yet. He just wanted to give me a heads up."

"Does Ruth know?" Blake asked tentatively.

"Yeah, Ruth knows. The ranch has been up for sale for a while now. We both knew this day was coming. Still, it's pretty sobering now that it's here."

"Where are you gonna go?"

"Ruth and I have a little savings. I'm sure I'll get picked up as a ranch hand somewhere. Won't pay as much, but we'll get by."

"And Allison?"

"As long as I can draw breath from these lungs, she and Trevor will have a roof over their heads, that I can promise you." Emmett sighed. "I just worry things won't be the same. Allison has lived on this ranch her whole life. How am I gonna tell her? She'll be heart broken." Emmett turned to Blake and said, "Would you mind keepin' this to yourself. I'd like to be the one to tell Allison."

"Yeah, sure thing Emmett," Blake said.

"Thanks. So anyway, how about you?"

"What'd you mean?"

"Well, Buddy seems to be healed up for the most part. Aren't you gonna finish your trip?" Emmett asked.

"That's a good question. I've been having such a good time here I've hardly thought about my trip over these last few weeks, but you're right…I guess it's probably time to get going."

"Now, don't get me wrong. I'm not tryin' to push ya out of here. In fact, if ya ask me, you'd be hard pressed to make it to Alaska now."

"You think?"

"Blake, did you ever consider, with everything that's gone on, just makin' another stab at it next year? I know Allison would love it if you stayed a little longer."

"Emmett, I couldn't do that. Not with the ranch selling and all the stress everyone's gonna be dealing with. You don't need me around getting in the way."

"Nonsense!" Emmett said as he put his hand on Blake's shoulder. "You're like family around here. Stay, and don't worry about the ranch. These things have a way of workin' themselves out."

"No promises Emmett, but I'll think about it," Blake said with a grin.

"That's what I like to hear," Emmett said slapping Blake on the back. "Now let's get back to work."

They walked around to the back of the pickup and grabbed a few tools. As Blake knelt down to inspect the fence, Emmett asked, "Did I ever tell you what *really* happened to Hitler's body during the last days of the war."

Blake smiled and said, "No, but I'd love to hear about it."

Later that afternoon Blake drove into town for his lunch rendezvous with Allison at the Pronghorn Bar & Grill. He pulled into the parking lot about a half hour early, walked in, and found Sam standing near the entrance. "Well, look what the cat dragged in." Sam said.

"Hey, Sam. How are things?"

"Things are great. What brings you in?"

"I'm meeting Allison for lunch. I'm a little early."

"Well I just got here myself, but we're not that busy. Sit wherever you want."

"Thanks."

"Sure thing. Hey, you want somethin' to drink while you're waiting? Maybe an iced tea?" Sam said with a wink.

Blake laughed. "I'm good for now, but thanks."

Blake walked over to the same table where he and Allison had dinner a month earlier. He pulled out a chair and sat down. Blake smiled as he caressed the top of the wooden table with his hand, feeling all the divots and scratches it had endured over the years. He looked across the table and envisioned Allison sitting on the other side smiling back at him, wearing that summer dress that complimented her figure so very well. He remembered vividly how beautiful she looked on that night. He had a warmth in his heart as he reminisced about how soft she felt in his arms as they tenderly swayed to the music.

As Blake sat at the table, he anxiously looked across the restaurant toward the entrance anticipating when she might walk through the doors. He could hardly wait to see her again.

"Mind if I sit?"

Blake looked up to see a strapping man about his age standing over the table holding two glasses of whiskey. He was tall, clean cut, and well dressed. He had short wavy brown hair that was styled in such a way that it looked like the small flames from a campfire. He wore a custom-cut black-label suit with a maroon tie that had been loosened from his neck to allow his unbuttoned shirt collar the freedom to breathe and had on black cowboy boots.

"Who are you?" Blake asked.

172

The man set one glass in front of Blake and the other across from him. He pulled a chair from the table, tipped it up on one leg, and spun it around. He defiantly sat down facing Blake, resting his forearms on the backrest of the chair and smugly said, "I'm Wade."

Blake, sensing hostility, asked, "What do you want, *Wade?*"

"No need to get in a twist friend. Just want to talk, that's all."

"So talk."

"Well, aren't you gonna take a drink of the whiskey I brought ya?"

Blake pushed the glass toward Wade. "I'm not thirsty."

Wade smirked and let out a laugh. "You know, it's considered bad manners around here not to except a drink that's bought for ya. You must not be from around here."

"What business is it of yours?" Blake asked becoming more agitated.

"Well, you not bein' from around here, I thought you might also like to know that it's considered bad manners to sleep with another man's wife."

"What are you talking about? Who the hell are you?"

Wade picked up his glass and chugged the remainder of his drink like he was downing a shot. He gently set the glass back down on the table, dabbed the corners of his mouth with the bottom of his tie, and looked up at Blake with a stern face. "Who the hell am I? I'm Allison's husband."

CHAPTER TWENTY-THREE

Do the Right Thing

Blake and Wade stared at each other for what seemed like an eternity, neither wanting to show weakness by being the first to break the silence. Finally, Blake flinched. "Husband? Allison said you walked out on her when she was pregnant."

"That's her side of the story but the fact remains that we're technically still married."

"I don't believe you."

"I don't really care if you do. I'm not here to prove anything."

"Then why are you here?" Blake asked.

"It's simple really...I'm here to start over with Allison. To do that, I need you out of the picture. She thinks the two of you are in love."

Blake leaned over the table with a cocky smirk. "Sorry to spoil your plans, but I'm not going anywhere."

Wade sneered. He reached toward the middle of the table and picked up the glass of whiskey he had brought for Blake. "You mind? I hate to see good whiskey go to waste."

"Have at it."

Wade picked up the glass and sipped on the whiskey. Then he asked, "Can I tell you a story, Blake?"

"I'm all ears," Blake said sarcastically.

"Allison and I were together all through high school. I never even looked at another girl. I loved her. I mean that. Anyway, right before I graduated from high school, I received a full academic scholarship from the University of Colorado."

"Congratulations," Blake said with a look of contempt.

"Well, thank you, Blake," Wade said. "Of course I was excited. So was Allison. But we had a little problem. Even with a scholarship, goin' to school out of state is a pretty expensive venture. Too expensive for her to have come out there and live with me. We decided that I'd go off to college and when I graduated, we'd get married. But before I even left for school, Allison found out she was pregnant with Trevor."

"So what happened?"

"Allison couldn't stand the thought of being an unwed mother. Guess she didn't want to embarrass her family with such a scandal. So, naturally we went to the justice of the peace and got married right away. But I couldn't see the point of giving up a college scholarship to flip burgers for a living, just because Allison was pregnant. So she stayed on at the ranch while I went to school in Colorado."

"Wow, you're so noble," Blake sarcastically said. "Way to put your family's future first. Were you also thinking of their future when you hooked up with little miss college skank and walked out on them?"

Wade leaned forward, slammed his hand on the table and said, "Don't you judge me you little prick!" Blake didn't flinch. He stared Wade down with the gruff scowl of a battle-hardened Marine that would make any man think twice before challenging further. Blake wanted nothing more than to reach across the table and rip this coward's throat out.

Wade backed down. He slowly leaned back from the table, smiled, and said, "I admit I was a little taken with college night life, if you know what I mean."

"I can't say I do."

"I suppose not," Wade said with an arrogant smirk. "Well, long story short, Allison drove down for a surprise visit at the most inopportune time

175

and caught me with…how'd you put it? *Little miss college skank?*" Wade picked up the glass of whiskey and took another sip. "Anyway, the gal meant nothing to me, but Allison was unforgiving. Said she could never trust me again. Said she wanted a divorce. I've been draggin' my feet with it in hopes that she'll come around, put that little incident behind her so me, her, and Trevor can finally be a family."

"Well, I guess that's not working out so well. So why don't you just let it go?" Blake said.

"Let me ask you something, Blake. You ever made a mistake? You ever let weakness get the best of you? You ever regret something *so* much, that not a day goes by where you wish you could go back and change it? Well, I have. I cheated on Allison. I admit that. But that was four years ago. I still love her and I deserve a second chance. I want to be a father to my son. I don't think a man should be judged on a single mistake for the rest of his life, unless he's a murderer or child molester or—whatever. Do you? Look, things were goin' good with us. I felt like Allison and I were finally making some headway. I felt like she might take me back." Wade flopped back in his seat and threw his arms up. "And then you came along. Pulled her from that car and suddenly she's back to givin' me the cold shoulder. Today I meet with her and all of the sudden, she insists we go through with the divorce."

Blake shook his head in disgust and said, "Excuse me all to hell for saving Allison's life."

"You see, that's just it. You think if you met her in bar or walkin' down the sidewalk that a girl as amazing as Allison would even give you the time of day? Come on my man! She's infatuated with you because you saved her from that car wreck. You're her hero…at least for the time being. Now how long do you think that whole *Florence Nightingale Effect* is gonna last? You've known her for what? A few weeks? We were together for years. We have a child together. I know nearly everything about that woman. Do you know how much I make a year? Ninety-eight thousand. And I'm still on the lower rung of the company I work for. I have a house in a good neighborhood near a good school for Trevor. I've got a solid career. Allison can finally get her degree and become a school teacher like she's always wanted. They have a bright future with me. What do you even do? What stability do you have to offer her? Do you have a job that can support a wife and a child? A place for them to live?"

Blake's scowl softened as he began to contemplate these questions. How could Blake take care of Allison and Trevor? He was unemployed. Outside the Corps, he had no marketable skills or education. For crying out loud, he still lived with his mother. The ranch had just sold. Allison and Trevor would soon be looking for a new place to live…a place Blake couldn't provide. He had to admit, Wade was right. What kind of life could he provide for Allison and Trevor? What kind of future would they have? All this time he'd selfishly been living in the moment, never thinking about where this relationship was truly going.

Blake considered for the first time the responsibility of raising a family. Was he even fit for it? He'd nearly killed himself a few months earlier. He was a depressed alcoholic. What claim did he have on someone as perfect as Allison? Blake's posture melted from one of a fierce alpha male marking his territory, to a submissive puppy who was ashamed for pissing on the carpet.

Wade looked up at the ceiling, let out a deep breath, and said, "I know you think I'm an asshole. But Blake, put yourself in my shoes. Wouldn't you fight for your family? Everybody I've talked to around here says you're a great guy. And don't get me wrong, I appreciate what you did for Allison and Trevor. But if you're really this great guy like people say, and you care about Allison's welfare, you'll end this fling as soon as possible. The longer you drag it out, the more you'll hurt Allison and Trevor when it inevitably fails."

Wade picked up the glass and drank the last swallow of whiskey, then gently set the glass down. He stood up, looked down at Blake, and said, "I know it sounds hard, but do the right thing…not for you…for them." Then he walked out of the restaurant.

Blake sat frozen at the table. Sam walked up and asked, "What was that about?"

"Nothing," Blake said.

"Don't mind him, Blake. He's an ass. Can I get you somethin' while you wait?"

"No—I—I've got to go," Blake said as he stood up and made his way to the entrance.

"Where are you going Blake? What about Allison?" Sam called out.

"Just tell her something came up. I'll call her later," Blake said as he walked out.

Blake got in his truck and raced back to the ranch. He pulled up to the cabin and started gathering his things up and packing his truck. He was nearly finished when Allison sped down the road in her pickup. She came to a sliding stop next to the cabin and jumped out of the truck slamming the door behind her. "What do think you're doing?" Allison asked.

"What's it look like? I'm heading out," Blake said as kept his back to her.

"Just like that?" Allison asked.

"Just like that."

"What did he say to you?"

"What are you talking about?"

"Don't give me that crap, Blake! Sam called and told me that Wade confronted you at the Pronghorn."

Blake continued packing his things.

"Blake! Look at me please!" Allison demanded.

Blake stopped packing, dropped his shoulders, and let out a sigh. He turned and faced Allison. "Why didn't you tell me you were still married?"

"It's just a formality. We haven't been together in over four years. Wade's been doing everything in his power to keep the divorce from going through. Where do you think I was this morning? I was in court with Wade trying to get our divorce finalized."

"Well, is it finalized?"

"Not exactly, but it will be soon. I promise."

"You know, Wade told me he still loves you. He wants to make things right. He wants you, Trevor, and him to be a family."

"But I don't love him, Blake."

"You did once. And he obviously loves Trevor."

"Blake, I'm in love with you, not Wade."

"How Allison? How can you love me? You hardly know me!" Blake said throwing his hands in the air. "I don't even have a job! Wade not only has a job, he's got a good job with a steady income. He's got his own house! Don't be stupid about this. I won't let you throw away a promising future on someone like me."

"Don't you think that should be my decision?"

"Well, it's not. I'm sorry," Blake said as he turned back toward the truck.

Tears ran down Allison's cheeks. "Why are you doing this? What did Wade say to you?"

"Only what I already knew. You and Trevor deserve a good life…and that's something I'm just not sure I could ever give you."

Allison began breathing heavy as her sorrow turned into anger. "Give me? Who the hell do you think you are? I have a good life right here! Don't think for a second that I need *you* to take care of me like I'm some charity case! And I certainly don't need Wade's money!"

Blake turned around. "That's just it, Allison! All this is an illusion! You don't have a good life here anymore…the ranch has been sold!" Blake immediately caught himself. In his fit of anger and sadness, he broke his promise to Emmett. He looked at Allison's shocked face trying to think of something to say.

Allison stared at Blake with a horrified look trying to process the news. Blake walked over to her. "Allison…I." Blake said as he reached out to her, holding her hands in his.

Allison asked, "How do you know that? Who told you the ranch was sold?"

"I'm so sorry. Emmett told me earlier today. He asked me not to say anything to you. Please forgive me," Blake said as he put his arm around her.

"So what then? You find out you're going to lose your free ride so it's time to move on?"

"Allison, it's not like that at all."

"Get away from me!" Allison yelled as she pushed Blake. Blake tried to approach her to comfort her. "I said get the hell away from me, Blake! You're a real son-of-a-bitch, you know that? Just go! Go finish your little fishing trip."

"Mommy?" Blake looked over by Allison's truck. Trevor was hiding halfway behind the truck with Buddy. Allison ran over to him and gave him a hug. "Why are you crying?"

"It's OK, Trevor. Let's go back over to the house," Allison said.

"Are Bwake and Buddy going to come over too?"

"No, honey, Blake's going away."

"Buddy too?"

"Yes, sweetheart," Allison said as she brushed Trevor's hair back.

"Are they coming back?"

"I don't think so, honey," Allison said as she looked up at Blake with a pained expression.

"But Mommy, Buddy's my best fwiend."

"I'm sorry, sweetheart. Give Buddy a hug and kiss goodbye."

"But I don't want to say goodbye," Trevor said, his bottom lip quivering.

"I know. Now say goodbye to Buddy so Blake can get going."

Trevor's big blue eyes welled up with tears as he grabbed Buddy around the neck and held him tight. Buddy could sense Trevor's sadness and whimpered. "Goodbye Buddy. I'm gonna miss you. Thanks for being my best fwiend," Trevor whispered.

Allison wiped the tears from her face with her forearms and stood up. "OK, let's go," Allison said as she took Trevor's hand and turned toward the ranch house.

"Bye, Bwake," Trevor called out.

"Take care sport," Blake said in a somber tone.

"Bye Buddy...I wuv you!" Trevor called out with a distressed voice one last time before he and Allison made it to the ranch house. Blake watched as they disappeared through the front door. Buddy sat in the dirt staring at the ranch house and whining.

"Come on Buddy, let's go," Blake said. Buddy stayed on the ground fixated on the house. "Buddy! Now!" Blake yelled as he stood by the open passenger door of his pickup. Buddy stayed in place, only looking over his shoulder at Blake for a moment, then focusing back on the ranch house.

"Buddy, come!" Blake said as he widened his stance and clenched his fists. Buddy let out a soft tormented whine as he began to crawl toward Blake.

Blake's scowl began to lift as he watched the frightened dog. Buddy had done nothing wrong. He was as confused about all of this as Trevor was. Blake knelt down and held out his hand. "Come here boy. I'm sorry for yelling." Buddy walked over to Blake and licked his palm. Blake pet Buddy on the head. "You're a good boy. You shouldn't have to leave if you don't want to," Blake said as he pulled Buddy's head to his chest.

Blake heard some shuffling in the dirt and looked up. He could see Emmett walking toward the cabin. "Blake," Emmett said.

"Emmett I'm sorry. I told Allison about the sale of the ranch."

"Yes, I know. Allison's pretty upset."

"I'm sorry for that too."

"Looks like you're all packed up. You leavin' right now?"

"I'm afraid so."

"It's none of my business of course, but I wish you'd stay, at least until tomorrow. Sometimes these arguments need time to heal. I'm sure whatever the trouble, it can be worked out once everyone has a good night's sleep."

"Thanks Emmett, but I've got to go."

Emmett gave a nod and held out his hand. "Just know, as long as we're here, you'll always be welcome."

Blake shook Emmett's hand and said, "Thanks." Blake turned toward his truck, then paused. He turned back to Emmett. "Emmett, I was wondering if I could ask a favor?"

"Anything."

182

"Could I leave Buddy here for Trevor? I've already caused so much damage, I think taking Buddy away from here would just break his heart."

"Of course. We'd be glad to have him."

"Thanks."

Blake knelt down and gave Buddy one last pet through his thick curly hair and said, "You be good, Buddy. Take good care of Allison and Trevor." Blake stood up and started walking toward his truck. Buddy jogged beside him and pushed his head underneath Blake's hand.

"Buddy… Buddy. Over here, boy," Emmett said as he slapped his hand against his leg. Buddy turned from Blake and ran over to Emmett.

Blake got into his truck and drove away. He watched in his rearview mirror as Buddy sat beside Emmett. Buddy suddenly burst from Emmett's side and began running down the road chasing after Blake. He accelerated to put more distance between them. Buddy tried to keep up but gradually tired, slowing to a light jog, then giving up. Blake sped past the ranch house as Allison watched from her bedroom window, a whipping trail of dust sweeping by as Blake's truck disappeared down the road.

CHAPTER TWENTY-FOUR

The Fire Hole

I t was mid-September. Blake had been gone from the ranch for over a week. He was a month behind schedule and had only just finished fishing the Snake River near Jackson Hole the day before. With that location scratched off his list, he was nearing the halfway point of his trip. He still had a long way to go and not much time. Over the past week he had been trying to move from river to river so fast that he was hardly enjoying himself; sometimes only staying long enough to wet a line before hitting the road in an attempt to outrun the looming Alaskan winter. He drove north from Jackson Hole trying to make his way beyond the Grand Tetons to gain access to Yellowstone National Park. His first planned destination on his trip through Yellowstone was the famous Fire Hole River.

The Fire Hole was named such, due to the giant pillars of white steam that resembled smoke ascending just off its banks, caused by the boiling water of nearby geysers draining into the river and violently colliding with the frigid water of the mountain stream. Blake and Aaron had read about the Fire Hole as children and had always dreamed of fishing this unique body of water. Today would be Blake's chance to fulfill that dream.

Blake looked out the window as he drove north down a two-lane highway. The grass-covered prairie was flat, barely rising beyond the height of a small hill even in the tallest of places. One could nearly see the curvature of the earth as the sedate landscape rolled to the West. Then, out of what seemed like the depths of hell, dark, jagged, snow-covered rocks resembling ancient flint-knapped arrowheads shot through the earth's crust like white-capped ocean waves crashing against a cliff side. It was the most magnificent mountain range Blake had ever seen...the Grand Tetons.

Blake had not taken many photos chronicling his trip thus far, but after seeing the vast splendor of the Tetons, he decided that was going to change. He pulled over to the side of the road and dug around the backseat looking for his backpack. He pulled the pack out and unzipped it. Aaron's fly box was still resting on top of the other items in the pack. He picked the box up and opened it. With everything that had happened, he had forgotten all about it. His mind and heart had been dwelling so much on Allison that he almost forgot why he was taking this trip to begin with. Blake decided he would put what happened at the ranch behind him and focus on what he had set out to do. With a new found vigor, Blake made a conscious effort to start fresh and to make the rest of his trip meaningful.

Blake dug deeper into the pack and pulled out his camera. After snapping a few photos, he took a couple minutes to clear his mind by taking in the majestic scenery before he continued down the highway.

It didn't take long for Blake to reach the southern entrance of Yellowstone. It was like no place he had ever been. The park was teeming with wildlife. Around one corner a small red fox would cause him to brake as it darted across the road. Around the next, a gridlock of cars yielded the right-of-way to a slow meandering herd of bison going by, unimpressed by the tourists. Nothing in the park was tame, but nothing seemed threatened by him. The mule deer didn't scamper away in fear as he drove through. No panicked critters were flushed from their activities at the sight of him. It was as if he had entered another dimension, where beast was king and the simple presence of man did not rate alarm.

Blake pulled into a parking space alongside the Fire Hole. He stepped out of his truck and surveyed the area before gearing up. The winding river snaked through grassy meadows that were outlined with a thick forest of iridescent pine trees. White and orange sulfuric stains painted a trail in the dirt as the nearby geysers boiled over, spilling scalding water that cut through the landscape and drained into the river. The potent smell of rotten eggs filled the air as the steam from the hot springs carried the emitting hydrogen sulfide gas into the atmosphere. Blake inhaled deeply through his nose, closed his eyes, and smiled. Today he would take it slow, do things right for a change…today he would fish for Aaron.

Blake walked to the back of his truck and opened the tailgate. After putting on his waders and boots, he pieced together Aaron's fly rod that Mr. Grady had given him before his trip, then attached Aaron's reel. He threaded the fly line through the eyelets and tied on a fresh leader and tippet. He walked down to the riverbank and studied the water. A hatch of blue-winged olive mayflies were skating along the surface of the river before softly resting atop the surface-film. Blake could see dimples in the water made from two rising trout that were taking turns devouring the duns that were being swept by the top current into the trout's feeding lane.

Blake opened Aaron's fly box and examined the patterns. He found one of Aaron's favorite topwater imitations, a meticulously tied *Parachute Adams*. The Parachute Adams was tied with hackle feathers twisted horizontally around a white calf hair post over a slim gray beaver fur-dubbed body. With brown filaments of feather barbules used as the tail, this tried and true pattern's underbelly silhouette would perfectly mimic the hatch of mayflies and with a delicate presentation would most likely fool the hungry trout.

Blake tied on the Adams and stood just off shore. He made a soft cast about three feet above the trout. The fly floated to the surface of the water and slowly drifted through the run. Blake could see through the glacier-clear water as one of the trout slowly rose toward the surface. The trout nosed up and closed its mouth over the fly. Blake set the hook and a solid connection was made with the fish. "Fish on!" Blake said with a grin. The fish darted upstream after feeling the sting of the hook in its jaw and when that did nothing to dislodge the hook, changed direction and swam downstream. Blake stripped the slack out of the line and quickly reeled in the excess. He played the trout like a seasoned angler and brought it to the net unharmed.

Blake looked down into his net to find a healthy brown trout with the Adams hooked to the roof of its mouth. Blake clamped onto the bend of the hook with his hemostats and with hardly any effort popped the fly from the trout's mouth. He released the fish back into the river. With a couple false casts the residual water was shaken free from the fly and Blake went back to working the water trying to get another fish to rise.

Later that evening, as the light was beginning to fade, Blake reeled in his line. He clipped the flies from his leader, and safely placed them back into Aaron's fly box. It had been a good day. A few fish caught but most importantly, not a single one of Aaron's flies were lost. Blake took a moment to admire Aaron's fly rod and reel as it balanced in his hand. The last time this rod had seen any action was on the Blue River. It was the same rod and reel that Aaron used to land the trophy rainbow right before they deployed to Iraq…the last time the two had ever fished together. With the memory of that day replaying in Blake's mind he smiled, as he now realized why it was so important to Mr. Grady that Blake use Aaron's rod and flies on this trip. He wanted Blake to have a way to reconnect with Aaron. He wanted him to have something tangible…something meaningful that could accompany him on his quest to find peace.

A rustling in the grass across the river startled Blake. He looked up and froze in place as he saw a deep brown mane contrast against the light tan hide of a giant bull elk. His antlers were thick like tree branches and towered nearly five feet above his head. The base of his horns were a dark burnt sienna, the tips of his impressive six-by-six rack where the elk had scratched it against the trees and dirt were polished to an ivory spike. His front legs waded in the river and his back legs anchored him to the shore while he drank from the water. A cloud of steam floated in the air behind him. It was an incredible sight. He had never been this close to a bull elk before.

Blake knelt down and placed Aaron's rod and fly box on the ground. He carefully opened his backpack to retrieve his camera. River water was dripping from the elk's mouth and the white steam floating behind him created a crisp contrast. The elk looked up right as Blake raised the camera. He snapped the photo and then another. Blake smiled in gratitude for the animal's cooperation. The elk plunged its snout back into the river for another drink. Blake carefully put the camera back into his pack and picked up the fly rod. Then, leaving the elk in peace, he slowly backed out of the area and hiked back to his truck.

With nightfall nearly upon him, Blake opened the tailgate of his truck, set his gear down, and began unlacing his boots. But before he could pull the first boot off he got a nagging feeling that something wasn't right. He sat there pondering it for a moment. Suddenly, dread fell over him. His eyes opened wide as he said, "Oh no! Oh, please no!" Blake grabbed his backpack and opened it. He dug through the inside frantically looking through its contents. He began to panic as he opened every pocket. He tossed the backpack to the side and with a flashlight in hand, searched around on the ground and inside the cab before surrendering to the horror that he had left Aaron's fly box on the river bank.

Blake ran as fast as he could back to the spot where he had seen the elk. When he arrived, he searched the river bank but didn't see anything. He flashed his light in all directions, but nothing. Was he at the right spot? Everything looked different in the dark.

"I swear it was right here…where the hell is it?" Blake questioned.

Blake turned in circles shuffling his feet as he scanned the ground. Suddenly he kicked something. He heard a splash in the water. He shined the light just off the bank and saw Aaron's fly box floating downstream in the fast-moving current. "Shit!" Blake yelled as he realized he had just unwittingly kicked the fly box into the water.

He jumped into the river, but it was too late. The fly box had already floated too far downstream for him to grab it. Blake quickly waded back to shore. He sprinted along the river, keeping the beam of his flashlight trained on the box. He heard heavy water ahead. He flashed his light downriver. The fly box was heading toward fast-moving rapids. If Blake was going to retrieve it, he needed to do it soon. He was just about parallel to the waterproof box as it started to dip and dive through the increasingly rough water like a tiny kayak. A couple more strides and he could cut in front of it, rescuing it from the rapids. Blake hurdled a small boulder. As his heel contacted the ground on the other side, his left foot unexpectedly sank into a shallow hole. The jolt from the unexpected drop caused him to stumble. A sharp pain shot from Blake's left calf and spiraled up to his hip like a zap of electricity. He suddenly felt the strength in his leg give out. He collapsed headfirst into the dirt. Blake yelled out as he grabbed his leg, feeling the stabbing pain that was coursing through the scar tissue of his war wound. Blake fought through the pain and forced himself back to his feet.

He hobbled down the river as fast as he could, refusing to give up. He had to get Aaron's fly box. He feverishly scanned the rapids and could see nothing. He limped along the shoreline making his way below the turbulent water in hopes that the container may have washed to shore or hung up on a rock in the calmer water. He desperately searched for the better part of an hour but never saw Aaron's fly box again.

With his leg still throbbing, Blake slowly made his way back to his truck completely demoralized. How could he have let this happen? How could he have been so careless? How could he ever explain this to Mr. Grady? Blake walked over to the tailgate of his truck and took his boots and waders off. As he was pulling his left leg out of his waders he lost his balance and stumbled, nearly falling to the ground. "Dammit! That's it!" Blake was enraged. Of all the times for his leg to fail him, it had to be that night. In a fit of anger, Blake crumpled his waders into a large ball and threw them as hard as he could into the bed of his truck. "Goddamn this fucking day!" He screamed as he reached under the tailgate with both hands and slammed it shut.

Blake heard a snap like a dry twig breaking and felt something ricochet off his leg. He looked down. There lay the broken tip of Aaron's fly rod, about a foot in length. Blake was horrified. He had slammed the tailgate shut before putting the rod away. His hand shook as he reached down to retrieve the broken piece. The impact from the tailgate shattered and splintered the graphite leaving that piece of the rod unrepairable. Blake was in disbelief. This couldn't be happening. How could an already nightmarish situation so quickly escalate into this? Everything in his life was falling apart…first Sgt. Tomlin, then his relationship with Allison, and now this. It was if he destroyed everything he touched, along with everyone he cared about. No matter how hard he tried, no matter how good his intentions…the end result was only pain.

Blake got into his truck and drove north out of the park and crossed the state line into Montana. He stopped off at the first town he came to, a little town called Livingston. He parked across the street from the first tavern he found. He walked inside and sat at the bar. The place was nearly empty. The bartender asked, "What can I get ya?"

"Jonnie Walker, straight up," Blake said. The bartender pulled a glass out and poured Blake a shot. Blake lifted the shot to his lips and chugged the whiskey in one gulp. He slammed the glass down on the bar and said, "Another."

CHAPTER TWENTY-FIVE

The Alleyway

B lake downed another whiskey in a single swallow. He savored the taste and closed his eyes feeling the alcohol coursing through his bloodstream like a haunting spirit possessing his body. He placed the glass down and signaled to the barkeep for a fresh one. The bartender slid another drink toward him. Blake eagerly picked it up and brought it to his mouth. "Slow down, guy," the bartender said. "Last call's not for another hour."

"Don't worry about me. Just keep 'em comin'," Blake said refusing to make eye contact as he set the glass down.

"Hard day at the office, champ?" said a stranger as he walked behind Blake, then sat down next to him. Blake didn't respond. The stranger shrugged, turned to the bartender and said, "I'll take a bourbon, neat." The bartender poured the bourbon into a cocktail glass and set it in front of the man.

The television over the bar was on, but the sound was muted. The local news was showing footage of the war in Iraq. Images of explosions and mangled heaps of metal that at one time were U.S. Humvees, the ticker at the bottom flashing the number of civilians and soldiers killed that week. "Can you believe this shit? What a waste," the man said with disgust as he watched the screen. "All those poor Iraqis. Why did we even go over there?"

"*We?*" Blake said.

"Oh, he can speak after all," the man joked. "Don't tell me you support this crap."

"And what crap is that?"

"Oh, I don't know, U.S. Soldiers killing and maiming innocent women and children in the name of *spreading democracy*. What a scam," the man said shaking his head.

"What are you talking about?" Blake said as he angrily turned and faced the man. "The only thing killing women and children over there is sectarian violence and fucking insurgents."

"Yeah, sure," the man said with a laugh. "You know that how?"

"I know cause I was there! I saw firsthand what they did! The civilians they blew up—the American service men and women they killed!" Blake said staring the man down.

"Spare me the self-righteous patriotic speech about the poor Soldiers who gave their lives for my freedom," the man said as he sipped his drink. "Any idiots foolish enough to join the Army and get themselves killed over there won't get any sympathy from me. They got what they deserved."

"You son-of-a-bitch!" Blake said as he stood up.

"Hey!" the bartender yelled out. "Sit down! I'll have none of that in my bar!" Blake glared at the man, breathing heavily. "Come on, son. He's not worth it," the bartender said trying to calm Blake down. Blake took a deep breath and reluctantly sat back down. The bartender walked over to the man, leaned against the bar, and said, "Finish your drink, then get the hell out of my bar."

"Oh, it's like that, huh? You hick hillbilly types are so predictable. You're all about free speech and liberty until someone says something you don't want to hear."

"Oh, I believe in free speech," the bartender said. "But I also believe in my right not to serve loudmouthed assholes that don't show respect to our men and women in uniform."

The man shrugged and said, "Sticks and stones my ignorant friend."

The bartender took a deep breath and walked away from the man. He poured Blake another drink, set it in front of him, and said, "This one's on the house." Blake nodded, picked up the glass, and began to drink.

"Yeah, drink up hero," the man said. "Maybe it'll help ease your murderous conscious."

Blake slammed his glass down on the bar. A sudden screech rang out as Blake kicked his barstool back and stood up. He reached over with his left hand and grabbed the man by the collar. The man's cocky smirk melted into a look of sheer terror as his beady eyes widened. Blake belted the man in the nose and blood shot out in all directions. The man fell back over his barstool and landed with a thud on the floor.

"No! What the hell are you doing?" the bartender yelled as he ran around the bar to check on the man.

"I—I don't know! The guy just pissed me off. I—I'm sorry." Blake said as he started to come to his senses. The bartender knelt down to check on the man.

"You knocked him out cold. Probably broke his nose," the bartender said.

"I'll call an ambulance," Blake said as he pulled out his cell phone.

"No, I'll do that. Just get out of here. You being here is just gonna make things worse."

"But—"

"Dammit! I don't need this trouble right now! Just get the hell out of here! Please!"

Blake looked down at his fist. It was spattered with the man's blood. He looked down at the man on the ground. His arms lay out to his sides and his eyes were rolled back. Blood was draining from his nostrils down the sides of his face. The man began to moan as he slowly started to regain consciousness.

"Go!" the bartender yelled. Blake stumbled backward and walked out of the bar.

He drunkenly staggered down the sidewalk, balancing himself on the buildings to keep upright. He walked around a street corner and turned down a dark alleyway. His stomach was tied in knots. It felt like something was yanking on his intestines. He could hardly breathe as he tried to hold back the urge to vomit. He collapsed to his knees splashing down in a shallow puddle of gutter water. Sharp pain like a giant hand gripping and twisting his guts forced him down onto his forearms. His neck stretched and his mouth opened wide as he lurched forward and heaved uncontrollably until the taste of burning stomach acid boiled over into his mouth. He spewed vomit onto the ground. During a reflexive break from the purge, he desperately gasped for a breath of air.

He wiped the dripping vomitus from his mouth with his forearm, then began to shiver as the darkness of night blanketed him in a chill. What had he become? How could this have happened? Was he always destined to end up this way? Was this where all roads eventually lead? Over a week ago he was happier than he had been in years. Now he lay face down in a pool of filth, alone, with not even the simple comfort of the stray dog he had rescued.

Blake crawled to the edge of the alley and sat with his back propped up against the side of a building. He hugged his knees up toward his chest to try to warm himself. He sat there, posed like a frightened child, trying to catch his breath. As his breathing slowed, his leg began to ache, and despair consumed him. He folded his arms and braced his elbows against his knees as he rested his head in shame against his forearms. There was no denying it now, his journey to Alaska ended here, cut short in the cold wet backstreet of an unfamiliar town. This intended pilgrimage of hope turned out to be nothing short of a curse, not only to him but to those he encountered along the way. Instead of helping things, he only left a path of destruction in his wake. Tears began to stream as he realized his utter failure. Not only to himself but to Allison, his mother, Mr. Grady, and the one he set out to honor in the first place, Aaron. He had nowhere to go, no one to turn to. The remorse and pain he thought he had outrun had now finally hunted him down and was suffocating the last wheezing breath of dignity still left in him.

A swift gust of wind blew through the alley, rolling a discarded soda can along the pavement near the main street. The hollowed clanking noise of the can startled Blake. He looked up. A light blue glow seemed to be hovering in the sky across the street. The tears in his eyes still clouded his vision like he was looking through a frosted window. He swiped his forearm across his eyes and looked again at the ghostly light. It was a white cross, illuminated by a blue-tinted spotlight mounted on top the roof of a Christian church. Blake gazed at the cross, his lips quivering. It was as if God was looking down on him. The same God that he had turned his back on the day Aaron was killed. The faith that had been instilled in him as a child by the Grady's, of an all forgiving and endless loving Lord, completely rotted away on the day his only brother was shot dead on that street in Ramadi. Not even after he was saved from suicide, did Blake ever welcome Him back into his heart. But now, sitting in the cold muck of the alley, Blake turned to the only refuge he had left…prayer.

He interlaced his fingers and squeezed them together. He forced his eyelids closed and his face crinkled as if he was enduring unimaginable physical pain. Although freezing outside, sweat began to filter from the pores of his skin. He didn't know what to say…he didn't know what to ask for. He had forgotten how to talk with God. He pounded his forehead against his folded hands until he could hear the thumping from the pulse of his heart echoing throughout his temples. He strained in search of the right words, but nothing came. Every muscle in his body tightened and shook. Who was he to ask for help? After what he had done, after what he had become…who was he to ask anything of God?

Blake's voice cracked. He whispered, "Please, help me…please. I know I don't deserve Your help…but I can't do this alone anymore."

A hush seemed to blanket the world. Blake felt a hand slowly reach down and touch his head. He gasped from surprise and jerked his head back as he looked up. A dark figure stood above him. A man's voice spoke, "Duh—duh—don't be scared. I'm not gonna hurt ya."

"Who are you?" Blake asked. "What do you want?"

"Muh—muh—my name is Gabe," the voice stuttered. "I heard you ask fur some help. Suh—so, I—I came to help."

CHAPTER TWENTY-SIX

My Name Is Gabe

G abe held out his dark leathery wind-beaten hand and said, "Let me hel—help you up."

Blake cautiously looked the man up and down. He looked worn out, dirty. Older in appearance than he probably was in age. He had a hunch in his posture and wore a black beanie which forced his frizzy shoulder-length salt-and-pepper hair to poof out around the sides like a circus clown. A short gnarly gray-and-black beard choked out most of the features of his neck and jowls, but receded enough to leave exposed his short paunchy nose and plump lower lip. He wore an old blue jacket that was frayed and ripped in many places, along with jeans that didn't fare much better. He smelled of old onions and cigarette smoke.

Blake reluctantly took his hand but stood up under his own power, while the weakened old man leaned back in a vain attempt to assist. "Thanks, old timer, but I'm OK," Blake said with his head down as he tried to wipe the tears from his eyes.

"Why were you crying?" Gabe asked.

"It's nothing. I'm better now, thanks. Where did you come from?" Blake asked, quickly trying to change the subject. Gabe pointed down the alley toward a crumpled-up refrigerator box. "I didn't even see you there," Blake said.

"Oh, I—I was laying down trying to sleep."

"Don't you have a place to stay?"

"Oh, yes," Gabe said. "I stay in all sorts of places."

"No, I mean are you homeless?"

"Muh—my father told me once that *your home is where your heart is*," Gabe said with a smile. "Yuh—yuh—you look cold," Gabe said taking off his blue coat. "Huh—here, take my jacket. It—it—it's warm."

"No thanks, I'm OK," Blake said. Blake noticed that Gabe had been wearing an old Vietnam era OD green battle dress blouse under his jacket. It had a faded blue patch in the shape of a knight's shield sewn on the shoulder. In the center of the shield was a red circle with white wings spread out over top. The number *11* was embroidered in white in the center of the red circle. Above the shield was sewn a curved military tab that read: *Air Assault*.

Blake looked at Gabe and asked, "Are you a vet?"

"Oh, no. I—I—I love animals, but I don't know how to fix 'em wuh—when their sick."

"No, I mean." Blake pointed at Gabe's patch. "Are you a veteran of the military?"

"Oh, yes," Gabe said. "The a—a—army…uh—11th Air Assault div—Division."

"I was in the Corps…Second Battalion, Fourth Marines."

Gabe's mouth opened wide. "Oh, wow! The mer—Marines?"

Blake could see that Gabe was of simple mind but large of heart. He grinned as he patted him on the back and asked, "You hungry?"

"Oh, yes," Gabe said rubbing his belly.

Blake laughed and said, "Let's get out of here and find some food. What do ya say?"

"The—the—there's a place around the corner that I like. Ruh—really good suh—soup."

They walked into an old diner that boasted 24-hour service on a red-glowing neon sign in the front window. The place was empty aside from a waitress and grill man who were sitting at the counter drinking coffee and watching the clock tick by. The waitress stood up. With a smile she said, "Well, hi there."

"Hey, how's it goin'?" Blake asked.

"Well, I'm doin' great. You two lookin' for food or coffee?"

Blake looked over at Gabe who was enthusiastically nodding. "Both, if that's OK?"

"We can do both. It'll take just a minute for the grill to heat up," the waitress said as she looked at the cook. He quickly took another sip of coffee and headed back to the kitchen. "Coffee to start?" the waitress asked.

Gabe smiled and said, "Oh, yes…please."

"Make it two," Blake said.

"Comin' right up," the waitress said. "Sit wherever ya please. I'll be over with your coffee and a couple menus here in a bit."

Blake and Gabe sat in a corner booth by the front window. The waitress walked over with two coffee mugs and a warm pitcher of fresh brew. She sat a coffee mug and menu in front of each of them.

Blake asked, "What kind of soup do you have?" Gabe's face lit up as he turned his attention to the waitress.

"All we've got tonight is chicken noodle," she said while filling their cups with steamy dark coffee. Gabe looked over at Blake and smiled.

"We'll each have a bowl to start," Blake said, winking at Gabe.

"Two bowls of chicken noodle, got it," the waitress said before walking back to the kitchen.

Blake opened his menu. "So Gabe, I've never heard of the 11th Air Assault Division. Were they an infantry unit?"

"The—they were once…back in Wuh—World War II. Back then they were called the 11ᵗʰ *Airborne* Division," Gabe said. "I was with 'em in '63 after they were changed to *air assault* instead of airborne. We were a special unit trying to develop new ways to duh—deploy infantry troops from helicopters."

"Did you ever deploy to Vietnam?"

"Oh, no. Wuh—we just trained, trying to come up with new ways of doin' stuff fur the Army, usin' those duh—darn choppers. But, it didn't matter, I got hurt just the same."

"What happened?" Blake asked.

"Oh, a helicopter crashed when I was training. I—I don't remember much about that day. The—doctors say I have severe brain trauma," Gabe said while lifting the front of his beanie, exposing a curved surgical scar that ran from the center of his forehead and extended through the top of his hairline. "They say I'm luh—lucky to be alive."

The waitress returned with two bowls of hot soup. She set a bowl in front of each of them and asked, "You guys know what else you want?"

"I—I'll have the tuna melt, please," Gabe said with a smile.

"The same," Blake said, handing the waitress the menu.

Blake turned back to Gabe who had his head bowed and his hands folded. He suddenly began to pray out loud. "Dear God," he said as Blake, caught off guard, quickly folded his hands and bowed his head. "Thuh—thank You fur this food and fur all Your blessings—especially those blessings we might not yet recognize. A—amen."

Blake looked curiously up at Gabe who was now lightly blowing on a hot spoonful of soup. "Mmm…" Gabe said as he savored the hot satisfying broth-soaked noodles. He sucked up a stray noodle that had been dangling from his lower lip. "Aren't ya gonna eat your suh—soup?" he asked as droplets of liquid dripped down his beard.

"Yeah. Sure," Blake said while watching Gabe slurp another bite. "Good grief Gabe. When was the last time you ate?"

"Nuh—night before last," Gabe said not breaking eye contact from his bowl.

"Don't you have any family or friends that can help take care of you?"

"No one that I know of. But that's OK, I—I don't need anyone to take care of me. I get by juh—just fine.

"Isn't there a shelter you can stay at?"

"Oh, not in this town, but maybe in the next."

"The next town? Are you just passing through?"

"Oh, yes, wuh—winter is almost here. I need to head south to Phoenix where it's warmer."

"What? Are you walking there?"

"Sometimes I get a luh—lift for a few miles, but mostly I just walk."

"Do you have any money?"

"I—I've got ten bucks," Gabe said proudly.

Blake wrestled his wallet out of his back pocket and pulled out a wad of cash. "Here's about 60 bucks. It's all the cash I have on me right now," he said handing the roll to Gabe. "You know what?" Blake said snapping his fingers. "I'll get us a hotel room for the night, here in town. We'll both get a good night sleep, a hot shower, and tomorrow I'll give you a lift to Denver. That'll at least cut a few hundred miles off your trip."

"Is thuh—that where you live?"

"Littleton actually, but it's near Denver," Blake said as he finally took a bite of soup.

"What ya doin' wuh—way out here?"

"I'm on a fishing trip. It's a long story."

Gabe stopped eating and placed his spoon on the table. He looked at Blake and said, "I've never known fishing to make anyone that upset before."

"Yeah, you kinda caught me at a bad time back there. Sorry about that."

"Yuh—you should never be sorry to ask for help. Especially when you're really sad."

"I—I wasn't asking *you* for help, Gabe. You just overheard me…"

"Oh, I—I know Who you were asking," Gabe said with a soft smile. "Don't be embarrassed. I talk to Him all the time. He helps me every day."

"Really? And what does He tell you?"

With steady voice and perfect clarity, Gabe answered, "He tells me not to dwell in anger. He reminds me that every day on this earth is a gift worthy of thanks." Gabe took a deep breath, looked Blake in the eyes, and said, "He shows me the good in this world…like today, when I found a young man in an alley who had fallen into the depths of despair but still had enough faith and kindness left in his heart to buy an old man a warm meal and to offer him a place to sleep. I can only pray that He shows you what He's shown me…that your life is a blessing not only to you, but to those around you."

Blake sat speechless, not knowing what to say. Who was this man that he had taken at first glance as someone who was helpless? Who was this simple stranger who lent him a helping hand at his darkest moment, lifting him from his knees and bringing him in from the cold?

"Here ya go, fellas. Two tuna melts," the waitress said, setting their plates down.

"Mmm. Suh—smells good. Thank you. I—I'm so sorry, but can I have this ruh—wrapped up to go? I—I've got to get going."

"Yours too?" the waitress asked Blake.

"No. Just mine, please," Gabe said.

"Sure thing. It'll just take a second," the waitress said as she took Gabe's plate.

"You're leaving?" Blake asked. "But what about the hotel and ride to Denver?"

"The offer meant more to me than you know, Blake. But it's time for me to leave."

A minute later, the waitress came back. "Here ya go, all wrapped up. I even brought you a coffee to go." The waitress placed a paper bag and a Styrofoam cup in front of Gabe.

"Thuh—thank you so very much. God bless you," Gabe said.

The waitress smiled and asked Blake, "Anything else I can bring you?"

"Just the check, please," Blake said.

The waitress put a receipt on the table and said, "Whenever you're ready."

"Thanks. Here ya go," Blake said handing her a credit card. The waitress walked back to the register and Gabe stood up and held out his hand. Blake shook his hand and said, "Gabe, are you sure I can't help you? You don't deserve to be out there, living in the cold."

Gabe smiled and said, "No Blake, it's you who shouldn't be living out in the cold."

Gabe picked up the paper sack and coffee and walked out the door. Blake was watching him pass by the front window of the diner when he noticed that Gabe had left the roll of cash Blake had given him on the table. Blake grabbed the money and ran out the front door. "Gabe! Gabe, wait!"

Blake yelled out, but the street and sidewalks were empty. He turned in circles looking for Gabe. Blake ran down the street and turned into the alley where he had first met him. The alley was empty. He was gone.

Blake walked back over to the diner. "Oh good, you're back," the waitress said when Blake walked through the door. "I thought you forgot your card."

"No, I'm back. I just forgot to give something to my friend." Blake crinkled his brow and thought for a second. "Hey, have you ever seen the guy I was eating with in here before? He mentioned he liked the soup here."

"No, but I work nights mostly."

"You've never seen him around town?"

"No, I live just down the street and I've never seen him before," she said handing Blake his card and two receipts. "Just sign my copy and leave it on the table."

"OK, thanks," Blake said as he took the card and receipts and sat back down at the table. Blake opened his wallet to return the credit card and wad of cash. As Blake placed the cash back, he saw a folded piece of paper sticking out of one of the pockets. He unfolded the paper and saw a number and address written on it. At the top was written the name, Tibbs.

Blake called to the waitress, "How far is Bozeman?"

CHAPTER TWENTY-SEVEN

A Message for Renee

The next morning Blake called Tibbs. "Yello? Emmanuel Tibbins here."

"Hey Tibbs, it's Blake."

"Marine! How the hell are ya?"

"I'm OK. I'm a few miles outside of Bozeman. How about that cup of coffee?"

"Love to Marine, but I'm bedded up here in the hospital right now."

"Really? You OK?"

"Oh, yeah, just fine. This was a scheduled visit. Heart valve replacement. The old ticker just ain't what she once was. Just got out of surgery two days ago. I'll be here for a couple more days till I can get my feet back under me. Come by for a visit if you like."

"I will."

Blake got directions from Tibbs and headed to the hospital. When he arrived he walked up to the nurses' station and said, "Excuse me. I'm looking for Emmanuel Tibbins. Do you know what room he's in?"

"Oh, you must be Blake," the middle-aged nurse sitting behind the counter said. "Tibbs told me to keep an eye out for you. He's in room 11…well, here, follow me, and I'll walk you back there," the nurse said as she walked around the counter and started down the hall. "Tibbs tells me you're on a fishing trip."

Blake laughed. "I am. Been a big part of the conversation around here, have I?"

"Only for about the last half hour or so," the nurse said as she lightly knocked on the door.

"Come on in Belle, I'm decent!" Tibbs called.

"Tibbs, your friend Blake is here."

"Marine! You made it. Belle, a cup of coffee for me and young Blake if you don't mind," Tibbs said while sitting, partially propped up in the hospital bed.

"Not on your life, Tibbs…doctor's orders. And stop calling me *Belle* you old flirt. The name's Nurse Terri and you know it," she said as she pulled the covers back up over Tibbs's chest.

"Sorry, Nurse Terri, for some reason you look like a Belle to me. Doesn't she Blake?"

Blake laughed and shook his head before telling Nurse Terri, "I have a sneaky suspicion they don't pay you nearly enough to put up with the likes of this guy."

"Ah…he's actually a sweetheart, just a little eccentric that's all," Nurse Terri said while examining a near-empty IV bag hanging from a hook over Tibbs's bed. "I'll be back to change this in a few minutes. In the meantime, you two behave yourselves."

"Thanks Belle—sorry, I mean, Nurse Terri." Tibbs said with a sly grin.

"Man, you sure are a character, Tibbs," Blake said. "So how are you feeling?"

"Like a million bucks. Thanks for swingin' by."

"No problem, devil dog. From the looks of it, I'm not your first guest," Blake said, seeing several floral arrangements and get-well-soon cards all over the room.

There was an oval pewter picture frame sitting on the nightstand next to his bed. The photo was a faded portrait of a soft-skinned lovely-eyed brunette who looked to be in her late twenties. "Who's this pretty lady?" Blake asked bent over examining the picture.

"That's my wife Gail, taken about the time we got married. She passed a couple years back."

"I'm sorry to hear that. She sure was beautiful, if you don't mind me saying. I wish I could've met her."

"Thanks Marine. She'd a liked you. She would've really liked Buddy."

"Oh, was she a dog person?"

"Not especially—more of an animal person, I'd say. I don't think there was a mammal on this earth she didn't think was cute. Even those godawful hairless cats," Tibbs said rolling his eyes and laughing. "Now, tell me, how the hell can you think a hairless cat's cute?"

Blake laughed. "I don't know."

"How is Buddy anyway?"

"As far as I know, he's OK. He's still back at Allison's ranch."

"She watchin' him for you while you fish?"

"No. She and I had a falling out. I left Buddy with her because her little boy Trevor just couldn't handle being away from him. I couldn't bring myself to do that to the little guy."

"He got pretty attached, did he? Well, I would've liked to see Buddy again, but I suppose he's lovin' that ranch life. Anyway, why'd you and Allison split up? I thought things were goin' good?"

"It's a long story, but essentially her ex confronted me and asked me to leave her alone. He was trying to make things right and I was getting in the way."

"What did Allison think about that?"

"It doesn't matter…her ex was right. She's better off without me."

"Now why in the world would you say somethin' like that?" Tibbs asked.

"Cause I'm a mess, Tibbs. I—I can't even manage myself, let alone anyone else."

"You seem pretty capable to me Marine."

"Well, I'm not Tibbs," Blake said running his hand through his hair and plopping down in a chair at the foot of the bed. "In the past week the only thing I've been able to *manage* is to alienate the only girl I've ever had feelings for, lose my dead friend's fly box on the river, and lose my temper and accidentally smash his fly rod in the tailgate of my damn truck. All it takes is a little bit of misfortune in my life and I fall apart. For crying out loud, I'm even back to drinking," Blake said throwing his hands up.

Tibbs laughed. "I've been down that road a few times."

Blake leaned forward. "That's right, you were a heavy drinker. How long have you been sober?"

"It's been over 20 years since I've had a drink but not even 20 seconds since I've wanted one. That's the curse of the drink for ya."

"That's for sure," Blake said gritting his teeth. "How'd you sober up in the first place?"

"Well, you remember me tellin' you about the 1/9 reunion?"

"Yeah."

"Well, what I didn't tell you was after I came home from the reunion I was feelin' pretty low, completely defeated. I didn't want to face another day on this godforsaken earth."

"Why not? You'd think seeing all those guys from your unit would help."

"Well, it didn't. It made things worse."

"Why?"

"I guess I was more jealous than anything. Envious that life was goin' just fine for everyone else, even the fellas who had gone through a lot more than me. I couldn't pull myself together, couldn't stop feelin' sorry for myself. Lookin' back, I guess it was pretty pathetic...a grown man, full of nothin' but self-pity." Tibbs shook his head. "I just couldn't figure out what the hell was wrong with me or how to fix it...couldn't pull out of the nose dive. In hindsight, I suppose there was a part of me that didn't really want to."

"Didn't want to? How could you not want to?"

"I guess when you're at your lowest, it seems like there's no point in tryin' to climb out."

"So what'd you do?"

"I knocked back a half bottle of blended scotch, put on my dress blues, stepped inside my bathtub, stood at attention like a good Marine, and shoved the barrel of my Colt 1911 in my mouth." Tibbs calmly described.

"Shit Tibbs! Are you serious? Well, you obviously didn't shoot yourself. What kept you from goin' through with it?"

"Oh, I went through with it. Pulled the trigger and everything. Problem was, the gun went click, but in the words of a Vietnamese *mama-san* tellin' a GI he's short on cash, *No boom-boom*," Tibbs said with a grin and a wink.

"Why didn't it go off?"

"Turned out the tip of the firing pin was broken. Don't ask me how it got busted, but it was. I drove out to the local outfitters store to try to locate a replacement pin, so I could finish the job."

"Did they have a replacement?"

"Sure did."

"So what kept you from *finishing the job?*"

"She did," Tibbs said pointing to the picture.

"Gail?"

Tibbs reached over and picked up the photo. He looked adoringly at it and answered, "Yes Marine, my precious Gail. It was the first time I ever saw her. She was standing at the front counter waiting in line to buy a fishing reel of all things. She was the loveliest thing I'd ever laid eyes on. For a moment I forgot all about my self-pity. I just stood there staring, lookin' her up and down." Tibbs's face lit up as he began to laugh. "I—I remember she looked back at me with this cross look on her face like I was some sort of pervert."

"Did you say anything to her?"

"The way she was lookin' at me I figured I better. It was either that or take a jab to the nose."

Blake grinned. "Well, what'd you say?"

"Probably the most romantic thing a young man could say to impress a young beautiful woman standing in line at a register. I looked deep into those big beautiful brown eyes of hers and asked, *You buyin' somethin'?*"

Blake laughed. "Boy, you really choked. So what'd she say?"

"She said, *How astute. Let me guess, you're a detective.*"

Blake laughed again. "She sure had your number! That's too funny."

"Yeah, she had definitely mastered the quick-witted sarcasm that a manically-depressed suicidal man would look for in a woman," Tibbs said with a sedate smile while staring at the photo and caressing his thumb over her image. "She was somethin'. Enough to make you rethink every decision you ever made. I gotta tell ya…I fell in love with her right there."

"What happened next?"

"Well, after my dimwitted comment broke the ice, we started talkin' and I asked her if I could buy her a cup of coffee. She agreed and next thing I knew we were dating. I sobered up, and about a year later I was down on one knee on the banks of the Missouri askin' her to marry me."

"You said she was buying a reel. By chance was that a fly fishing reel?"

"It sure was young Blake. In fact, I'd never picked up a rod before I met Gail. She'd been an angler since she was a child. She was an avid fly fisher and most of our dates were centered on her teaching me the sport on the local waters here in Montana."

"So that's how you got into fly fishing? Who would have thought?"

"Yep, Gail was the real deal. She taught me most everything about fly fishin'—from tyin' bugs, to casting…hell, she even knew how to row a damn drift boat, something I still haven't figured out," Tibbs said grinning while gently biting his lower lip. "We must have gone on a thousand fishing trips over the years. Even now, it seems like it wasn't enough."

"How long were you married?"

"25 wonderful years," Tibbs said before leaning his head back and taking a deep breath.

"Any kids?"

"One. My little girl, Renee."

"She live around here?"

Tibbs's tone softened. "Well, she lives with our Father in Heaven now."

"Tibbs, I—I'm sorry," Blake said.

"Don't be, Marine. God takes us all when He sees fit, that's just the way of it."

"Do you mind if I ask what happened?"

"No I—I don't mind. There's really not a lot to it," Tibbs said rubbing his chin while staring at the ceiling. "But where to begin?" he asked himself. "Well, I guess I should back up a little. When I say *25 wonderful years* of marriage, that's not exactly true. Ya see, Gail had always dreamt of being a mother, but things weren't working out the way she'd planned. After we got married, we spent the first couple years trying to have a child but were comin' up short. Gail's inability to get pregnant added a lot of stress. To make matters worse, I wasn't quite dealin' with my issues from Nam very well. I had gone back to drinking, was struggling at work, and our marriage was sufferin' because of it. It was just a roller coaster of emotions at the house—some days really good—some days, downright awful. We kept trying to have a baby, but with every failed attempt, it seemed we were becoming more and more distant from each other. Just when I thought we may be on the verge of divorce, fate stepped in and…well, she finally got pregnant."

"Wow, no kidding?" Blake said leaned over in his chair paying full attention.

"Everything went fine at first. All the check-ups were normal and everything was on track as far as development and whatnot," Tibbs said. "But Gail started having minor contractions about two months before the baby was due. Initially, the doc told us not to worry. Said that these things were common. But a couple nights later she woke up having the most painful contractions. They were so intense that she screamed out in pain. It was obvious something was seriously wrong. I rushed Gail to the hospital and she gave birth that night—two months premature. The doctor called me into the room and introduced me to my daughter. They had her in this special crib that was connected to some futuristic-lookin' apparatus. Poor little thing was so tiny, she could fit in the palm of your hand. She had all kinds of tubes comin' out of her. Even with all that, I remember lookin' at her and thinking, *this child is the most beautiful thing I've ever seen.* Just like the first time I saw her mother…I fell in love with that little girl on the spot."

"They wheeled the crib into the recovery room where Gail was resting. The doctor asked her if she'd like to hold her baby. I remember Gail asking if the baby would be hurt if they took her out of the crib. The doctor told us it didn't matter, there was nothing he could do. The child wouldn't survive more than a few hours. The doc picked her up and gently placed her in Gail's arms. He asked her, *Have you thought of a name?* Gail just looked at this precious child with the most tender gaze of love and with tears in her eyes, smiled and said, *Renee, her name's Renee.* I remember smiling cause we never discussed baby names. I suppose Gail figured it would be her call. But in all actuality, I—I couldn't have thought of a more suitable name. Turns out Renee means, *reborn.* And after seeing the beauty of my wife holdin' my little girl, that's exactly what I became. I could hardly believe it…I was a father. The miserable retch that held a gun in his mouth only a few years earlier now had a beautiful daughter. It was the most indescribable feeling. All the pain and despair that haunted me from Nam was eclipsed by the absolute joy I felt in that moment. And although I knew our time together would be short, standing in that hospital room, seeing my wife and child together, was the single greatest moment of my life. Nothing before and nothing since has come close."

"Did Renee die that day like the doctors thought?" Blake asked.

"Nah, that little tyke had too much of her mom in her—tough as nails. She held on for three days before the Lord took her. I don't think Gail slept a wink during those three days. I guess she didn't want to miss a single minute of her little girl's life. Who could blame her? She spent that time telling Renee stories about the world she would never live to see, humming lullabies to her and studying every feature on her little body so Renee's beauty would be forever etched into her memory. On that third day, I'd nodded off in a chair next to Gail's bed. She whispered for me to wake up. I looked over at her and I'll never forget the words that came out of her mouth. She said, *It's time, Emanuel. Come tell your little girl goodbye.*"

For the first time since Blake had met Tibbs he saw his impassive carefree walls come crashing down as the raw emotion of this painful memory overtook his strong demeanor, allowing a single tear to escape from his eye and race down his cheek.

"How Gail knew Renee was in her final moments…I'll never know," Tibbs said. "A mother's bond with her child, I suppose. Anyway, I leaned over and kissed her on top of her head and said, *Goodbye, sweet Renee, your mom and I love you so very much. Thank you for the greatest three days of my life.*"

There was absolute silence in the room for several seconds as Tibbs stared at Gail's picture. Blake finally broke the silence by timidly asking, "Did Gail say anything to her?"

Tibbs smiled and without looking up from Gail's portrait, said, "She gave Renee a soft kiss on the forehead and whispered, *Sleep well, little angel. I'll meet you in Heaven and hold you in my arms again one day…I promise.*" Tibbs took a deep breath and looked up at Blake. "And with that…my only child slipped away."

Knock, knock, knock came from the door. "Come on in Belle!" Tibbs called out while quickly wiping away the residue left behind by the tear.

"Sorry to interrupt," Nurse Terri said as she walked over to replace the IV bag hanging over Tibbs's bed.

"You're not interruptin' a thing," Tibbs said. "Any word on that coffee?"

"The word is no, Tibbs," Nurse Terri said with a playful grimace.

"Ouch! That's one hell of a war face, Belle. You sure you weren't a Marine?"

"No, I wasn't. But if I find out you've snuck a cup of coffee in this room you'll need an army to save you from my wrath," she said with a stern look.

"Understood Nurse Terri…understood," Tibbs said with a smile before Nurse Terri walked out of the room. Tibbs's smile melted away the second the door closed and his eyes drifted back to Gail's photograph.

"Tibbs, I—I don't really know what to say."

"You don't have to say anything Marine. That's just life. No matter how hard we might try, there's nothing we can do to change it."

"How did you and Gail handle things after Renee passed?"

"Well, I'll tell ya, I don't care how strong you are Marine, when you lose a child, you grieve…and grieve we both did. But Gail was a woman of faith; faith in God, faith in the goodness of mankind. She believed in the warmth the world had to offer. Felt that life, no matter how short or long, was meaningful…a belief I'd given up on after the war. She was the kinda person who would always look at what she had, not at what she didn't. It was that attitude that made her such a beautiful person. Even though Renee lived only a few days, Gail looked at her life as the greatest gift she'd ever received. She was sad that Renee had died but rejected the notion that her death was a tragedy. Sure, would she have wanted to see her little girl grow up and live a long life? Of course. But Renee wasn't supposed to live but three hours and God blessed us with three whole days with her. Twenty-four times longer than what was projected. I guess in Gail's eyes it was like comparing three years to three decades…a true miracle. And in those three days, Gail turned out to be one of the best mothers this world would ever know."

Tibbs brushed his thumb across his nose and sniffed, then looked up at Blake. "Although Gail never had another child, she was a mother and believed she and Renee would meet again. That belief did a lot to assuage the anguish of Renee's loss by giving her something to look forward to. As for me, after Renee's birth, life seemed more meaningful. I stopped dwelling in hate and began to see life through different eyes. I did my best to be a good husband and tried helping out veterans goin' through rough times. You see? Renee helped me experience true happiness for the first time in a long time. It was because of her and also seeing Gail's courage, that I finally snapped out of my funk. I finally stopped regretting my life and began embracing it. I truly was *reborn*."

The rhythmic cadence of beeping machines filled the empty void of silence as Blake absorbed the incredibly personal story. Blake asked, "When did Gail pass away?"

"Two years ago last month."

"She was still in her what…mid to late fifties? Was she sick or…was it some kind of accident?"

"Well, we were on a fishin' trip at Grey Reef of all places," Tibbs said. "On day two of the trip, she wasn't feeling very good. Said she felt weak, like she was comin' down with somethin'. By the time we got home things had gotten worse. I thought it best to take her to the doctor. He ran some tests and found she had cancer. Stage four. His plan was to attack it pretty hard right out of the gate with radiation. Doc said it was her only chance. But in the end, it would seem not even an atomic bomb had enough radiation to kill off this cancer…we just caught it way too late. Three months later she was lying in bed at this very hospital, holdin' on by a thread," Tibbs said, shaking his head. "Once she was admitted, it didn't take long. I remember I was reading her a book…she liked that. She was so weak she couldn't raise her voice above a whisper. She looked at me and tried to talk. I put the book down and leaned in to hear what she was saying." Tibbs tilted his head back and stared up at the ceiling, trying to force back the tears. "She asked me if I had a message I'd like delivered to Renee. It was then, I was the happiest for my Gail. I could tell she wasn't afraid. She knew her life had run its course and now she looked forward to being with her little girl again. And just like typical Gail, always lookin' on the bright side, she saw her death as an opportunity for me to say hi to my sweet little girl."

Tibbs closed his eyes and brushed away the tears. "I leaned in and whispered my message to Renee in Gail's ear. She looked at me and smiled before closing her eyes for the last time. She fell into a deep sleep…and took her last breath two hours later."

"Tibbs, may I ask…what your message was to Renee?"

"I said, *Sleep well little angels. I'll meet you both in Heaven and hold you in my arms again one day…I promise.*"

CHAPTER TWENTY-EIGHT

The Letter

A knock on the door. "Come on in Belle," Tibbs said.

"Hey guys, sorry to interrupt," Nurse Terri said as she walked into the room. "Tibbs, everything OK?"

"Oh, yes," Tibbs said wiping his eyes. "Blake was just tellin' me *the* most hilarious boot camp story I think I've ever heard. Haven't laughed that hard in years."

"Well, laughter might be good for the soul, but it isn't necessarily good for the heart. Especially one trying to recover from surgery. Now, I think it's time you got some rest."

"Agreed," Tibbs said. "Where you stayin' tonight Marine?"

"Probably a hotel," Blake said.

"Nonsense!" Tibbs said while leaning over to the side of his bed and rummaging in the nightstand. "Here's the keys to my house. There's a guest room right across from the master bedroom. I always keep that room clean and ready. There's plenty of food in the fridge, so help yourself."

"Thanks devil dog. I'll take good care of the place," Blake said taking the keys.

Tibbs reached over to a stationary tablet that was sitting on the nightstand and wrote down his address. "Here ya go young Blake—directions on how to get there. And uh, excuse the mess. I didn't have a chance to pick up."

"Thanks. I'll be by in the morning to return these to you before I go."

"Go? You headn' to Alaska then?"

"No, that ship has sailed. I'm heading back to Wyoming tomorrow. There's a young lady there that deserves an apology. It's time for me to start looking at life…like you said…through different eyes."

"Oorah Marine…that pleases me more than you know," Tibbs said with a smile. "I'll look forward to seein' you in the morning."

"Semper Fi, devil dog," Blake said holding out his hand.

"Semper Fi, Marine," Tibbs said taking Blake's hand in a strong grip.

Blake began walking out of the room and noticed the number *11* posted on the door of Tibbs's room. He stopped, turned around, and said, "Hey, Tibbs."

"Yes?"

"I met this vet in Livingston last night. He really helped me after I…well, *fell off the wagon*. Helped me pick myself up and get here, actually. Anyway, he said he was with the 11th Air Assault Division. You ever heard of that unit?"

"Sounds like an Army outfit, but I'm not familiar with them." Tibbs thought for a second, raised his eyebrows as he snapped his fingers, and said, "You know what you should do? Ask Allison's dad. You said he was an amateur military historian, didn't you? I bet he'd know."

"That's a pretty good idea. I'll do that."

"Also Blake, I was thinkin'. If you lost your friend's fly box on a river around these parts, you might try a few of the fly shops in the area. Most of them have a *lost and found*. I don't know how things are in Colorado, but in Montana, anglers are pretty good about turnin' those kinda things in. I guess they hope the favor's returned if they ever lose somethin'. Hell, I've turned in my fair share of fly boxes over the years. Can't hurt to check."

"Thanks Tibbs, I will. Try to get some rest."

"Will do my friend."

Blake left the hospital and drove to Tibbs's house. It was a modest well-kept ranch home, probably built in the early 80s. The siding was painted tan with brown trim. A large deep-colored American Flag, without a single fray, hung on a brass staff topped with a golden eagle finial attached at an angle to a porch pillar near the front entrance. The flawless bright-green lawn was freshly cut and the edges around the driveway and sidewalk were meticulously trimmed. Without a doubt, the house was the crown jewel of the neighborhood.

Blake walked inside and laughed. He shook his head. "*Excuse the mess*...what a character." The inside was immaculately clean. Even the white-glove treatment couldn't have produced a spec of dirt or dust. It reminded Blake of his days in boot camp, where the recruits were required to keep everything clean and organized, neatly tucked away in its rightful place.

Blake scanned the interior from the front door and noticed something on the wall above the couch in the living room. It was an arrangement of framed photographs chronicling the life of Tibbs and Gail. Blake turned on the light and walked over. The pictures seemed to be archived chronologically, from left to right.

The first few pictures near the top were of Tibbs and the bottom of Gail, presumably before they met. The only serious-looking photo of Tibbs on the wall was a Marine Corps boot camp graduation portrait, showing a young Private Emmanuel Tibbins in his dress blues with a battle-hardened look on his face. Next to it were several framed photos of him in Vietnam, screwing around with guys from his unit.

Most of the photos of Gail were of her out on the river fly fishing. Some of her holding up large trout, others of her fishing with a man, probably her father, taken when she was a young girl.

As Blake looked through the pictures, the photos gradually merged from *his* and *hers*...to *theirs*. About a third of the way down the wall there was hardly a picture without the two of them together, lovingly holding each other on some distant riverbank or some exotic foreign city, wearing smiles so big, they had to be genuine. And although the theme of the pictures stayed consistent, the faces gradually aged. Blake witnessed the two grow old together. What an incredible love story those pictures told. What a great life would have been missed if Tibbs had taken his prematurely.

Blake now truly understood what Tibbs had been trying to get across all this time. Life could be unmercifully cruel, for that there was no doubt. Not only to men in combat but also to mothers like Gail, to fathers like Mr. Grady, and to countless others who, by no fault of their own, were plagued with the pain of unexpected loss. But that loss, that sadness could be overcome. Joy and purpose could still be found if one could muster the courage to search for it.

Blake had set out on this journey to find peace. But he knew now that true peace couldn't have been found by fulfilling his fishing trip to Alaska. It wasn't until that moment, looking at the pictures of Tibbs and Gail, that he realized he had found what he was looking for only a few hours into his trip…not on a distant river but in the burning wreckage of a sedan on the side of an interstate just outside Casper, Wyoming. For the first time in his life, Blake knew exactly what he wanted. He wanted her…he wanted Allison. He was through with all the toil and torment he carried. He decided right then that he was going to accept what had happened and live the way Aaron would have wanted him to. He was going to put this darkness behind him. He wanted to be with Allison…he was in love with her. He wanted to start their own wall of memories. Just like Tibbs, he too felt a sense of rebirth. But he could only hope that the damage he caused could be forgiven. He could only hope it wasn't too late to make things right.

The next morning while Blake was driving back to the hospital, he spotted a small fly shop at the corner of an intersection and pulled into the parking lot.

There was an old white-haired man leaning against the front counter of the store with his head buried in a bird-hunting magazine. He looked up at Blake. "How's it goin'?"

"Pretty good. And you?"

"Other than bein' a little on the slow side things are good. What can I help you with?"

"Do you ever have anyone turn in items they find while they're out on the river?"

"Did you lose somethin'?"

"Yeah, a fly box."

"Where were you fishin'?"

"The Fire Hole, a couple days ago."

"Yeah, somebody came in yesterday and gave me a box he found. Although, he said he found it while fishing in Yellowstone. What's it look like?" The man asked while bent over rummaging through a cardboard box underneath the counter.

"It's one of those longer-sized hard plastic waterproof boxes," Blake said leaning over the counter trying to peer into the cardboard box.

"Color?" The man asked.

"It's tan…almost white from being sun-bleached."

"This it?" The man asked, holding up Aaron's fly box.

"Yes! Holy cow! Yes!" Blake said as he took the box from the man and quickly opened it. All the flies were there, undamaged. Blake could not believe this stroke of luck. Blake shook the man's hand with a huge grin and said, "You don't know how much this box means to me. Oh, I can't believe it! Thank you!"

"Sure thing, no problem," the man said. "It's pretty rare for us to reunite this lost stuff with the owners so I'm happy it worked out for ya."

"Do you know how to get in touch with the guy who dropped it off?" Blake asked.

"I don't remember his name. He didn't leave his info and I haven't seen him in here before. He was a colored fella with a blue jacket," the man said nonchalantly.

Blake wondered to himself, *Colored fella? Blue jacket? Could it be? No, that was far too improbable. In fact, it couldn't even be possible. It had to be someone else.* Looking a little vacant, Blake asked, "You don't happen to remember—if he said his name was Gabe? Do you?"

"Couldn't tell ya, even if he did. I'm horrible with rememberin' names."

"Well, did he talk with a stutter?"

"Not that I recall, but he wasn't in here for more than a minute. It was pretty busy at the time and I was in the middle of helpin' a customer. He just came in, said he found the box in Yellowstone, and asked if he could leave it in our lost and found. I told him to leave the box on the counter and I'd take care of it. He left after that."

Blake shook the man's hand again and said, "Well anyway, thanks so much. If you happen to see that guy again, will you relay to him my thanks?"

"Will do. Take care," The man said before going back to reading his magazine.

Blake drove through town to the hospital with a grin painted on his face. He coasted into the hospital parking lot, parked in the first spot available, swiftly jumped out of his truck, and jogged through the lot to the entrance. He walked briskly through the halls and without knocking, went straight into Tibbs's room. "Tibbs! You'll never guess what I—," Blake stopped midsentence. The bed was empty, the flowers and cards gone. A janitor was mopping the floor.

Blake left the room and walked up to the nurses' station. Nurse Terri was sitting behind the counter, typing. "Excuse me, Nurse Terri."

She looked up. "Oh, Blake. How are you?"

"I—I'm fine. Where's Tibbs?"

"No one told you?" She asked, standing up from her seat.

"Told me what?" Blake asked as the excited look on his face dissolved.

Nurse Terri looked at Blake with a tilted head and a pained look of empathy. "Blake, um, Tibbs suffered a massive stroke last night while he was sleeping."

"What? A stroke? Is he going to be OK? Can I see him?"

"Blake, please believe me when I tell you we did everything we could…I'm so sorry, but Tibbs passed last night."

"Wha—what do you mean? He was fine yesterday. He didn't even seem like he was in any pain."

"Blake, I know—"

"Hold on! He was supposed to go home in a couple days! How could you let this happen? He was in a hospital for crying out loud and nothing could be done?"

"I'm so sorry," Nurse Terri said softly. "All the staff here really liked Tibbs. But these things sometimes happen…even in a hospital. Strokes are impossible to predict and are often fatal." She reached over the counter and put a comforting hand on his shoulder.

"I'm sorry for yelling at you," Blake said hanging his head. "I'm just trying to process all this."

"I know. It's OK."

Blake took a couple deep breaths. "But his house? I mean, I've got his keys. Who's gonna take care of him? Wha—what happens to him now?"

"If it helps, here's the name and number of his cousin who's handling all of his affairs," Nurse Terri said while scribbling on a posted note.

Blake took the paper and said, "Thanks…I—I appreciate it."

Blake turned and began walking toward the exit when he heard Nurse Terri call out, "Blake! Wait!" Blake turned around to see her lightly jogging up to him. She pulled a piece of folded stationary from her pocket. "I found this on the nightstand next to his bed. He must have written this right before he went to sleep. I think he meant to give it to you."

Blake took the paper and unfolded it. He looked at the first couple lines and examined the writing for a few seconds before folding the paper back. He looked up at Nurse Terri and said, "It was meant for me…thank you."

Blake turned and walked out of the hospital. He sat down on a nearby bench and opened up the letter. He savored every word as he carefully read it in its entirety. When he finished, he gently folded it back up and placed it in his shirt pocket. With tears in his eyes he leaned forward, rested his forehead against his folded hands, and prayed…that his friend Tibbs, who had helped him so very much, had finally found peace…once again holding his wife and daughter in his arms.

CHAPTER TWENTY-NINE

A Better Me

I t was a Saturday morning, an hour before the service was scheduled to start. The church, which had a relatively large chapel, was already packed. Even arriving an hour early couldn't yield a decent seat. By the time the service started, the congregation swelled to over 300. For someone whose closest living relative was his cousin, the showing was a heartwarming tribute to a man, known by most, simply as Tibbs.

There was no flag-draped coffin on display, only a framed portrait of Tibbs, late in life, sitting beside the pulpit on a small table that was decorated with flowers. Although having earned the sacred privilege to be buried with full military honors, Tibbs instead specified in his will that he be cremated just as Gail and Renee had. He instructed that his ashes be scattered at a specific spot along the headwaters of the Missouri River in the Rocky Mountains of Western Montana, so to rest beside his wife and daughter.

The memorial service started much like Sgt. Tomlin's with a minister giving a short sermon followed by the relinquishment of the pulpit over to the congregation, affording friends the chance to give testament to their relationship with Emmanuel Tibbins. But unlike Tomlin's funeral, the mood in the chapel was not melancholy. There was a spirit of gratefulness that warmed the atmosphere as the people in attendance celebrated the life and accomplishments of their dear friend.

As Blake listened to the many eulogies, he learned what a truly great man had befriended him. Tales of Tibbs's selfless courage in Vietnam, his adoring love for his wife and daughter, and his unflinching loyalty to service members suffering from the physiological and psychological scars of war, were truly inspiring.

But the most inspiring came from a young man about Blake's age. He was the last to speak. Blake studied him as he walked up to the pulpit. He had a distinctive limp in his step which favored his left leg and the right sleeve of his suit was pinned up to the shoulder revealing a missing arm. The man introduced himself, "Hey—a, I'm Collin. I'm an Army vet. I met Tibbs almost two years ago at the Billings VFW. I was in a real bad place back then. Ya see, I was really into playing sports, ya know, before the war…baseball, mostly. Anyway, after I lost my good arm in Baghdad, I wasn't me anymore. I couldn't swing a bat, couldn't throw a ball right…couldn't hardly run the bases. I spent most of my days sitting alone drinking at the VFW. I remember one day this guy walks in and sits down at my table. I'd seen him in there a few times before but never talked to him. Anyway, he tells me his name's Tibbs and that he's a fly fisherman. He invites me to go fishing with him the next day. I just stared at him with this goofy look like, *Is this guy for real?*"

The congregation let out a laugh.

"I told him thanks but said I didn't think that was such a good idea, what with my arm and all." Collin paused and, trying not to laugh, continued, "Tibbs says to me, 'Oh, you're a defeatist. Let me guess, you served in the Air Force.'"

The congregation irrupted in laugher. Collin couldn't hold back after the response from the crowd and began to laugh along with them with a big toothy grin.

"That was Tibbs for ya," He said still snickering. "He somehow knew the right buttons to push to motivate you to get off your ass and stop feeling sorry for yourself. We went out to the river the next day and right out the gate he put a fly rod in my hand and said, 'Give it a shot.' I said, *Well, aren't you gonna show me how to do this?* He says, 'I don't know how you're gonna do it. I've never fished with only one arm. Do your best and we'll figure it out together.' After about 10 minutes of fumbling through a few sloppy casts and nearly hooking myself in the back, I got really frustrated. I popped off at him and asked how in the hell I was supposed to cast a fly rod while managing the slack in the line with an awkward left hand and a 10-inch stump for a right arm." Collin started to smile and said, "So Tibbs tells me, 'Use what God's given you.' *Like what?* I ask. Tibbs says, 'Well, I know God gave you a mouth, cause that's all I've been listening to all mornin'.'"

The crowd chuckled.

"He said, 'Instead of using your yap for whining, lift that rod up to your face, grab that slack line in your teeth, dip your chin, pull it close to your armpit, and pinch that slack against your chest with that nub of yours.' Reluctantly, I gave it a try. And you know what? It kinda worked. With a little fine tuning, some rod and reel modifications, and months of practice, I actually started catching fish that way. I don't play baseball anymore, but I'm happy to report that I've turned into one hell of an angler." Collin paused and looked down at the podium. His eyes began to tear up. He raised his head, and with a kind smile said, "I'll never be the man I use to be and that's OK…because that's the way life goes sometimes and all the wishing in the world won't change that. Tibbs helped me find a different me…a better me. Tibbs did more than teach me how to fish, he taught me how to live again. He showed me the strength that was still inside of me and what amazing things I could accomplish with that strength, as long as I had the courage to use it."

A single tear finally broke and ran down Collin's cheek. "Tibbs saved me. As long as I live I'll never forget what he did for me. He was as good of a man as I will ever know…as good of a man as this *world* will ever know." Collin took in a deep breath. He wiped the tears from his eyes with his knuckles, cleared his throat, and said, "I—I just thought you all should know that." He walked down from the podium and back to his seat.

Although most people were crying, none seemed to be grieving. They wore soft smiles as they absorbed the heartfelt story.

As the service came to a close, Blake didn't show a single sign of sadness. He stood there with a look of contentment, gazing at the portrait of Tibbs with genuine admiration. He was proud of Tibbs, for the man he was and the man he had become, despite all the trials and loss in his life. A true example of courage and strength, Tibbs was able to turn a life of pain into a life of meaning, not only for himself but for others. Tibbs had touched so many, he had accomplished so much. He embodied the code and was the true estimation of a husband, father, friend, and Marine.

Blake pulled a folded piece of stationary paper from his pocket and held it tightly. He looked down at his hand, gently opened the note, and silently read the last message from a man he barely knew who had helped change his life forever. Even in his last hours on earth, Tibbs had remained *always faithful.* Once finished, Blake folded the note and put it back into his pocket for safekeeping. Looking at Tibbs's portrait, he whispered, *Semper Fi, devil dog...rest in peace.*

CHAPTER THIRTY

The Angels

The golden glow of the sunset had nearly disappeared over the western horizon. Blake had driven all afternoon and well into the evening to get back to Casper. He bounced around in his seat as he drove down that familiar dusty road that lead to the Grace's ranch house as the rumbling from the washboard ruts in the dirt vibrated throughout the truck. As he pulled up, he could see Trevor and Buddy playing in front of the house.

Blake stopped the truck and turned off the engine but did not get out. He gazed out the window at them when they stopped playing and stared at the pickup. Blake took a deep breath and opened the door.

After seeing Blake emerge, Trevor yelled out, "It's Bwake! It's Bwake! Gwampa! Gwampa! Bwake's back!"

Trevor ran enthusiastically up to Blake. Buddy ran past Trevor at a full sprint and jumped into Blake's outstretched arms. The two fell to the ground and Buddy whined and yelped with excitement as he licked Blake's face. "OK! OK, Buddy! I'm glad to see you too boy!" Blake said laying on his back pushing Buddy away just far enough to steal a breath between licks.

"Bwake, you're back!" Trevor said joining in the reunion as he jumped onto Blake and gave him a warm hug.

"Yeah, I'm back sport. Where's your mom?"

"She's not here," a deep voice said.

He looked up to see Emmett, standing on the porch. Blake quickly stood and brushed himself off before saying, "Emmett, how are you?"

"Oh, I'm just fine. What brings you back? I figured you'd be in Alaska by now."

"Yeah, about that…I should have never left that way. It was a mistake. I—I realize that now. I'm here to apologize, and although I don't deserve it, I'd like the chance to make things right again."

"Trevor, take Buddy inside and watch a little TV while Blake and I talk. OK?" Emmett said.

"OK, Gwampa. Buddy, come on," Trevor said slapping his hand against his leg and running up the porch steps with Buddy at his heels.

Emmett walked up to Blake and said, "Ya know, I told you you'd always be welcome here as long as I ran this place and I meant it."

"I know and I appreciate it."

"Well, that being said, I accept your apology. Although I suppose my acceptance isn't what really matters here, is it?"

"It does matter to me Emmett, but I know what you're getting at. Do you know where Allison is? Can I talk to her?"

"Well, in light of the news of the ranch selling, she's been picking up a few shifts here and there waitin' tables at the Pronghorn to try to scrape together some extra cash. I'm not sure what time she'll be back. Probably late, like most nights."

"So are you going to lose your job here?"

"Well, up until a couple hours ago it looked like that's what might happen. But I just got a call from the new owner who said he'd like to keep me on, runnin' things around here. I've got a meeting with him tomorrow morning. If all goes well, maybe we'll be able to stay after all."

"That's great news! Have you told Allison yet?"

"No, and this time you'd better keep your mouth shut. I don't want to get her hopes up in case it doesn't work out."

"Of course. I won't say anything. But—if she's working at the Pronghorn, trying to make extra money, then sh—she's not?"

"Gettin back with Wade?" Emmett asked. "Let me tell you somethin' about that little twerp. The only reason he was holdin' out on the divorce was so he could figure out a way to get rid of Allison and Trevor without it costing him an arm and a leg."

"Huh, who knew? He seemed so genuine. Like he truly wanted to get back with her," Blake said in disbelief.

"The only thing genuine about Wade is that he's a genuine manipulator and liar. He wasn't makin' any headway with Allison in court. She was fighting him tooth and nail to get as much as she could, for Trevor's sake. Wade played you like a fiddle. Used you to try to break Allison's spirit. I think he figured without you in the picture, she'd give up."

"So what happened?"

"She got what was rightfully comin' to her and Trevor. Back payments for child support for all the years he'd abandoned them plus some alimony. Not to mention a college fund for Trevor. After the judge's divorce decree was final, Wade was so pissed off that he split and went back to his life in the city without even saying goodbye to Trevor. Like I said, *he couldn't care less about those two.*"

"I'm such a fool," Blake said shaking his head.

"You're not a fool, Blake. Your intentions were noble, just your judgment was a little off, that's all."

"Is she still pretty angry with me?"

"I suspect you should talk to her about that. But if you're gonna talk to her, sooner would probably be better than later."

"Understood. Thanks Emmett," Blake said with a nod. He turned and started walking toward the truck, then he stopped and turned back around. "Emmett?"

"Yes?"

"I know this might seem strange, but have you ever heard of the 11th Air Assault Division?"

"Oh yes, the old 11th Air Assault," Emmett said looking up into the sky trying to recall the details. "They were a U.S. Army helicopter infantry division if I remember right. An off shoot of the old 11th Airborne Division. They called themselves, *The Angels*."

Blake smiled. "*The Angels*, huh? Why am I not surprised?"

"What made you think of them?" Emmett asked.

"It's a pretty long story. One of these days I'll have to tell you."

"I'll look forward to hearin' it. Good luck, Blake. I hope to see you here again real soon."

Blake left the ranch and drove to the Pronghorn. He walked up the steps of the outside deck and stood in the lonely darkness of night looking through the front window of the restaurant. The warm glow of the light escaping from inside the bar touched his face and reminded him of the night they spent dancing in each other's arms. The smells and sounds from the restaurant echoed so strong in his senses that it brought back the vivid memory of that moment; he could almost see the ghostly image of them holding each other on the dance floor. What he wouldn't give to have that feeling again.

Allison appeared through the crowd of people. She was serving drinks to a table for two…the same table they had sat at that night. She was just as beautiful as when he last saw her. Although something was missing…she didn't have the same beam in her eyes. Her smile seemed forced. She seemed vacant, tired, almost awkward as she bounced around checking in on the customers at her tables. Blake feared he had hurt her beyond repair. How could he ever convince her that he had changed? That he was committed to her? That he loved her? Would she ever forgive him? Would she ever love him?

Blake looked down at his feet contemplating what he might say and how he might say it. He decided he was just going to march through that front door, walk right up to her in front of everyone, and lay it all out there, everything he was feeling. He was going to tell her how much he needed her and how much she needed him. They were right for each other. They were going to be happy. Everything that happened up to that point, all the indecision and worry was over. Nothing mattered to him except her, and they were going to make a great life together, no matter how hard they had to work…no matter how long it took.

Blake took a couple deep breaths. *This was it*, he thought. *It's now or never. Get in there and show her how much you—*

"Blake?"

Startled, Blake looked up to see Allison standing outside. Blake just stared at her.

"I saw you through the window. What are you doing here?"

Blake took a couple steps toward her. He looked at her with boldness in his eyes and simply said, "I'm in love with you."

Allison began to tear up and her face looked confused and pained. "What?"

Blake took a couple more steps closer and softly repeated, "I'm in love with you."

The pain in her face began to melt. Her eyes opened wide. "One more time, if you don't mind. I don't know if I heard you right," Allison said.

Blake cupped his hand under her cheek. He wiped away a tear with his thumb, just like he had that night on the dance floor. With the other hand he gently brushed her bangs from her eyes then held her softly behind her neck. He looked deep into her beautiful blue eyes and whispered, "I'm in love with you Allison Grace."

Allison smiled and said, "That's what I thought you said."

They leaned into each other and softly kissed.

THIRTY-ONE

Precious Life

It was September 11, 2007. Blake and Allison pulled into a newly paved parking lot off of a two-lane Colorado highway. Blake pulled into one of the parking spaces and they stepped out of Blake's truck. Allison pulled forward the front passenger seat to let Trevor out while Blake walked around to the back and opened the tailgate. Buddy jumped out from the truck bed, ran over to the edge of the parking lot, and began sniffing the grass and trees. "Buddy! Wait for me!" Trevor called as he ran over.

"Is this the trailhead to Cheesman Canyon?" Allison asked.

"Yeah, I'm pretty sure," Blake said.

"Pretty sure? I thought you use to fish here all the time."

Blake smiled. "I did. Come on, cut me some slack, it's been a few years. This parking lot wasn't here before." Blake turned in a circle looking around. He pointed toward the opposite side of the parking lot. "Look, right there. There's the trailhead."

"Ooooh, you mean the path with the sign posted next to it that says, *Trail Head?*" Allison said with a smirk. "Nothing escapes you Blake Jacobs."

"You know what?" Blake said with a crazy grin on his face.

"No. What?" Allison said with a wide-eyed smile.

"You're gonna get it, that's what!" Blake said as he grabbed Allison's arm pirouetting her around then wrapping his arms around her waist from behind in a playful hug.

"I just realized something." Blake whispered in her ear.

"What?"

"You're a little snot, but for some reason, I can't help but love you."

"Love you too," she said turning around in his arms and giving him a kiss. "Now, let's get going already."

Blake began putting on his waders and piecing together his fly rod. He held the butt end of the rod up to his eye, making sure the eyelets lined up. "You sure you don't want to fish while we're in there? I brought a spare rod."

"No thanks, I'm good," said Allison. "Besides, somebody has to keep an eye on Trevor and Buddy. You know how they love to disappear."

"Good point. You got the pack with our lunch in it, right?"

"Yep, it's right here," Allison said as she fed her arms through the straps of the backpack, hoisted it on her shoulders, and cinched the straps tight.

"Now all we're missing is Trevor and Buddy," Blake said looking around.

"Trevor! Buddy! Come on, we're leaving," Allison called out. Trevor enthusiastically ran toward Allison with Buddy in chase and the four of them set off down the Gill Trail.

Although the first hundred yards had been rerouted from the original path, it eventually merged into the same route that Blake and Aaron had walked so many times before. Blake was filled with warmth as each bend brought back fond memories of the countless childhood fishing adventures he and Aaron had taken. Trevor and Buddy ran along the path eagerly wanting to get to the river. Buddy kept gently colliding with Trevor as his excitement to play with the boy got the better of him. "It's OK to run, just don't leave my sight," Allison told Trevor.

"I won't Mommy...promise," Trevor said pushing Buddy down as he jumped up and tried to lick Trevor's face.

"That dog watches over him like nothin' I've ever seen," Allison said.

"Yeah, I know. I'm a little jealous. When Trevor's around, Buddy treats me like chopped liver," Blake said.

"I think Buddy just gets tired of watching you fish, whereas Trevor actually plays with him."

"You don't get tired of watching me fish, do you?"

Allison rolled her eyes and said, "No Blake, it's my favorite thing in the world. In fact, I'd probably die of boredom if not for the white-knuckle excitement of watching you fish."

"See? I knew it wasn't just my dashing good looks that won your heart," Blake said with a silly grin. "In all seriousness though, I do appreciate you coming along."

"It's no problem. I've been wanting to see this place. You talk about it like it's heaven."

"Well, now that you're here, it will be."

"Oh Blake Jacobs, you silver-tongued devil," Allison said as she playfully stepped in front of him, grabbed him by the collar, pulled him toward her, and gave him another kiss.

"Mommy! Mommy! It's the river!" Trevor yelled out as he and Buddy made a mad dash down the trail.

"OK, Trevor! Hold up and wait for us, please!" Allison yelled as she lightly ran downhill to keep up.

As Allison chased Trevor and Buddy down to the water, Blake stood at the top of the hill and took a panoramic gaze at the river while inhaling a deep breath. There was a slight breeze that whispered through the long needles of the ponderosa pines and with it carried a deep woody fragrance. The once-green willow bushes that sporadically grew near the river's edge had turned auburn and burnt yellow as they prepared to cast their leaves from their branches come the first sign of winter. The bright lemon hue of the aspen leaves glowed after first being kissed by the afternoon sun and glistened as they flickered in the delicate breeze. He could not have imagined a more perfect day.

While the others played, Blake walked up to the river and began reading the water. As he stood there, studying the ecosystem, a small insect landed on his hand. It was a good-sized mayfly with a dark olive body, a forked tail, and tall cobalt wings. Blake recognized the bug immediately. It was the unmistakable profile of the South Platte River's most famous mayfly, the infamous *baetis*. Most commonly known as the *Blue Winged Olive*.

Blake looked across the river and could see a small circular dimple appear in a pocket of slow-moving water. He looked closely and could see that a trout was hovering just below the surface, feeding on unsuspecting BWOs as they drifted on the top of the water.

Blake tied on a dry fly pattern that closely matched the BWO hatch and made a few casts to the rising fish. Within a couple minutes of casting to the trout, it finally took his fly. Blake called out, "Hey, Allison...Trevor! I got one!"

"Already?" Allison asked as she walked over holding Trevor by the hand. "That was pretty fast."

Blake fought the fish for a minute before scooping it from the river with his net. Trevor and Buddy leaned over the opening of Blake's net carefully examining the trout as it splashed and flipped in the partially submerged net. "Should we let him go sport?" Blake asked.

"Yes!" Trevor said as Buddy began to playfully hop and twirl. "Can I touch him before he goes?"

"Sure pal. In fact, why don't you let him go."

"Really?"

"Sure, just let me get the fly out of his mouth," Blake said as he pulled the hook from the trout's jaw. "Now, just reach under his belly with both hands and scoop him up."

"He's slimy," Trevor giggled while lifting the small rainbow trout from the net.

"Now, gently put him back in the water, let him catch his breath, and he'll swim away."

Trevor did as Blake asked and within a few seconds the trout thrust its tail and swam off. "Look Mommy, he's swimming away," Trevor said with an astonished smile as Buddy hopped into the river and chased the trout.

"He sure is. Good job Trevor!" Allison said rubbing her hand through his scruffy hair. Trevor ran off down the river. "What do you tell Blake?"

"Thanks Bwake!" Trevor yelled in midstride as he and Buddy ran down the river together.

"So why do you do that? Let 'em go, I mean?" Allison asked.

"What else would I do with them?"

"Oh, I don't know…eat 'em? Or don't you like to eat fish?"

"No, I love the taste of fish."

"Then why do you spend so much time tying the flies and researching all these different places, not to mention spending all that money on rods and such…just to release the darn fish back into the river?"

Blake looked up at the sky with a pondering look on his face. "Hmm, that's a good question. Let's just say I'm a believer in second chances."

Allison smiled. "*Second chances*. I like that."

"Mommy! Mommy!" Trevor called out. "Come look at these little bwack wocks I found!"

"I guess I better get over there," Allison said.

238

Blake chuckled and said, "I'd hurry if I were you. With all the deer and elk around here, those might not actually be *rocks* that he found, if ya know what I mean."

"Oh, yuck! You're gross," Allison said as she stood up. "Have fun," she said as she walked toward Trevor.

Blake continued down the riverbank, scanning the water in search of a feeding trout. After walking for a few minutes, he found himself standing in a large shadow. He looked up. The object casting the shadow was the same giant boulder Aaron had fallen off of on that same unforgettable September day six years earlier. Blake laughed thinking of the comical tumble and shook his head. He still couldn't believe Aaron wasn't hurt after the plunge into the icy waters of the South Platte.

As Blake walked closer, his foot stubbed something on the ground, stopping him short of the boulder. He looked down and kicked at a small manmade impediment hidden in the vegetation. It was the river rock fire pit he and Aaron sat around as they wrote down the plans for their fishing trip to Alaska. He couldn't believe the fire pit was still there. Over the years, most of the stones had sunken into the soft dirt, and the dark stain of ash could barely be seen through the thick blades of wild grass and fallen leaves. A ghostly relic from a day that would forever live in Blake's memory.

Facing the river, he sat down by the fire pit and unzipped his backpack. He pulled out Aaron's fly box, the same box he carried with him on his journey to Wyoming. He opened the small case. In it, was a piece of paper folded in half. Blake unfolded the paper and read the handwritten note.

Marine,

Sorrow for his fallen brothers and the guilt for not dying in their stead, is a nemesis that haunts a man's dreams and gnaws at his soul. The more he avoids facing it, the more it torments him. This pain…this regret that men like us feel, will never stop chasing us. No matter how hard we try, we will never truly escape it. The more we run from it, the faster it destroys us and those around us. We must turn and confront it, courageously stare it down and refuse to surrender to it.

With God's help, the wounds of the past will heal but a deep scar will always remain. A scar that we must accept and learn to live with; if not for us, then for the sake of those who love us.

In time, we will come to value it. For it is that scar that distinguishes our life from the lives of average men and serves as a living monument that honors the sacrifice of the friends we have lost. Once we realize that, we will never again wish to live without it.

Semper Fidelis,

Tibbs

Blake folded the note, placed it inside Aaron's fly box and closed the small plastic case. "What's that?" Allison asked as she walked up to Blake and sat down beside him.

Blake looked at Allison with a loving smile while he put his arm behind her lower back and gently squeezed her up against his side. "A letter."

"What's it say?"

"It's a reminder from a friend of how precious life truly is."

Allison closed her eyes and took a deep restful breath. When she opened her eyes, she smiled and said, "It truly is, Blake Jacobs…it truly is."

She leaned to the side and rested her head on Blake's shoulder. Blake laid his head against hers and they watched as the enchanting gleam of light from the evening sun was captured by the riffles of the water and shot back out in a hundred different directions like a bright beam redirected by a prism. Trevor and Buddy ran back and forth along the riverbank, their bodies silhouetted by the reflected sunlight. Blake and Allison sat in silence, not daring to interrupt the comforting sounds of the rushing water. They listened, as the breaking swells from the rippling current swallowed the oxygen from the atmosphere and churned it into a breathable libation for the finned princes of the deep. The river gave birth to a hatch of mayflies that danced in the air before parachuting back down to the water where the trout feasted, gently sipping them from the surface of their aqueous kingdom. The river was teeming with life...precious life.

— end —

Your Road Trip List